THE CUCKOO CLOCK

AND

THE TAPESTRY ROOM

BY

MRS. MOLESWORTH

THE MACMILLAN CHILDREN'S CLASSICS

*Illustrated by the most famous American and English artists.
With ages recommended for first reading.*

AGES 4-6

The Fables of Aesop
English Fairy Tales

AGES 6-8

Household Tales by the Brothers
Grimm
The Cuckoo Clock and The Tap-
estry Room
Grimm's Fairy Tales

AGES 8-10

The Story of Reynard the Fox
East of the Sun and West of the
Moon
Pinocchio
Andersen's Fairy Tales and
Stories
Granny's Wonderful Chair
The Princess and the Goblin
The Princess and Curdie
Dickens' Captain Boldheart. A
Holiday Romance
Alice's Adventures in Wonderland
and Through the Looking Glass
The Prince and the Page
The Listening Child
The Bears of Blue River
Lady Green Satin and Her Maid
Rosette

AGES 8-10 (*Continued*)

The Pilgrim's Progress
The Iliad for Boys and Girls
The Odyssey for Boys and Girls
Games for Every Day (8-12)
Mopsa the Fairy
Simple Susan

AGES 10-12

Juniper Farm
Johnny Appleseed
The Older Children's Bible
At the Back of the North Wind
Treasure Island
Tales from Shakespeare
A Christmas Carol
Rip Van Winkle and The Legend
of Sleepy Hollow
The Little Duke
A Book of Golden Deeds

AGES 12-15

The Arabian Nights
The Dove in the Eagle's Nest
The Alhambra
Two Years Before the Mast
Feats on the Fiord
Kidnapped
Olaf the Glorious
The Lances of Lynwood

Onwards quietly stepped the Little Procession. — p. 66.

THE CUCKOO CLOCK

AND

THE TAPESTRY ROOM

BY

MRS. MOLESWORTH

Author of
"Carrots," "Edmée," "Fairies
Afield," etc.

ILLUSTRATIONS BY
WALTER CRANE

First published in Edinburg,
1877. Reissued, with the same
pictures as in the original editions,
for The Children's Classics, 1925.

New York
THE MACMILLAN COMPANY
1947

CONTENTS.

THE CUCKOO CLOCK.

CHAPTER VII.

CHAPTER VIII.

CHAPTER IX.

CHAPTER X.

CHAPTER XI.

CONTENTS.

THE TAPESTRY ROOM.

CHAPTER VII.

CHAPTER VIII.

CHAPTER IX.

CHAPTER X.

CHAPTER XI.

CHAPTER XII.

THE CUCKOO CLOCK

"Now, these little folks, like most girls and boys,
Loved fairy tales even better than toys.

And they knew that in flowers on the spray
Tiny spirits are hidden away,
That frisk at night on the forest green,
When earth is bathed in dewy sheen —
And shining halls of pearl and gem,
The Regions of Fancy — were open to them."

". . . just as any little child has been guided towards the true paradise
by its fairy dreams of bliss." — E. A. ABBOTT.

BY

MRS. MOLESWORTH

THE CUCKOO CLOCK.

CHAPTER I.

THE OLD HOUSE.

> "Somewhat back from the village street
> Stands the old-fashioned country seat."

ONCE upon a time in an old town, in an old street, there stood a very old house. Such a house as you could hardly find nowadays, however you searched, for it belonged to a gone-by time — a time now quite passed away.

It stood in a street, but yet it was not like a town house, for though the front opened right on to the pavement, the back windows looked out upon a beautiful, quaintly terraced garden, with old trees growing so thick and close together that in summer it was like living on the edge of a forest to be near them; and even in winter the web of their interlaced branches hid all clear view behind.

There was a colony of rooks in this old garden. Year after year they held their parliaments and cawed and chattered and fussed; year after year they built their nests and hatched their eggs; year

1

after year, I *suppose*, the old ones gradually died off and the young ones took their place, though, but for knowing this *must* be so, no one would have suspected it, for to all appearance the rooks were always the same — ever and always the same.

Time indeed seemed to stand still in and all about the old house, as if it and the people who inhabited it had got *so* old that they could not get any older, and had outlived the possibility of change.

But one day at last there did come a change. Late in the dusk of an autumn afternoon a carriage drove up to the door of the old house, came rattling over the stones with a sudden noisy clatter that sounded quite impertinent, startling the rooks just as they were composing themselves to rest, and setting them all wondering what could be the matter.

A little girl was the matter! A little girl in a gray merino frock and gray beaver bonnet, gray tippet and gray gloves — all gray together, even to her eyes, all except her round rosy face and bright brown hair. Her name even was rather gray, for it was Griselda.

A gentleman lifted her out of the carriage and disappeared with her into the house, and later that same evening the gentleman came out of the house and got into the carriage which had come back for him again, and drove away. That was all that the rooks saw of the change that had come to the old house. Shall we go inside to see more?

A Carriage Drove up to the Old House

Up the shallow, wide, old-fashioned staircase, past the wainscoted walls, dark and shining like a mirror, down a long narrow passage with many doors, which but for their gleaming brass handles one would not have known were there, the oldest of the three old servants led little Griselda, so tired and sleepy that her supper had been left almost untasted, to the room prepared for her. It was a queer room, for everything in the house was queer; but in the dancing light of the fire burning brightly in the tiled grate, it looked cheerful enough.

"I am glad there's a fire," said the child. "Will it keep alight till the morning, do you think?"

The old servant shook her head.

"'Twould not be safe to leave it so that it would burn till morning," she said. "When you are in bed and asleep, little missie, you won't want the fire. Bed's the warmest place."

"It isn't for that I want it," said Griselda; "it's for the light I like it. This house all looks so dark to me, and yet there seem to be lights hidden in the walls too, they shine so."

The old servant smiled.

"It will all seem strange to you, no doubt," she said; "but you'll get to like it, missie. 'Tis a *good* old house, and those that know best love it well."

"Whom do you mean?" said Griselda. "Do you mean my great-aunts?"

"Ah, yes, and others beside," replied the old

woman. "The rooks love it well, and others beside.
Did you ever hear tell of the 'good people,' missie,
over the sea where you come from?"

"Fairies, do you mean?" cried Griselda, her eyes
sparkling. "Of course I've *heard* of them, but I
never saw any? Did you ever?"

"I couldn't say," answered the old woman. "My
mind is not young like yours, missie, and there are
times when strange memories come back to me as of
sights and sounds in a dream. I am too old to see
and hear as I once could. We are all old here,
missie. 'Twas time something young came to the
old house again."

"How strange and queer everything seems!"
thought Griselda, as she got into bed. "I don't feel
as if I belonged to it a bit. And they are all *so*
old; perhaps they won't like having a child among
them?"

The very same thought that had occurred to the
rooks! They could not decide as to the fors and
againsts at all, so they settled to put it to the vote
the next morning, and in the meantime they and
Griselda all went to sleep.

I never heard if *they* slept well that night; after
such unusual excitement it was hardly to be expected
they would. But Griselda, being a little girl and
not a rook, was so tired that two minutes after she
had tucked herself up in bed she was quite sound
asleep, and did not wake for several hours.

"I wonder what it will all look like in the morning," was her last waking thought. "If it was summer now, or spring, I shouldn't mind — there would always be something nice to do then."

As sometimes happens, when she woke again, very early in the morning, long before it was light, her thoughts went straight on with the same subject.

"If it was summer now, or spring," she repeated to herself, just as if she had not been asleep at all — like the man who fell into a trance for a hundred years just as he was saying "it is bitt—" and when he woke up again finished the sentence as if nothing had happened — "erly cold." "If only it was spring," thought Griselda.

Just as she had got so far in her thoughts, she gave a great start. What was it she heard? Could her wish have come true? Was this fairyland indeed that she had got to, where one only needs to *wish*, for it to *be?* She rubbed her eyes, but it was too dark to see; *that* was not very fairyland-like, but her ears she felt certain had not deceived her: she was quite, quite sure that she had heard the cuckoo!

She listened with all her might, but she did not hear it again. Could it, after all, have been fancy? She grew sleepy at last, and was just dropping off when — yes, there it was again, as clear and distinct as possible — "Cuckoo, cuckoo, cuckoo!" three, four, *five* times, then perfect silence as before.

"What a funny cuckoo," said Griselda to herself.

"I could almost fancy it was in the house. I won-der if my great-aunts have a tame cuckoo in a cage? I don't *think* I ever heard of such a thing, but this is such a queer house; everything seems different in it — perhaps they have a tame cuckoo. I'll ask them in the morning. It's very nice to hear, whatever it is."

And, with a pleasant feeling of companionship, a sense that she was not the only living creature awake in this dark world, Griselda lay listening, contentedly enough, for the sweet, fresh notes of the cuckoo's friendly greeting. But before it sounded again through the silent house she was once more fast asleep. And this time she slept till daylight had found its way into all but the *very* darkest nooks and crannies of the ancient dwelling.

She dressed herself carefully, for she had been warned that her aunts loved neatness and precision; she fastened each button of her gray frock, and tied down her hair as smooth as such a brown tangle *could* be tied down; and, absorbed with these weighty cares, she forgot all about the cuckoo for the time. It was not till she was sitting at breakfast with her aunts that she remembered it, or rather was reminded of it, by some little remark that was made about the friendly robins on the terrace walk outside.

"Oh, aunt," she exclaimed, stopping short half-way the journey to her mouth of a spoonful of bread and milk, "have you got a cuckoo in a cage?"

"A cuckoo in a cage," repeated her elder aunt, Miss Grizzel; "what is the child talking about?"

"In a cage!" echoed Miss Tabitha, "a cuckoo in a cage!"

"There is a cuckoo somewhere in the house," said Griselda; "I heard it in the night. It couldn't have been out-of-doors, could it? It would be too cold."

The aunts looked at each other with a little smile. "So like her grandmother," they whispered. Then said Miss Grizzel—

"We have a cuckoo, my dear, though it isn't in a cage, and it isn't exactly the sort of cuckoo you are thinking of. It lives in a clock."

"In a clock," repeated Miss Tabitha, as if to confirm her sister's statement.

"In a clock!" exclaimed Griselda, opening her gray eyes very wide.

It sounded something like the three bears, all speaking one after the other, only Griselda's voice was not like Tiny's; it was the loudest of the three.

"In a clock!" she exclaimed; "but it can't be alive, then?"

"Why not?" said Miss Grizzel.

"I don't know," replied Griselda, looking puzzled.

"I knew a little girl once," pursued Miss Grizzel, "who was quite of opinion the cuckoo *was* alive, and nothing would have persuaded her it was not. Finish your breakfast, my dear, and then if you like you shall come with me and see the cuckoo for yourself."

"Thank you, Aunt Grizzel," said Griselda, going on with her bread and milk.

"Yes," said Miss Tabitha, "you shall see the cuckoo for yourself."

"Thank you, Aunt Tabitha," said Griselda. It was rather a bother to have always to say "thank you," or "no, thank you," twice, but Griselda thought it was polite to do so, as Aunt Tabitha always repeated everything that Aunt Grizzel said. It wouldn't have mattered so much if Aunt Tabitha had said it *at once* after Miss Grizzel, but as she generally made a little pause between, it was sometimes rather awkward. But of course it was better to say "thank you" or "no, thank you" twice over than to hurt Aunt Tabitha's feelings.

After breakfast Aunt Grizzel was as good as her word. She took Griselda through several of the rooms in the house, pointing out all the curiosities, and telling all the histories of the rooms and their contents; and Griselda liked to listen, only in every room they came to, she wondered *when* they would get to the room where lived the cuckoo.

Aunt Tabitha did not come with them, for she was rather rheumatic. On the whole, Griselda was not sorry. It would have taken such a *very* long time, you see, to have had all the histories twice over, and possibly, if Griselda had got tired, she might have forgotten about the "thank you's" or "no, thank you's" twice over.

The old house looked quite as queer and quaint by daylight as it had seemed the evening before; almost more so indeed, for the view from the windows added to the sweet, odd "old-fashionedness" of everything.

"We have beautiful roses in summer," observed Miss Grizzel, catching sight of the direction in which the child's eyes were wandering.

"I wish it was summer. I do love summer," said Griselda. "But there is a very rosy scent in the rooms even now, Aunt Grizzel, though it is winter, or nearly winter."

Miss Grizzel looked pleased.

"My pot-pourri," she explained.

They were just then standing in what she called the "great saloon," a handsome old room, furnished with gold-and-white chairs, that must once have been brilliant, and faded yellow damask hangings. A feeling of awe had crept over Griselda as they entered this ancient drawing-room. What grand parties there must have been in it long ago! But as for dancing in it *now* — dancing, or laughing, or chattering — such a thing was quite impossible to imagine!

Miss Grizzel crossed the room to where stood in one corner a marvellous Chinese cabinet, all black and gold and carving. It was made in the shape of a temple, or a palace — Griselda was not sure which. Any way, it was very delicious and wonderful. At the door stood, one on each side, two solemn mandarins; or, to speak more correctly, perhaps I should say, a mandarin and his wife, for the right-hand figure was evidently intended to be a lady.

Miss Grizzel gently touched their heads. Forthwith, to Griselda's astonishment, they began solemnly to nod.

"Oh, how do you make them do that, Aunt Grizzel?" she exclaimed.

"Never you mind, my dear; it wouldn't do for *you* to try to make them nod. They wouldn't like it," replied Miss Grizzel mysteriously. "Respect to your elders, my dear, always remember that. The mandarins are *many* years older than you — older than I myself, in fact."

Griselda wondered, if this were so, how it was that Miss Grizzel took such liberties with them herself, but she said nothing.

"Here is my last summer's pot-pourri," continued Miss Grizzel, touching a great china jar on a little stand, close beside the cabinet. "You may smell it, my dear."

Nothing loth, Griselda buried her round little nose in the fragrant leaves.

"It's lovely," she said. "May I smell it whenever I like, Aunt Grizzel?"

"We shall see," replied her aunt. "It isn't *every*

little girl, you know, that we could trust to come into the great saloon alone."

"No," said Griselda meekly.

Miss Grizzel led the way to a door opposite to that by which they had entered. She opened it and passed through, Griselda following, into a small ante-room.

"It is on the stroke of ten," said Miss Grizzel, consulting her watch; "now, my dear, you shall make acquaintance with our cuckoo."

The cuckoo "that lived in a clock!" Griselda gazed round her eagerly. Where was the clock? She could see nothing in the least like one, only up on the wall in one corner was what looked like a miniature house, of dark brown carved wood. It was not so *very* like a house, but it certainly had a roof — a roof with deep projecting eaves; and, looking closer, yes, it *was* a clock, after all, only the figures, which had once been gilt, had grown dim with age, like everything else, and the hands at a little distance were hardly to be distinguished from the face.

Miss Grizzel stood perfectly still, looking up at the clock; Griselda beside her, in breathless expectation. Presently there came a sort of distant rumbling. *Something* was going to happen. Suddenly two little doors above the clock face, which Griselda had not known were there, sprang open with a burst and out flew a cuckoo, flapped his wings, and uttered his pretty cry, "Cuckoo! cuckoo!

cuckoo!" Miss Grizzel counted aloud, "Seven, eight, nine, ten." "Yes, he never makes a mistake," she added triumphantly. "All these long years I have never known him wrong. There are no such clocks made nowadays, I can assure you, my dear."

"But *is* it a clock? Isn't he alive?" exclaimed Griselda. "He looked at me and nodded his head, before he flapped his wings and went into his house again — he did indeed, aunt," she said earnestly; "just like saying, 'How do you do?' to me."

Again Miss Grizzel smiled, the same odd yet pleased smile that Griselda had seen on her face at breakfast. "Just what Sybilla used to say," she murmured. "Well, my dear," she added aloud, "it is quite right he *should* say, 'How do you do?' to you. It is the first time he has seen *you*, though many a year ago he knew your dear grandmother, and your father, too, when he was a little boy. You will find him a good friend, and one that can teach you many lessons."

"What, Aunt Grizzel?" inquired Griselda, looking puzzled.

"Punctuality, for one thing, and faithful discharge of duty," replied Miss Grizzel.

"May I come to see the cuckoo — to watch for him coming out, sometimes?" asked Griselda, who felt as if she could spend all day looking up at the clock, watching for her little friend's appearance.

"You will see him several times a day," said her

aunt, "for it is in this little room I intend you to prepare your tasks. It is nice and quiet, and nothing to disturb you, and close to the room where your Aunt Tabitha and I usually sit."

So saying, Miss Grizzel opened a second door in the little ante-room, and, to Griselda's surprise, at the foot of a short flight of stairs through another door, half open, she caught sight of her Aunt Tabitha, knitting quietly by the fire, in the room in which they had breakfasted.

"What a *very* funny house it is, Aunt Grizzel," she said, as she followed her aunt down the steps. "Every room has so many doors, and you come back to where you were just when you think you are ever so far off. I shall never be able to find my way about."

"Oh yes, you will, my dear, very soon," said her aunt encouragingly.

"She is very kind," thought Griselda; "but I wish she wouldn't call my lessons tasks. It makes them sound so dreadfully hard. But, any way, I'm glad I'm to do them in the room where that dear cuckoo lives."

CHAPTER II.

". . . fairies but seldom appear ;
If we do wrong we must expect
That it will cost us dear ! "

IT was all very well for a few days. Griselda
found plenty to amuse herself with while the novelty
lasted, enough to prevent her missing *very* badly the
home she had left "over the sea," and the troop of
noisy merry brothers who teased and petted her. Of
course she *missed* them, but not "dreadfully." She
was neither homesick nor "dull."

It was not quite such smooth sailing when lessons
began. She did not dislike lessons; in fact, she had
always thought she was rather fond of them. But
the having to do them alone was not lively, and her
teachers were very strict. The worst of all was the
writing and arithmetic master, a funny little old man
who wore knee-breeches and took snuff, and called
her aunt "Madame," bowing formally whenever he
addressed her. He screwed Griselda up into such
an unnatural attitude to write her copies, that she
really felt as if she would never come straight
and loose again; and the arithmetic part of his in-

14

structions was even worse. Oh! what sums in addition he gave her! Griselda had never been partial to sums, and her rather easy-going governess at home had not, to tell the truth, been partial to them either. And Mr. — I can't remember the little old gentleman's name. Suppose we call him Mr. Kneebreeches — Mr. Kneebreeches, when he found this out, conscientiously put her back to the very beginning.

It was dreadful, really. He came twice a week, and the days he didn't come were as bad as those he did, for he left her a whole *row* I was going to say, but you couldn't call Mr. Kneebreeches' addition sums "rows," they were far too fat and wide across to be so spoken of! — whole slatefuls of these terrible mountains of figures to climb wearily to the top of. And not to climb *once* up merely. *The* terrible thing was Mr. Kneebreeches' favourite method of what he called "proving." I can't explain it — it is far beyond my poor powers — but it had something to do with cutting off the top line, after you had added it all up and had actually done the sum, you understand — cutting off the top line and adding the long rows up again without it, and then joining it on again somewhere else.

"I wouldn't mind so much," said poor Griselda, one day, "if it was any good. But you see, Aunt Grizzel, it isn't. For I'm just as likely to do the *proving* wrong as the sum itself — more likely, for I'm always so tired when I get to the proving — and so all that's proved is that *something's* wrong, and I'm sure that isn't any good, except to make me cross."

"Hush!" said her aunt gravely. "That is not the way for a little girl to speak. Improve these golden hours of youth, Griselda; they will never return."

"I hope not," muttered Griselda, "if it means doing sums."

Miss Grizzel fortunately was a little deaf; she did not hear this remark. Just then the cuckoo clock struck eleven.

"Good little cuckoo," said Miss Grizzel. "What an example he sets you. His life is spent in the faithful discharge of duty;" and so saying she left the room.

The cuckoo was still telling the hour — eleven took a good while. It seemed to Griselda that the bird repeated her aunt's last words. "Faith — ful, dis — charge, of — your, du — ty," he said, "faith — ful."

"You horrid little creature!" exclaimed Griselda in a passion; "what business have you to mock me?"

She seized a book, the first that came to hand, and flung it at the bird who was just beginning his eleventh cuckoo. He disappeared with a snap, disappeared without flapping his wings, or, as Griselda always fancied he did, giving her a friendly nod, and in an instant all was silent.

Griselda felt a little frightened. What had she done? She looked up at the clock. It seemed just the same as usual, the cuckoo's doors closely shut, no sign of any disturbance. Could it have been her fancy only that he had sprung back more hastily than he would have done but for her throwing the book at him? She began to hope so, and tried to go on with her lessons. But it was no use. Though she really gave her best attention to the long addition sums, and found that by so doing she managed them much better than before, she could not feel happy or at ease. Every few minutes she glanced up at the clock, as if expecting the cuckoo to come out, though she knew quite well there was no chance of his doing so till twelve o'clock, as it was only the hours, not the half hours and quarters, that he told.

"I wish it was twelve o'clock," she said to herself anxiously more than once.

If only the clock had not been so very high up on the wall, she would have been tempted to climb up and open the little doors, and peep in to satisfy herself as to the cuckoo's condition. But there was no possibility of this. The clock was far, very far above her reach, and there was no high piece of furniture standing near, upon which she could have climbed to get to it. There was nothing to be done but to wait for twelve o'clock.

And, after all, she did not wait for twelve o'clock, for just about half-past eleven, Miss Grizzel's voice was heard calling to her to put on her hat and cloak quickly, and come out to walk up and down the terrace with her.

"It is fine just now," said Miss Grizzel, "but there is a prospect of rain before long. You must leave your lessons for the present, and finish them in the afternoon."

"I have finished them," said Griselda, meekly.

"*All?*" inquired her aunt.

"Yes, all," replied Griselda.

"Ah, well, then, this afternoon, if the rain holds off, we shall drive to Merrybrow Hall, and inquire for the health of your dear godmother, Lady Lavander," said Miss Grizzel.

Poor Griselda! There were few things she disliked more than a drive with her aunts. They went in the old yellow chariot, with all the windows up, and of course Griselda had to sit with her back to the horses, which made her very uncomfortable when she had no air, and had to sit still for so long.

Merrybrow Hall was a large house, quite as old and much grander, but not nearly so wonderful as the home of Griselda's aunts. It was six miles off, and it took a very long time indeed to drive there in the rumbling old chariot, for the old horses were fat and wheezy, and the old coachman fat and wheezy too. Lady Lavander was, of course, old too — very old indeed, and rather grumpy and very deaf.

Miss Grizzel and Miss Tabitha had the greatest respect for her; she always called them "My dear," as if they were quite girls, and they listened to all she said as if her words were of gold. For some mysterious reason she had been invited to be Griselda's godmother; but, as she had never shown her any proof of affection beyond giving her a prayer-book, and hoping, whenever she saw her, that she was "a good little miss," Griselda did not feel any particular cause for gratitude to her.

The drive seemed longer and duller than ever this afternoon, but Griselda bore it meekly; and when Lady Lavander, as usual, expressed her hopes about her, the little girl looked down modestly, feeling her cheeks grow scarlet. "I am not a good little girl at all," she felt inclined to call out. "I'm very bad and cruel. I believe I've killed the dear little cuckoo."

What *would* the three old ladies have thought if she had called it out? As it was, Lady Lavander patted her approvingly, said she loved to see young people modest and humble-minded, and gave her a slice of very highly-spiced, rather musty gingerbread, which Griselda couldn't bear.

All the way home Griselda felt in a fever of impatience to rush up to the ante-room and see if the cuckoo was all right again. It was late and dark when the chariot at last stopped at the door of the old house. Miss Grizzel got out slowly, and still more slowly Miss Tabitha followed her. Griselda was obliged to restrain herself and move demurely.

"It is past your supper-time, my dear," said Miss Grizzel. "Go up at once to your room, and Dorcas shall bring some supper to you. Late hours are bad for young people."

Griselda obediently wished her aunts good-night, and went quietly upstairs. But once out of sight, at the first landing, she changed her pace. She turned to the left instead of to the right, which led to her own room, and flew rather than ran along the dimly-lighted passage, at the end of which a door led into the great saloon. She opened the door. All was quite dark. It was impossible to fly or run across the great saloon! Even in daylight this would have been a difficult matter. Griselda *felt* her way as best she could, past the Chinese cabinet and the pot-pourri jar, till she got to the ante-room door. It was open, and now, knowing her way better, she hurried in. But what was the use? All was silent, save the tick-tick of the cuckoo clock in the corner. Oh, if *only* the cuckoo would come out and call the hour as usual, what a weight would be lifted off Griselda's heart!

She had no idea what o'clock it was. It might be close to the hour, or it might be just past it. She stood listening for a few minutes, then hearing Miss Grizzel's voice in the distance, she felt that she dared not stay any longer, and turned to feel her way out of the room again. Just as she got to the door it seemed to her that something softly brushed her cheek, and a very, very faint "cuckoo" sounded as it were in the air close to her.

Startled, but not frightened, Griselda stood perfectly still.

"Cuckoo," she said, softly. But there was no answer.

Again the tones of Miss Grizzel's voice coming upstairs reached her ear.

"I *must* go," said Griselda; and finding her way across the saloon without, by great good luck, tumbling against any of the many breakable treasures with which it was filled, she flew down the long passage again, reaching her own room just before Dorcas appeared with her supper.

Griselda slept badly that night. She was constantly dreaming of the cuckoo, fancying she heard his voice, and then waking with a start to find it was *only* fancy. She looked pale and heavy-eyed when she came down to breakfast the next morning; and her Aunt Tabitha, who was alone in the room when she entered, began immediately asking her what was the matter.

"I am sure you are going to be ill, child," she said, nervously. "Sister Grizzel must give you some medicine. I wonder what would be the best. Tansy tea is an excellent thing when one has taken cold, or —"

But the rest of Miss Tabitha's sentence was never heard, for at this moment Miss Grizzel came hurriedly into the room — her cap awry, her shawl disarranged, her face very pale. I hardly think any one had ever seen her so discomposed before.

"Sister Tabitha!" she exclaimed, "what can be going to happen? The cuckoo clock has stopped."

"The cuckoo clock has stopped!" repeated Miss Tabitha, holding up her hands; "*im*possible!"

"But it has, or rather I should say — dear me, I am so upset I cannot explain myself — the *cuckoo* has stopped. The clock is going on, but the cuckoo has not told the hours, and Dorcas is of opinion that he left off doing so yesterday. What can be going to happen? What shall we do?"

"What can we do?" said Miss Tabitha. "Should we send for the watch-maker?"

Miss Grizzel shook her head.

"'Twould be worse than useless. Were we to search the world over, we could find no one to put it right. Fifty years and more, Tabitha, fifty years and more, it has never missed an hour! We are getting old, Tabitha, our day is nearly over; perhaps 'tis to remind us of this."

Miss Tabitha did not reply. She was weeping silently. The old ladies seemed to have forgotten the presence of their niece, but Griselda could not bear to see their distress. She finished her breakfast as quickly as she could, and left the room.

On her way upstairs she met Dorcas.

"Have you heard what has happened, little missie?" said the old servant.

"Yes," replied Griselda.

"My ladies are in great trouble," continued Dorcas, who seemed inclined to be more communicative than usual, "and no wonder. For fifty years that clock has never gone wrong."

"Can't it be put right?" asked the child.

Dorcas shook her head.

"No good would come of interfering," she said. "What must be, must be. The luck of the house hangs on that clock. Its maker spent a good part of his life over it, and his last words were that it would bring good luck to the house that owned it, but that trouble would follow its silence. It's my belief," she added solemnly, "that it's a *fairy* clock, neither more nor less, for good luck it has brought there's no denying. There are no cows like ours, missie — their milk is a proverb hereabouts; there are no hens like ours for laying all the year round; there are no roses like ours. And there's always a friendly feeling in this house, and always has been. 'Tis not a house for wrangling and jangling, and sharp words. The 'good people' can't stand that. Nothing drives them away like ill-temper or anger."

Griselda's conscience gave her a sharp prick. Could it be *her* doing that trouble was coming upon the old house? What a punishment for a moment's fit of ill-temper.

"I wish you wouldn't talk that way, Dorcas," she said; "it makes me so unhappy."

"What a feeling heart the child has!" said the old servant as she went on her way downstairs. "It's true —she is very like Miss Sybilla."

That day was a very weary and sad one for Griselda. She was oppressed by a feeling she did not understand. She knew she had done wrong, but she had sorely repented it, and "I do think the cuckoo might have come back again," she said to herself, "if he *is* a fairy; and if he isn't, it can't be true what Dorcas says."

Her aunts made no allusion to the subject in her presence, and almost seemed to have forgotten that she had known of their distress. They were more grave and silent than usual, but otherwise things went on in their ordinary way. Griselda spent the morning "at her tasks," in the ante-room, but was thankful to get away from the tick-tick of the clock in the corner and out into the garden.

But there, alas! it was just as bad. The rooks seemed to know that something was the matter; they set to work making such a chatter immediately Griselda appeared that she felt inclined to run back into the house again.

"I am sure they are talking about me," she said to herself. "Perhaps they are fairies too. I am beginning to think I don't like fairies."

She was glad when bed-time came. It was a

sort of reproach to her to see her aunts so pale and troubled; and though she tried to persuade herself that she thought them very silly, she could not throw off the uncomfortable feeling.

She was so tired when she went to bed — tired in the disagreeable way that comes from a listless, un-easy day — that she fell asleep at once and slept heavily. When she woke, which she did suddenly, and with a start, it was still perfectly dark, like the first morning that she had wakened in the old house. It seemed to her that she had not wakened of herself — something had roused her. Yes! there it was again, a very, *very* soft distant "cuckoo." *Was* it distant? She could not tell. Almost she could have fancied it was close to her.

"If it's that cuckoo come back again, I'll catch him!" exclaimed Griselda.

She darted out of bed, felt her way to the door, which was closed, and opening it let in a rush of moonlight from the unshuttered passage window. In another moment her little bare feet were patter-ing along the passage at full speed, in the direction of the great saloon.

For Griselda's childhood among the troop of noisy brothers had taught her one lesson — she was afraid of nothing. Or rather perhaps I should say she had never learnt that there was anything to be afraid of! And is there?

CHAPTER III.

"Little girl, thou must thy part fulfil,
    If we're to take kindly to ours :
Then pull up the weeds with a will,
    And fairies will cherish the flowers."

THERE was moonlight, though not so much, in the
saloon and the ante-room, too; for though the windows, like those in Griselda's bed-room, had the shutters closed, there was a round part at the top, high
up, which the shutters did not reach to, and in crept.
through these clear uncovered panes, quite as many
moonbeams, you may be sure, as could find their
way.

Griselda, eager though she was, could not help
standing still a moment to admire the effect.

"It looks prettier with the light coming in at those
holes at the top than even if the shutters were open,"
she said to herself. "How goldy-silvery the cabinet
looks ; and, yes, I do declare, the mandarins are nodding! I wonder if it is out of politeness to me, or
does Aunt Grizzel come in last thing at night and
touch them to make them keep nodding till morning? I *suppose* they're a sort of policemen to the
palace ; and I dare say there are all sorts of beautiful

26

"WHY WON'T YOU SPEAK TO ME?"—p. 27.

things inside.   How I should like to see all through it!"

But at this moment the faint tick-tick of the cuckoo clock in the next room, reaching her ear, reminded her of the object of this midnight expedition of hers.   She hurried into the ante-room.

It looked darker than the great saloon, for it had but one window.   But through the uncovered space at the top of this window there penetrated some brilliant moonbeams, one of which lighted up brightly the face of the clock with its queer overhanging eaves.

Griselda approached it and stood below, looking up.

"Cuckoo," she said softly — very softly.

But there was no reply.

"Cuckoo," she repeated rather more loudly. "Why won't you speak to me?   I know you are there, and you're not asleep, for I heard your voice in my own room.   Why won't you come out, cuckoo?"

"Tick-tick" said the clock, but there was no other reply.

Griselda felt ready to cry.

"Cuckoo," she said reproachfully, "I didn't think you were so hard-hearted.   I have been *so* unhappy about you, and I was so pleased to hear your voice again, for I thought I had killed you, or hurt you very badly; and I didn't *mean* to hurt you, cuckoo.

I was sorry the moment I had done it, *dreadfully* sorry. Dear cuckoo, won't you forgive me?"

There was a little sound at last — a faint *coming* sound, and by the moonlight Griselda saw the doors open, and out flew the cuckoo. He stood still for a moment, looked round him as it were, then gently flapped his wings, and uttered his usual note — " Cuckoo."

Griselda stood in breathless expectation, but in her delight she could not help very softly clapping her hands.

The cuckoo cleared his throat. You never heard such a funny little noise as he made ; and then, in a very clear, distinct, but yet " cuckoo-y " voice, he spoke.

" Griselda," he said, " are you truly sorry?"

"I told you I was," she replied. "But I didn't *feel* so very naughty, cuckoo. I didn't, really. I was only vexed for one moment, and when I threw the book I seemed to be a very little in fun, too. And it made me so unhappy when you went away, and my poor aunts have been dreadfully unhappy too. If you hadn't come back I should have told them to-morrow what I had done. I would have told them before, but I was afraid it would have made them more unhappy. I thought I had hurt you dreadfully."

" So you did," said the cuckoo.

"But you *look* quite well," said Griselda.

"It was my *feelings*," replied the cuckoo; "and I couldn't help going away. I have to obey orders like other people."

Griselda stared. "How do you mean?" she asked.

"Never mind. You can't understand at present," said the cuckoo. "You can understand about obeying *your* orders, and you see, when you don't, things go wrong."

"Yes," said Griselda humbly, "they certainly do. But, cuckoo," she continued, "I never used to get into tempers at home — *hardly* never, at least; and I liked my lessons then, and I never was scolded about them."

"What's wrong here, then?" said the cuckoo. "It isn't often that things go wrong in this house."

"That's what Dorcas says," said Griselda. "It must be with my being a child — my aunts and the house and everything have got out of children's ways."

"About time they did," remarked the cuckoo drily.

"And so," continued Griselda, "it is really very dull. I have lots of lessons, but it isn't so much that I mind. It is that I've no one to play with."

"There's something in that," said the cuckoo. He flapped his wings and was silent for a minute or two. "I'll consider about it," he observed at last.

" Thank you," said Griselda, not exactly knowing what else to say.

" And in the meantime," continued the cuckoo, " you'd better obey present orders and go back to bed."

" Shall I say good-night to you, then?" asked Griselda somewhat timidly.

" You're quite welcome to do so," replied the cuckoo. " Why shouldn't you?"

" You see I wasn't sure if you would like it," returned Griselda, " for of course you're not like a person, and — and — I've been told all sorts of queer things about what fairies like and don't like."

" Who said I was a fairy?" inquired the cuckoo.

" Dorcas did, and, *of course*, my own common sense did too," replied Griselda. " You must be a fairy — you couldn't be anything else."

" I might be a fairyfied cuckoo," suggested the bird.

Griselda looked puzzled.

" I don't understand," she said, " and I don't think it could make much difference. But whatever you are, I wish you would tell me one thing."

" What?" said the cuckoo.

" I want to know, now that you've forgiven me for throwing the book at you, have you come back for good?"

" Certainly not for evil," replied the cuckoo.

Griselda gave a little wriggle. " Cuckoo, you're

laughing at me," she said. "I mean, have you come
back to stay and cuckoo as usual and make my aunts
happy again?"

"You'll see in the morning," said the cuckoo.
"Now go off to bed."

"Good-night," said Griselda, "and thank you, and
please don't forget to let me know when you've considered."

"Cuckoo, cuckoo," was her little friend's reply.
Griselda thought it was meant for good-night, but
the fact of the matter was that at that exact second
of time it was two o'clock in the morning.

She made her way back to bed. She had been
standing some time, talking to the cuckoo, but,
though it was now well on in November, she did not
feel the least cold, nor sleepy! She felt as happy
and light-hearted as possible, and she wished it was
morning, that she might get up. Yet the moment
she laid her little brown curly head on the pillow,
she fell asleep; and it seemed to her that just as she
dropped off a soft feathery wing brushed her cheek
gently and a tiny "Cuckoo" sounded in her ear.

When she woke it was bright morning, really
bright morning, for the wintry sun was already
sending some clear yellow rays out into the pale
gray-blue sky.

"It must be late," thought Griselda, when she had
opened the shutters and seen how light it was. "I
must have slept a long time. I feel so beautifully

unsleepy now. I must dress quickly — how nice it
will be to see my aunts look happy again! I don't
even care if they scold me for being late."

But, after all, it was not so much later than usual;
it was only a much brighter morning than they had
had for some time. Griselda did dress herself very
quickly, however. As she went downstairs two or
three of the clocks in the house, for there were several, were striking eight. These clocks must have
been a little before the right time, for it was not till
they had again relapsed into silence that there rang
out from the ante-room the clear sweet tones, eight
times repeated, of "Cuckoo."

Miss Grizzel and Miss Tabitha were already at the
breakfast-table, but they received their little niece
most graciously. Nothing was said about the clock,
however, till about half-way through the meal, when
Griselda, full of eagerness to know if her aunts were
aware of the cuckoo's return, could restrain herself
no longer.

"Aunt Grizzel," she said, "isn't the cuckoo all
right again?"

"Yes, my dear. I am delighted to say it is,"
replied Miss Grizzel.

"Did you get it put right, Aunt Grizzel?" inquired Griselda, slyly.

"Little girls should not ask so many questions,"
replied Miss Grizzel, mysteriously. "It *is* all right
again, and that is enough. During fifty years that

cuckoo has never, till yesterday, missed an hour. If you, in your sphere, my dear, do as well during fifty years, you won't have done badly."

"No, indeed, you won't have done badly," repeated Miss Tabitha.

But though the two old ladies thus tried to improve the occasion by a little lecturing, Griselda could see that at the bottom of their hearts they were both so happy that, even if she had been very naughty indeed, they could hardly have made up their minds to scold her.

She was not at all inclined to be naughty this day. She had something to think about and look forward to, which made her quite a different little girl, and made her take heart in doing her lessons as well as she possibly could.

"I wonder when the cuckoo will have considered enough about my having no one to play with?" she said to herself, as she was walking up and down the terrace at the back of the house.

"Caw, caw!" screamed a rook just over her head, as if in answer to her thought.

Griselda looked up at him.

"Your voice isn't half so pretty as the cuckoo's, Mr. Rook," she said. "All the same, I dare say I should make friends with you, if I understood what you meant. How funny it would be to know all the languages of the birds and the beasts, like the prince in the fairy tale! I wonder if I should wish for that, if a fairy gave me a wish? No, I don't think I would. I'd *far* rather have the fairy carpet that would take you anywhere you liked in a minute. I'd go to China to see if all the people there looked like Aunt Grizzel's mandarins; and I'd first of all, of course, go to fairyland."

"You must come in now, little missie," said Dorcas's voice. "Miss Grizzel says you have had play enough, and there's a nice fire in the ante-room for you to do your lessons by."

"Play!" repeated Griselda indignantly, as she turned to follow the old servant. "Do you call walking up and down the terrace 'play,' Dorcas? I mustn't loiter even to pick a flower, if there were any, for fear of catching cold, and I mustn't run for fear of overheating myself. I declare, Dorcas, if I don't have some play soon, or something to amuse me, I think I'll run away."

"Nay, nay, missie, don't talk like that. You'd never do anything so naughty, and you so like Miss Sybilla, who was so good."

"Dorcas, I'm tired of being told I'm like Miss Sybilla," said Griselda, impatiently. "She was my grandmother; no one would like to be told they were like their grandmother. It makes me feel as if my face must be all screwy up and wrinkly, and as if I should have spectacles on and a wig."

"*That* is not like what Miss Sybilla was when I first saw her," said Dorcas. "She was younger than you, missie, and as pretty as a fairy."

"*Was* she?" exclaimed Griselda, stopping short.

"Yes, indeed she was. She might have been a fairy, so sweet she was and gentle — and yet so merry. Every creature loved her; even the animals about seemed to know her, as if she was one of themselves. She brought good luck to the house, and it was a sad day when she left it."

"I thought you said it was the cuckoo that brought good luck?" said Griselda.

"Well, so it was. The cuckoo and Miss Sybilla came here the same day. It was left to her by her mother's father, with whom she had lived since she was a baby, and when he died she came here to her sisters. She wasn't *own* sister to my ladies, you see, missie. Her mother had come from Germany, and it was in some strange place there, where her grandfather lived, that the cuckoo clock was made. They make wonderful clocks there, I've been told, but none more wonderful that our cuckoo, I'm sure."

"No, I'm *sure* not," said Griselda, softly. "Why didn't Miss Sybilla take it with her when she was married and went away?"

"She knew her sisters were so fond of it. It was like a memory of her left behind for them. It was like a part of her. And do you know, missie, the night she died — she died soon after your father was born, a year after she was married — for a whole hour, from twelve to one, that cuckoo went on cuckooing in a soft, sad way, like some living creature in trouble. Of course, we did not know anything was wrong with her, and folks said something had caught some of the springs of the works; but *I* didn't think so, and never shall. And — "

But here Dorcas's reminiscences were abruptly brought to a close by Miss Grizzel's appearance at the other end of the terrace.

" Griselda, what are you loitering so for? Dorcas, you should have hastened, not delayed Miss Griselda."

So Griselda was hurried off to her lessons, and Dorcas to her kitchen. But Griselda did not much mind. She had plenty to think of and wonder about, and she liked to do her lessons in the ante-room, with the tick-tick of the clock in her ears, and the feeling that *perhaps* the cuckoo was watching her through some invisible peep-hole in his closed doors.

" And if he sees," thought Griselda, " if he sees how hard I am trying to do my lessons well, it will perhaps make him be quick about ' considering.' "

So she did try very hard. And she didn't speak to the cuckoo when he came out to say it was four o'clock. She was busy, and he was busy. She felt it was better to wait till he gave her some sign of being ready to talk to her again.

For fairies, you know, children, however charming, are sometimes *rather* queer to have to do with.

They don't like to be interfered with, or treated except with very great respect, and they have their own ideas about what is proper and what isn't, I can assure you.

I suppose it was with working so hard at her lessons — most people would say it was with having been up the night before, running about the house in the moonlight; but as she had never felt so "fresh" in her life as when she got up that morning, it could hardly have been that — that Griselda felt so tired and sleepy that evening, she could hardly keep her eyes open. She begged to go to bed quite half an hour earlier than usual, which made Miss Tabitha afraid again that she was going to be ill. But as there is nothing better for children than to go to bed early, even if they *are* going to be ill, Miss Grizzel told her to say good-night, and to ask Dorcas to give her a wine-glassful of elder-berry wine, nice and hot, after she was in bed.

Griselda had no objection to the elderberry wine, though she felt she was having it on false pretences. She certainly did not need it to send her to sleep, for almost before her head touched the pillow she was as sound as a top. She had slept a good long while, when again she wakened suddenly — just as she had done the night before, and again with the feeling that something had wakened her. And the queer thing was that the moment she was awake she felt so *very* awake — she had no inclination to stretch and yawn and hope it wasn't quite time to get up, and think how nice and warm bed was, and how cold it was outside! She sat straight up, and peered out into the darkness, feeling quite ready for an adventure.

"Is it you, cuckoo?" she said softly.

There was no answer, but listening intently, the child fancied she heard a faint rustling or fluttering in the corner of the room by the door. She got up and, feeling her way, opened it, and the instant she had done so she heard, a few steps only in front of her it seemed, the familiar notes, very, *very* soft and whispered, "Cuckoo, cuckoo."

It went on and on, down the passage, Griselda trotting after. There was no moon to-night, heavy clouds had quite hidden it, and outside the rain was falling heavily. Griselda could hear it on the window-panes, through the closed shutters and all. But dark as it was, she made her way along without any difficulty, down the passage, across the great saloon, in through the ante-room door, guided only by the little voice now and then to be heard in front of her. She came to a standstill right before the clock, and stood there for a minute or two patiently waiting.

She had not very long to wait. There came the usual murmuring sound, then the doors above the clock face opened — she heard them open, it was far too dark to see — and in his ordinary voice, clear and distinct (it was just two o'clock, so the cuckoo was killing two birds with one stone, telling the hour and greeting Griselda at once), the bird sang out, "Cuckoo, cuckoo."

"Good evening, cuckoo," said Griselda, when he had finished.

"Good morning, you mean," said the cuckoo.

"Good morning, then, cuckoo," said Griselda. "Have you considered about me, cuckoo?"

The cuckoo cleared his throat.

"Have you learnt to obey orders yet, Griselda?" he inquired.

"I'm trying," replied Griselda. "But you see, cuckoo, I've not had very long to learn in — it was only last night you told me, you know."

The cuckoo sighed.

"You've a great deal to learn, Griselda."

"I dare say I have," she said. "But I can tell you one thing, cuckoo — whatever lessons I have, I *couldn't* ever have any worse than those addition sums of Mr. Kneebreeches'. I have made up my mind about that, for to-day, do you know, cuckoo —"

"Yesterday," corrected the cuckoo. "Always be exact in your statements, Griselda."

"Well, yesterday, then," said Griselda, rather tartly; "though when you know quite well what I mean, I don't see that you need be so *very* particular. Well, as I was saying, I tried and *tried*, but still they were fearful. They were, indeed."

"You've a great deal to learn, Griselda," repeated the cuckoo.

"I wish you wouldn't say that so often," said Griselda. "I thought you were going to *play* with me."

"There's something in that," said the cuckoo, "there's something in that. I should like to talk about it. But we could talk more comfortably if you would come up here and sit beside me."

Griselda thought her friend must be going out of his mind.

"Sit beside you up there!" she exclaimed. "Cuckoo, how *could* I? I'm far, far too big."

"Big!" returned the cuckoo. "What do you mean by big? It's all a matter of fancy. Don't you know that if the world and everything in it, counting yourself of course, was all made little enough to go into a walnut, you'd never find out the difference?"

"*Wouldn't* I?" said Griselda, feeling rather muddled; "but, *not* counting myself, cuckoo, I would then, wouldn't I?"

"Nonsense," said the cuckoo hastily; "you've a great deal to learn, and one thing is, not to *argue*. Nobody should argue; it's a shocking bad habit, and ruins the digestion. Come up here and sit beside me comfortably. Catch hold of the chain; you'll find you can manage if you try."

"But it'll stop the clock," said Griselda. "Aunt

Grizzel said I was never to touch the weights or the chains."

"Stuff," said the cuckoo; "it won't stop the clock. Catch hold of the chains and swing yourself up. There now — I told you you could manage it."

CHAPTER IV.

THE COUNTRY OF THE NODDING MANDARINS.

" We're all nodding, nid-nid-nodding."

How she managed it she never knew; but, somehow or other, it *was* managed. She seemed to slide up the chain just as easily as in a general way she would have slidden down, only without any disagreeable anticipation of a bump at the end of the journey. And when she got to the top how wonderfully different it looked from anything she could have expected! The doors stood open, and Griselda found them quite big enough, or herself quite small enough — which it was she couldn't tell, and as it was all a matter of fancy she decided not to trouble to inquire — to pass through quite comfortably.

And inside there was the most charming little snuggery imaginable. It was something like a saloon railway carriage — it seemed to be all lined and carpeted and everything, with rich mossy red velvet; there was a little round table in the middle and two arm-chairs, on one of which sat the cuckoo — " quite like other people," thought Griselda to herself — while the other, as he pointed out to Griselda by a little nod, was evidently intended for her.

"Thank you," said she, sitting down on the chair as she spoke.

"Are you comfortable?" inquired the cuckoo.

"Quite," replied Griselda, looking about her with great satisfaction. "Are all cuckoo clocks like this when you get up inside them?" she inquired. "I can't think how there's room for this dear little place between the clock and the wall. Is it a hole cut out of the wall on purpose, cuckoo?"

"Hush!" said the cuckoo, "we've got other things to talk about. First, shall I lend you one of my mantles? You may feel cold."

"I don't just now," replied Griselda; "but perhaps I *might*."

She looked at her little bare feet as she spoke, and wondered why *they* weren't cold, for it was very chilblainy weather.

The cuckoo stood up, and with one of his claws reached from a corner where it was hanging a cloak which Griselda had not before noticed. For it was hanging wrong side out, and the lining was red velvet, very like what the sides of the little room were covered with, so it was no wonder she had not noticed it.

Had it been hanging the *right* side out she must have done so; this side was so very wonderful!

It was all feathers — feathers of every shade and colour, but beautifully worked in, somehow, so as to lie quite smoothly and evenly, one colour melting away into another like those in a prism, so that you could hardly tell where one began and another ended.

"What a *lovely* cloak!" said Griselda, wrapping it round her and feeling even more comfortable than before, as she watched the rays of the little lamp in the roof — I think I was forgetting to tell you that the cuckoo's boudoir was lighted by a dear little lamp set into the red velvet roof like a pearl in a ring — playing softly on the brilliant colours of the feather mantle.

"It's better than lovely," said the cuckoo, "as you shall see. Now, Griselda," he continued, in the tone of one coming to business — "now, Griselda, let us talk."

"We have been talking," said Griselda, "ever so long. I am very comfortable. When you say 'let us talk' like that, it makes me forget all I wanted to say. Just let me sit still and say whatever comes into my head."

"That won't do," said the cuckoo; "we must have a plan of action."

"A what?" said Griselda.

"You see you *have* a great deal to learn," said the cuckoo triumphantly. "You don't understand what I say."

"But I didn't come up here to learn," said Griselda; "I can do that down there;" and she nodded her head in the direction of the ante-room table "I want to play."

"Just so," said the cuckoo; "that's what I want to talk about. What do you call 'play' — blind-man's-buff and that sort of thing?"

"No," said Griselda, considering. "I'm getting rather too big for that kind of play. Besides, cuckoo, you and I alone couldn't have much fun at blindman's-buff; there'd be only me to catch you or you to catch me."

"Oh, we could easily get more," said the cuckoo. "The mandarins would be pleased to join."

"The mandarins!" repeated Griselda. "Why, cuckoo, they're not alive! How could they play?"

The cuckoo looked at her gravely for a minute, then shook his head.

"You have a *great* deal to learn," he said solemnly. "Don't you know that *everything's* alive?"

"No," said Griselda, "I don't; and I don't know what you mean, and I don't think I want to know what you mean. I want to talk about playing."

"Well," said the cuckoo, "talk."

"What I call playing," pursued Griselda, "is — I have thought about it now, you see — is being amused. If you will amuse me, cuckoo, I will count that you are playing with me."

"How shall I amuse you?" inquired he.

"Oh, that's for you to find out!" exclaimed Griselda. "You might tell me fairy stories, you know: if you're a fairy you should know lots; or — oh yes, of course that would be far nicer — if you are a fairy you might take me with you to fairyland."

Again the cuckoo shook his head.

"That," said he, "I cannot do."

"Why not?" said Griselda. "Lots of children have been there."

"I doubt it," said the cuckoo. "*Some* may have been, but not lots. And some may have thought they had been there who hadn't really been there at all. And as to those who have been there, you may be sure of one thing — they were not *taken*, they found their own way. No one ever was *taken* to fairyland — to the real fairyland. They may have been taken to the neighbouring countries, but not to fairyland itself."

"And how is one ever to find one's own way there?" asked Griselda.

"That I cannot tell you either," replied the cuckoo. "There are many roads there; you may find yours some day. And if ever you do find it, be sure you keep what you see of it well swept and clean, and then you may see further after a while. Ah, yes, there are many roads and many doors into fairy-land!"

"Doors!" cried Griselda. "Are there any doors into fairyland in this house?"

"Several," said the cuckoo; "but don't waste your time looking for them at present. It would be no use."

"Then how will you amuse me?" inquired Griselda, in a rather disappointed tone.

"Don't you care to go anywhere except to fairy-land?" said the cuckoo.

"Oh yes, there are lots of places I wouldn't mind seeing. Not geography sort of places — it would be just like lessons to go to India and Africa and all those places — but *queer* places, like the mines where the goblins make diamonds and precious stones, and the caves down under the sea where the mermaids live. And — oh, I've just thought — now I'm so nice and little, I *would* like to go all over the mandarins' palace in the great saloon."

"That can be easily managed," said the cuckoo; "but — excuse me for an instant," he exclaimed suddenly. He gave a spring forward and disappeared. Then Griselda heard his voice outside the doors. "Cuckoo, cuckoo, cuckoo." It was three o'clock.

The doors opened again to let him through, and he re-settled himself on his chair. "As I was saying," he went on, "nothing could be easier. But that palace, as you call it, has an entrance on the other side, as well as the one you know."

"Another door, do you mean?" said Griselda. "How funny! Does it go through the wall? And where does it lead to?"

"It leads," replied the cuckoo, "it leads to the country of the Nodding Mandarins."

"*What* fun!" exclaimed Griselda, clapping her hands. "Cuckoo, do let us go there. How can we get down? You can fly, but must I slide down the chain again?"

"Oh dear, no," said the cuckoo, "by no means. You have only to stretch out your feather mantle, flap it as if it was wings — so " — he flapped his own wings encouragingly — "wish, and there you'll be."

"Where?" said Griselda bewilderedly.

"Wherever you wish to be, of course," said the cuckoo. "Are you ready? Here goes."

"Wait — wait a moment," cried Griselda. "Where am I to wish to be?"

"Bless the child!" exclaimed the cuckoo. "Where *do* you wish to be? You said you wanted to visit the country of the Nodding Mandarins."

"Yes; but am I to wish first to be in the palace in the great saloon?"

"Certainly," replied the cuckoo. "That is the entrance to Mandarin Land, and you said you would like to see through it. So — you're surely ready now?"

"A thought has just struck me," said Griselda. "How will you know what o'clock it is, so as to come back in time to tell the next hour? My aunts will get into such a fright if you go wrong again! Are you sure we shall have time to go to the mandarins' country to-night?"

MANDARINS NODDING. — p. 49.

"Time!" repeated the cuckoo; "what is time? Ah, Griselda, you have a *very* great deal to learn! What do you mean by time?"

"I don't know," replied Griselda, feeling rather snubbed. "Being slow or quick — I suppose that's what I mean."

"And what is slow, and what is quick?" said the cuckoo. "*All* a matter of fancy! If everything that's been done since the world was made till now, was done over again in five minutes, you'd never know the difference."

"Oh, cuckoo, I wish you wouldn't!" cried poor Griselda; "you're worse than sums, you do so puzzle me. It's like what you said about nothing being big or little, only it's worse. Where would all the days and hours be if there was nothing but minutes? Oh, cuckoo, you said you'd amuse me, and you do nothing but puzzle me."

"It was your own fault. You wouldn't get ready," said the cuckoo. "*Now*, here goes! Flap and wish."

Griselda flapped and wished. She felt a sort of rustle in the air, that was all — then she found herself standing with the cuckoo in front of the Chinese cabinet, the door of which stood open, while the mandarins on each side, nodding politely, seemed to invite them to enter. Griselda hesitated.

"Go on," said the cuckoo, patronizingly; "ladies first."

Griselda went on. To her surprise, inside the cabinet it was quite light, though where the light came from that illuminated all the queer corners and recesses and streamed out to the front, where stood the mandarins, she could not discover.

The "palace" was not quite as interesting as she had expected. There were lots of little rooms in it opening on to balconies commanding, no doubt, a splendid view of the great saloon; there were ever so many little staircases leading to more little rooms and balconies; but it all seemed empty and deserted.

"I don't care for it," said Griselda, stopping short at last; "it's all the same, and there's nothing to see. I thought my aunts kept ever so many beautiful things in here, and there's nothing."

"Come along, then," said the cuckoo. "I didn't expect you'd care for the palace, as you called it, much. Let us go out the other way."

He hopped down a sort of little staircase near which they were standing, and Griselda followed him willingly enough. At the foot they found themselves in a vestibule, much handsomer than the entrance at the other side, and the cuckoo, crossing it, lifted one of his claws and touched a spring in the wall. Instantly a pair of large doors flew open in the middle, revealing to Griselda the prettiest and most curious sight she had ever seen.

A flight of wide shallow steps led down from this

doorway into a long, long avenue bordered by stiffly growing trees, from the branches of which hung innumerable lamps of every colour, making a perfect network of brilliance as far as the eye could reach.

"Oh, how lovely!" cried Griselda, clapping her hands. "It'll be like walking along a rainbow. Cuckoo, come quick."

"Stop," said the cuckoo; "we've a good way to go. There's no need to walk. Palanquin!"

He flapped his wings, and instantly a palanquin appeared at the foot of the steps. It was made of carved ivory, and borne by four Chinese-looking figures with pigtails and bright-coloured jackets. A feeling came over Griselda that she was dreaming, or else that she had seen this palanquin before. She hesitated. Suddenly she gave a little jump of satisfaction.

"I know," she exclaimed. "It's exactly like the one that stands under a glass shade on Lady Lavander's drawing-room mantelpiece. I wonder if it is the very one? Fancy me being able to get *into* it!"

She looked at the four bearers. Instantly they all nodded.

"What do they mean?" asked Griselda, turning to the cuckoo.

"Get in," he replied.

"Yes, I'm just going to get in," she said; "but

what do *they* mean when they nod at me like
that?"

"They mean, of course, what I tell you — 'Get
in,'" said the cuckoo.

"Why don't they say so, then?" persisted Griselda, getting in, however, as she spoke.

"Griselda, you have a *very* great — " began the
cuckoo, but Griselda interrupted him.

"Cuckoo," she exclaimed, "if you say that again,
I'll jump out of the palanquin and run away home to
bed. Of course I've a great deal to learn — that's
why I like to ask questions about everything I see.
Now, tell me where we are going."

"In the first place," said the cuckoo, "are you
comfortable?"

"Very," said Griselda, settling herself down
among the cushions.

It was a change from the cuckoo's boudoir. There
were no chairs or seats, only a number of very, *very*
soft cushions covered with green silk. There were
green silk curtains all round, too, which you could
draw or not as you pleased, just by touching a spring.
Griselda stroked the silk gently. It was not "fruz-
zley" silk, if you know what that means; it did not
make you feel as if your nails wanted cutting, or as
if all the rough places on your skin were being
rubbed up the wrong way; its softness was like that
of a rose or pansy petal.

"What nice silk!" said Griselda. "I'd like a

dress of it. I never noticed that the palanquin was
lined so nicely," she continued, "for I suppose it *is*
the one from Lady Lavander's mantelpiece? There
couldn't be two so exactly like each other."

The cuckoo gave a sort of whistle.

"What a goose you are, my dear!" he exclaimed.
"Excuse me," he continued, seeing that Griselda
looked rather offended; "I didn't mean to hurt your
feelings, but you won't let me say the other thing,
you know. The palanquin from Lady Lavander's!
I should think not. You might as well mistake one
of those horrible paper roses that Dorcas sticks in
her vases for one of your aunt's Gloires de Dijon!
The palanquin from Lady Lavander's — a clumsy
human imitation not worth looking at!"

"I didn't know," said Griselda humbly. "Do
they make such beautiful things in Mandarin
Land?"

"Of course," said the cuckoo.

Griselda sat silent for a minute or two, but very
soon she recovered her spirits.

"Will you please tell me where we are going?"
she asked again.

"You'll see directly," said the cuckoo; "not that
I mind telling you. There's to be a grand reception
at one of the palaces to-night. I thought you'd like
to assist at it. It'll give you some idea of what a
palace is like. By-the-by, can you dance?"

"A little," replied Griselda.

"Ah, well, I dare say you will manage. I've ordered a court dress for you. It will be all ready when we get there."

"Thank you," said Griselda.

In a minute or two the palanquin stopped. The cuckoo got out, and Griselda followed him.

She found that they were at the entrance to a *very* much grander palace than the one in her aunt's saloon. The steps leading up to the door were very wide and shallow, and covered with a gold embroidered carpet, which *looked* as if it would be prickly to her bare feet, but which, on the contrary, when she trod upon it, felt softer than the softest moss. She could see very little besides the carpet, for at each side of the steps stood rows and rows of mandarins, all something like, but a great deal grander than, the pair outside her aunt's cabinet; and as the cuckoo hopped and Griselda walked up the staircase, they all, in turn, row by row, began solemnly to nod. It gave them the look of a field of very high grass, through which, any one passing, leaves for the moment a trail, till all the heads bob up again into their places.

"What do they mean?" whispered Griselda.

"It's a royal salute," said the cuckoo.

"A salute!" said Griselda. "I thought that meant kissing or guns."

"Hush!" said the cuckoo, for by this time they had arrived at the top of the staircase; "you must be dressed now."

Two mandariny-looking young ladies, with porcelain faces and three-cornered head-dresses, stepped forward and led Griselda into a small ante-room, where lay waiting for her the most magnificent dress you ever saw. But how *do* you think they dressed her? It was all by nodding. They nodded to the blue and silver embroidered jacket, and in a moment it had fitted itself on to her. They nodded to the splendid scarlet satin skirt, made very short in front and very long behind, and before Griselda knew where she was, it was adjusted quite correctly. They nodded to the head-dress, and the sashes, and the necklaces and bracelets, and forthwith they all arranged themselves. Last of all, they nodded to the dearest, sweetest little pair of high-heeled shoes imaginable — all silver, and blue, and gold, and scarlet, and everything mixed up together, *only* they were rather a stumpy shape about the toes, and Griselda's bare feet were encased in them, and, to her surprise, quite comfortably so.

"They don't hurt me a bit," she said aloud; "yet they didn't look the least the shape of my foot."

But her attendants only nodded; and turning round, she saw the cuckoo waiting for her. He did not speak either, rather to her annoyance, but gravely led the way through one grand room after another to the grandest of all, where the entertainment was evidently just about to begin. And everywhere there were mandarins, rows and rows, who all set to work nodding as fast as Griselda appeared. She began to be rather tired of royal salutes, and was glad when, at last, in profound silence, the procession, consisting of the cuckoo and herself, and about half a dozen "mandarins," came to a halt before a kind of daïs, or raised seat, at the end of the hall.

Upon this daïs stood a chair — a throne of some kind, Griselda supposed it to be — and upon this was seated the grandest and gravest personage she had yet seen.

"Is he the king of the mandarins?" she whispered. But the cuckoo did not reply; and before she had time to repeat the question, the very grand and grave person got down from his seat, and coming towards her, offered her his hand, at the same time nodding — first once, then two or three times together, then once again. Griselda seemed to know what he meant. He was asking her to dance.

"Thank you," she said. "I can't dance *very* well, but perhaps you won't mind."

The king, if that was his title, took not the slightest notice of her reply, but nodded again — once, then two or three times together, then once alone, just as before. Griselda did not know what to do, when suddenly she felt something poking her head. It was the cuckoo — he had lifted his claw, and was tapping her head to make her nod. So she nodded — once, twice together, then once — that appeared to be enough. The king nodded once again; an invisible band suddenly struck up the loveliest music, and off they set to the places of honour reserved for them in the centre of the room, where all the mandarins were assembling.

What a dance that was! It began like a minuet and ended something like the hay-makers. Griselda had not the least idea what the figures or steps were, but it did not matter. If she did not know, her shoes or something about her did; for she got on famously. The music was lovely — "so the mandarins can't be deaf, though they are dumb," thought Griselda, "which is one good thing about them." The king seemed to enjoy it as much as she did, though he never smiled or laughed; any one could have seen he liked it by the way he whirled and twirled himself about. And between the figures, when they stopped to rest for a little, Griselda got on very well too. There was no conversation, or rather, if there was, it was all nodding.

So Griselda nodded too, and though she did not know what her nods meant, the king seemed to understand and be quite pleased; and when they had nodded enough, the music struck up again, and off they set, harder than before.

And every now and then tiny little mandariny boys appeared with trays filled with the most delicious fruits and sweetmeats. Griselda was not a greedy child, but for once in her life she really *did* feel rather so. I cannot possibly describe these delicious things; just think of whatever in all your life was the most "lovely" thing you ever eat, and you may be sure they tasted like that. Only the cuckoo would not eat any, which rather distressed Griselda. He walked about among the dancers, apparently quite at home; and the mandarins did not seem at all surprised to see him, though he did look rather odd, being nearly, if not quite, as big as any of them. Griselda hoped he was enjoying himself, considering that she had to thank him for all the fun *she* was having, but she felt a little conscience-stricken when she saw that he wouldn't eat anything.

"Cuckoo," she whispered; she dared not talk out loud — it would have seemed so remarkable, you see. "Cuckoo," she said, very, very softly, "I wish you would eat something. You'll be so tired and hungry."

"No, thank you," said the cuckoo; and you can't think how pleased Griselda was at having succeeded in making him speak. "It isn't my way. I hope you are enjoying yourself?"

"Oh, *very* much," said Griselda. "I — "

"Hush!" said the cuckoo; and looking up, Griselda saw a number of mandarins, in a sort of procession, coming their way.

When they got up to the cuckoo they set to work nodding, two or three at a time, more energetically than usual. When they stopped, the cuckoo nodded in return, and then hopped off towards the middle of the room.

"They're very fond of good music, you see," he whispered as he passed Griselda; "and they don't often get it."

CHAPTER V.

" And she is always beautiful,
   And always is eighteen ! "

WHEN he got to the middle of the room the cuckoo
cleared his throat, flapped his wings, and began to
sing. Griselda was quite astonished. She had had
no idea that her friend was so accomplished. It
wasn't "cuckooing" at all; it was real singing, like
that of the nightingale or the thrush, or like something prettier than either. It made Griselda think
of woods in summer, and of tinkling brooks flowing
through them, with the pretty brown pebbles sparkling up through the water; and then it made her
think of something sad — she didn't know what;
perhaps it was of the babes in the wood and the
robins covering them up with leaves — and then
again, in a moment, it sounded as if all the merry
elves and sprites that ever were heard of had escaped
from fairyland, and were rolling over and over with
peals of rollicking laughter. And at last, all of a
sudden, the song came to an end.

"Cuckoo! cuckoo! cuckoo!" rang out three
times, clear and shrill. The cuckoo flapped his

wings, made a bow to the mandarins, and retired to his old corner.

There was no buzz of talk, as is usual after a performance has come to a close, but there was a great buzz of nodding, and Griselda, wishing to give the cuckoo as much praise as she could, nodded as hard as any of them. The cuckoo really looked quite shy at receiving so much applause. But in a minute or two the music struck up and the dancing began again — one, two, three: it seemed a sort of mazurka this time, which suited the mandarins very well, as it gave them a chance of nodding to mark the time.

Griselda had once learnt the mazurka, so she got on even better than before — only she would have liked it more if her shoes had had sharper toes; they looked so stumpy when she tried to point them. All the same, it was very good fun, and she was not too well pleased when she suddenly felt the little sharp tap of the cuckoo on her head, and heard him whisper —

" Griselda, it's time to go."

" Oh dear, why?" she asked. "I'm not a bit tired. Why need we go yet?"

" Obeying orders," said the cuckoo; and after that, Griselda dared not say another word. It was very nearly as bad as being told she had a great deal to learn.

" Must I say good-bye to the king and all the people?" she inquired; but before the cuckoo had time to answer, she gave a little squeal. "Oh, cuckoo," she cried, "you've trod on my foot."

"I beg your pardon," said the cuckoo.

"I must take off my shoe; it does so hurt," she went on.

"Take it off, then," said the cuckoo.

Griselda stooped to take off her shoe. "Are we going home in the pal——?" she began to say; but she never finished the sentence, for just as she had got her shoe off she felt the cuckoo throw something round her. It was the feather mantle.

And Griselda knew nothing more till she opened her eyes the next morning, and saw the first early rays of sunshine peeping in through the chinks of the closed shutters of her little bedroom.

She rubbed her eyes, and sat up in bed. Could it have been a dream?

"What could have made me fall asleep so all of a sudden?" she thought. "I wasn't the least sleepy at the mandarins' ball. What fun it was! I believe that cuckoo made me fall asleep on purpose to make me fancy it was a dream. *Was* it a dream?"

She began to feel confused and doubtful, when suddenly she felt something hurting her arm, like a little lump in the bed. She felt with her hand to see if she could smooth it away, and drew out — one of the shoes belonging to her court dress! The very one she had held in her hand at the moment the cuckoo spirited her home again to bed.

"Ah, Mr. Cuckoo!" she exclaimed, "you meant to play me a trick, but you haven't succeeded, you see."

She jumped out of bed and unfastened one of the window-shutters, then jumped in again to admire the little shoe in comfort. It was even prettier than she had thought it at the ball. She held it up and looked at it. It was about the size of the first joint of her little finger. "To think that I should have been dancing with you on last night!" she said to the shoe. "And yet the cuckoo says being big or little is all a matter of fancy. I wonder what he'll think of to amuse me next?"

She was still holding up the shoe and admiring it when Dorcas came with the hot water.

"Look, Dorcas," she said.

"Bless me, it's one of the shoes off the Chinese dolls in the saloon," exclaimed the old servant. "How ever did you get that, missie? Your aunts wouldn't be pleased."

"It just isn't one of the Chinese dolls' shoes, and if you don't believe me, you can go and look for yourself." said Griselda. "It's my very own shoe, and it was given me to my own self."

Dorcas looked at her curiously, but said no more, only as she was going out of the room Griselda heard her saying something about "so very like Miss Sybilla."

"I wonder what 'Miss Sybilla' *was* like?"

thought Griselda. "I have a good mind to ask the cuckoo. He seems to have known her very well."

It was not for some days that Griselda had a chance of asking the cuckoo anything. She saw and heard nothing of him — nothing, that is to say, but his regular appearance to tell the hours as usual.

"I suppose," thought Griselda, "he thinks the mandarins' ball was fun enough to last me a good while. It really was very good-natured of him to take me to it, so I mustn't grumble."

A few days after this poor Griselda caught cold. It was not a very bad cold, I must confess, but her aunts made rather a fuss about it. They wanted her to stay in bed, but to this Griselda so much objected that they did not insist upon it.

"It would be so dull," she said piteously. "Please let me stay in the ante-room, for all my things are there; and, then, there's the cuckoo."

Aunt Grizzel smiled at this, and Griselda got her way. But even in the ante-room it was rather dull. Miss Grizzel and Miss Tabitha were obliged to go out, to drive all the way to Merrybrow Hall, as Lady Lavander sent a messenger to say that she had an attack of influenza, and wished to see her friends at once.

Miss Tabitha began to cry — she was so tender-hearted.

"Troubles never come singly," said Miss Grizzel, by way of consolation.

"No, indeed, they never come singly," said Miss Tabitha, shaking her head and wiping her eyes.

So off they set; and Griselda, in her arm-chair by the ante-room fire, with some queer little old-fashioned books of her aunts', which she had already read more than a dozen times, beside her by way of amusement, felt that there was one comfort in her troubles — she had escaped the long weary drive to her godmother's.

But it was very dull. It got duller and duller. Griselda curled herself up in her chair, and wished she could go to sleep, though feeling quite sure she couldn't, for she had stayed in bed much later than usual this morning, and had been obliged to spend the time in sleeping, for want of anything better to do.

She looked up at the clock.

"I don't know even what to wish for," she said to herself. "I don't feel the least inclined to play at anything, and I shouldn't care to go to the mandarins again. Oh, cuckoo, cuckoo, I am so dull; couldn't you think of anything to amuse me?"

It was not near "any o'clock." But after waiting a minute or two, it seemed to Griselda that she heard the soft sound of "coming" that always preceded the cuckoo's appearance. She was right. In another moment she heard his usual greeting, "Cuckoo, cuckoo!"

"Oh, cuckoo!" she exclaimed, "I am so glad you have come at last. I *am* so dull, and it has nothing to do with lessons this time. It's that I've got such a bad cold, and my head's aching, and I'm so tired of reading, all by myself."

"What would you like to do?" said the cuckoo. "You don't want to go to see the mandarins again?"

"Oh no; I couldn't dance."

"Or the mermaids down under the sea?"

"Oh, dear, no," said Griselda, with a little shiver, "it would be far too cold. I would just like to stay where I am, if some one would tell me stories. I'm not even sure that I could listen to stories. What could you do to amuse me, cuckoo?"

"Would you like to see some pictures?" said the cuckoo. "I could show you pictures without your taking any trouble."

"Oh yes, that would be beautiful," cried Griselda. "What pictures will you show me? Oh, I know. I would like to see the place where you were born — where that very, very clever man made you and the clock, I mean."

"Your great-great-grandfather," said the cuckoo. "Very well. Now, Griselda, shut your eyes. First of all, I am going to sing."

Griselda shut her eyes, and the cuckoo began his song. It was something like what he had sung at the mandarins' palace, only even more beautiful. It was so soft and dreamy, Griselda felt as if she could have sat there for ever, listening to it.

The first notes were low and murmuring. Again they made Griselda think of little rippling brooks in summer, and now and then there came a sort of hum as of insects buzzing in the warm sunshine near. This humming gradually increased, till at last Griselda was conscious of nothing more — *everything* seemed to be humming, herself too, till at last she fell asleep.

When she opened her eyes, the ante-room and everything in it, except the arm-chair on which she was still curled up, had disappeared — melted away into a misty cloud all round her, which in turn gradually faded, till before her she saw a scene quite new and strange. It was the first of the cuckoo's "pictures."

An old, quaint room, with a high, carved mantel-piece, and a bright fire sparkling in the grate. It was not a pretty room — it had more the look of a workshop of some kind; but it was curious and interesting. All round, the walls were hung with clocks and strange mechanical toys. There was a fiddler slowly fiddling, a gentleman and lady gravely dancing a minuet, a little man drawing up water in a bucket out of a glass vase in which gold fish were swimming about — all sorts of queer figures; and the clocks were even queerer. There was one intended to represent the sun, moon, and planets, with one face for the sun and another for the moon, and gold and silver stars slowly circling round them; there was another clock with a tiny trumpeter perched on a ledge above the face, who blew a horn for the hours. I cannot tell you half the strange and wonderful things there were.

Griselda was so interested in looking at all these queer machines, that she did not for some time observe the occupant of the room. And no wonder; he was sitting in front of a little table, so perfectly still, much more still than the un-living figures around him. He was examining, with a magnifying glass, some small object he held in his hand, so closely and intently that Griselda, forgetting she was only looking at a "picture," almost held her breath for fear she should disturb him. He was a very old man, his coat was worn and threadbare in several places, looking as if he spent a great part of his life in one position. Yet he did not look *poor*, and his face, when at last he lifted it, was mild and intelligent and very earnest.

While Griselda was watching him closely there came a soft tap at the door, and a little girl danced into the room. The dearest little girl you ever saw, and *so* funnily dressed! Her thick brown hair, rather lighter than Griselda's, was tied in two long plaits down her back. She had a short red skirt with silver braid round the bottom, and a white chemisette with beautiful lace at the throat and wrists, and over that again a black velvet bodice, also trimmed with silver. And she had a great many trinkets, necklaces, and bracelets, and ear-rings, and a sort of little silver coronet; no, it was not like a coronet, it was a band with a square piece of silver fastened so as to stand up at each side of her head something like a horse's blinkers, only they were not placed over her eyes.

She made quite a jingle as she came into the room, and the old man looked up with a smile of pleasure.

"Well, my darling, and are you all ready for your *fête?*" he said; and though the language in which he spoke was quite strange to Griselda, she understood his meaning perfectly well.

"Yes, dear grandfather; and isn't my dress lovely?" said the child. "I should be *so* happy if only you were coming too, and would get yourself a beautiful velvet coat like Mynheer van Huyten."

The old man shook his head.

"I have no time for such things, my darling," he replied; "and besides, I am too old. I must work — work hard to make money for my pet when I am gone, that she may not be dependent on the bounty of those English sisters."

"But I won't care for money when you are gone, grandfather," said the child, her eyes filling with tears. "I would rather just go on living in this little house, and I am sure the neighbours would

give me something to eat, and then I could hear all
your clocks ticking, and think of you. I don't want
you to sell all your wonderful things for money for
me, grandfather. They would remind me of you,
and money wouldn't."

"Not all, Sybilla, not all," said the old man.
"The best of all, the *chef-d'œuvre* of my life, shall
not be sold. It shall be yours, and you will have in
your possession a clock that crowned heads might
seek in vain to purchase."

His dim old eyes brightened, and for a moment he
sat erect and strong.

"Do you mean the cuckoo clock?" said Sybilla,
in a low voice.

"Yes, my darling, the cuckoo clock, the crowning
work of my life — a clock that shall last long after I,
and perhaps thou, my pretty child, are crumbling
into dust; a clock that shall last to tell my great-
grandchildren to many generations that the old
Dutch mechanic was not altogether to be despised."

Sybilla sprang into his arms.

"You are not to talk like that, little grandfather,"
she said. "I shall teach my children and my grandchildren to be so proud of you — oh, so proud! — as
proud as I am of you, little grandfather."

"Gently, my darling," said the old man, as he
placed carefully on the table the delicate piece of
mechanism he held in his hand, and tenderly
embraced the child. "Kiss me once again, my pet,

and then thou must go; thy little friends will be waiting."

* * * * *

As he said these words the mist slowly gathered again before Griselda's eyes — the first of the cuckoo's pictures faded from her sight.

* * * * *

When she looked again the scene was changed, but this time it was not a strange one, though Griselda had gazed at it for some moments before she recognised it. It was the great saloon, but it looked very different from what she had ever seen it. Forty years or so make a difference in rooms as well as in people!

The faded yellow damask hangings were rich and brilliant. There were bouquets of lovely flowers arranged about the tables; wax lights were sending out their brightness in every direction, and the room was filled with ladies and gentlemen in gay attire.

Among them, after a time, Griselda remarked two ladies, no longer very young, but still handsome and stately, and something whispered to her that they were her two aunts, Miss Grizzel and Miss Tabitha.

"Poor aunts!" she said softly to herself; "how old they have grown since then."

But she did not long look at them; her attention was attracted by a much younger lady — a mere girl she seemed, but oh, so sweet and pretty! She was dancing with a gentleman whose eyes looked as if they saw no one else, and she herself seemed brimming over with youth and happiness. Her very steps had joy in them.

"Well, Griselda," whispered a voice, which she knew was the cuckoo's; "so you don't like to be told you are like your grandmother, eh?"

Griselda turned round sharply to look for the speaker, but he was not to be seen. And when she turned again, the picture of the great saloon had faded away.

*   *   *   *   *

One more picture.

Griselda looked again. She saw before her a country road in full summer time; the sun was shining, the birds were singing, the trees covered with their bright green leaves — everything appeared happy and joyful. But at last in the distance she saw, slowly approaching, a group of a few people, all walking together, carrying in their centre something long and narrow, which, though the black cloth covering it was almost hidden by the white flowers with which it was thickly strewn, Griselda knew to be a coffin.

It was a funeral procession, and in the place of chief mourner, with pale, set face, walked the same young man whom Griselda had last seen dancing with the girl Sybilla in the great saloon.

The sad group passed slowly out of sight; but as

it disappeared there fell upon the ear the sounds of sweet music, lovelier far than she had heard before — lovelier than the magic cuckoo's most lovely songs — and somehow, in the music, it seemed to the child's fancy there were mingled the soft strains of a woman's voice.

"It is Sybilla singing," thought Griselda dreamily, and with that she fell asleep again.

*   *   *   *   *

When she woke she was in the arm-chair by the ante-room fire, everything around her looking just as usual, the cuckoo clock ticking away calmly and regularly. Had it been a dream only? Griselda could not make up her mind.

"But I don't see that it matters if it was," she said to herself. "If it was a dream, the cuckoo sent it to me all the same, and I thank you very much indeed, cuckoo," she went on, looking up at the clock. "The last picture was rather sad, but still it was very nice to see it, and I thank you very much, and I'll never say again that I don't like to be told I'm like my dear pretty grandmother."

The cuckoo took no notice of what she said, but Griselda did not mind. She was getting used to his " ways."

"I expect he hears me quite well," she thought; "and even if he doesn't, it's only civil to *try* to thank him."

She sat still contentedly enough, thinking over what she had seen, and trying to make more " pictures " for herself in the fire. Then there came faintly to her ears the sound of carriage wheels, opening and shutting of doors, a little bustle of arrival.

"My aunts must have come back," thought Griselda; and so it was. In a few minutes Miss Grizzel, closely followed by Miss Tabitha, appeared at the ante-room door.

"Well, my love," said Miss Grizzel anxiously, "and how are you? Has the time seemed very long while we were away?"

"Oh no, thank you, Aunt Grizzel," replied Griselda, "not at all. I've been quite happy, and my cold's ever so much better, and my headache's *quite* gone."

"Come, that is good news," said Miss Grizzel. "Not that I'm exactly *surprised*," she continued, turning to Miss Tabitha, "for there really is nothing like tansy tea for a feverish cold."

"Nothing," agreed Miss Tabitha; "there really is nothing like it."

"Aunt Grizzel," said Griselda, after a few moments' silence, "was my grandmother quite young when she died?"

"Yes, my love, very young," replied Miss Grizzel with a change in her voice.

"And was her husband *very* sorry?" pursued Griselda.

"My Aunts must have come back!"—p. 74.

"Heart-broken," said Miss Grizzel. "He did not live long after, and then you know, my dear, your father was sent to us to take care of. And now he has sent *you* — the third generation of young creatures confided to our care."

"Yes," said Griselda. "My grandmother died in the summer, when all the flowers were out; and she was buried in a pretty country place, wasn't she?"

"Yes," said Miss Grizzel, looking rather bewildered.

"And when she was a little girl she lived with her grandfather, the old Dutch mechanic," continued Griselda, unconsciously using the very words she had heard in her vision. "He was a nice old man; and how clever of him to have made the cuckoo clock, and such lots of other pretty, wonderful things. I don't wonder little Sybilla loved him; he was so good to her. But, oh, Aunt Grizzel, *how* pretty she was when she was a young lady! That time that she danced with my grandfather in the great saloon. And how very nice you and Aunt Tabitha looked then, too."

Miss Grizzel held her very breath in astonishment; and no doubt if Miss Tabitha had known she was doing so, she would have held hers too. But Griselda lay still, gazing at the fire, quite unconscious of her aunt's surprise.

"Your papa told you all these old stories, I suppose, my dear," said Miss Grizzel at last.

"Oh no," said Griselda dreamily. "Papa never told me anything like that. Dorcas told me a very little, I think; at least, she made me want to know, and I asked the cuckoo, and then, you see, he showed me it all. It was so pretty."

Miss Grizzel glanced at her sister.

"Tabitha, my dear," she said in a low voice, "do you hear?"

And Miss Tabitha, who really was not very deaf when she set herself to hear, nodded in awestruck silence.

"Tabitha," continued Miss Grizzel in the same tone, "it is wonderful! Ah, yes, how true it is, Tabitha, that 'there are more things in heaven and earth than are dreamt of in our philosophy'" (for Miss Grizzel was a well-read old lady, you see); "and from the very first, Tabitha, we always had a feeling that the child was strangely like Sybilla."

"Strangely like Sybilla," echoed Miss Tabitha.

"May she grow up as good, if not quite as beautiful—*that* we could scarcely expect; and may she be longer spared to those that love her," added Miss Grizzel, bending over Griselda, while two or three tears slowly trickled down her aged cheeks. "See, Tabitha, the dear child is fast asleep. How sweet she looks! I trust by to-morrow morning she will be quite herself again; her cold is so much better."

CHAPTER VI.

RUBBED THE WRONG WAY.

"For now and then there comes a day
 When everything goes wrong."

GRISELDA'S cold *was* much better by "to-morrow morning." In fact, I might almost say it was quite well.

But Griselda herself did not feel quite well, and saying this reminds me that it is hardly sense to speak of a *cold* being better or well — for a cold's being "well" means that it is not there at all, out of existence, in short, and if a thing is out of existence how can we say anything about it? Children, I feel quite in a hobble — I cannot get my mind straight about it — please think it over and give me your opinion. In the meantime, I will go on about Griselda.

She felt just a little ill — a sort of feeling that sometimes is rather nice, sometimes "very extremely" much the reverse! She felt in the humour for being petted, and having beef-tea, and jelly, and sponge cake with her tea, and for a day or two this was all very well. She *was* petted, and she had lots of beef-tea, and jelly, and grapes, and sponge cakes, and everything nice, for her aunts, as you must have seen by this time, were really very, very kind to her in every way in which they understood how to be so.

But after a few days of the continued petting, and the beef-tea and the jelly and all the rest of it, it occurred to Miss Grizzel, who had a good large bump of "common sense," that it might be possible to overdo this sort of thing.

"Tabitha," she said to her sister, when they were sitting together in the evening after Griselda had gone to bed, "Tabitha, my dear, I think the child is quite well again now. It seems to me it would be well to send a note to good Mr. Kneebreeches, to say that she will be able to resume her studies the day after to-morrow."

"The day after to-morrow," repeated Miss Tabitha. "The day after to-morrow — to say that she will be able to resume her studies the day after to-morrow — oh yes, certainly. It would be very well to send a note to good Mr. Kneebreeches, my dear Grizzel."

"I thought you would agree with me," said Miss Grizzel, with a sigh of relief (as if poor Miss Tabitha during all the last half-century had ever ventured to do anything else), getting up to fetch her writing materials as she spoke. "It is such a satisfaction to consult together about what we do. I was only a little afraid of being hard upon the child, but as you agree with me, I have no longer any misgiving."

"Any misgiving, oh dear, no!" said Miss Tabitha.

" You have no reason for any misgiving, I am sure, my dear Grizzel."

So the note was written and despatched, and the next morning when, about twelve o'clock, Griselda made her appearance in the little drawing-room where her aunts usually sat, looking, it must be confessed, very plump and rosy for an invalid, Miss Grizzel broached the subject.

" I have written to request Mr. Kneebreeches to resume his instructions to-morrow," she said quietly. "I think you are quite well again now, so Dorcas must wake you at your usual hour."

Griselda had been settling herself comfortably on a corner of the sofa. She had got a nice book to read, which her father, hearing of her illness, had sent her by post, and she was looking forward to the tempting plateful of jelly which Dorcas had brought her for luncheon every day since she had been ill. Altogether, she was feeling very "lazy-easy" and contented. Her aunt's announcement felt like a sudden downpour of cold water, or rush of east wind. She sat straight up in her sofa, and exclaimed in a tone of great annoyance —

" *Oh*, Aunt Grizzel ! "

" Well, my dear ? " said Miss Grizzel, placidly.

" I *wish* you wouldn't make me begin lessons again just yet. I *know* they'll make my head ache again, and Mr. Kneebreeches will be *so* cross. I know he will, and he is so horrid when he is cross."

"Hush!" said Miss Grizzel, holding up her hand in a way that reminded Griselda of the cuckoo's favourite "obeying orders." Just then, too, in the distance the ante-room clock struck twelve. "Cuckoo! cuckoo! cuckoo!" on it went. Griselda could have stamped with irritation, but *somehow*, in spite of herself, she felt compelled to say nothing. She muttered some not very pretty words, coiled herself round on the sofa, opened her book, and began to read.

But it was not as interesting as she had expected. She had not read many pages before she began to yawn, and she was delighted to be interrupted by Dorcas and the jelly.

But the jelly was not as nice as she had expected, either. She tasted it, and thought it was too sweet; and when she tasted it again, it seemed too strong of cinnamon; and the third taste seemed too strong of everything. She laid down her spoon, and looked about her discontentedly.

"What is the matter, my dear?" said Miss Grizzel. "Is the jelly not to your liking?"

"I don't know," said Griselda shortly. She ate a few spoonfuls, and then took up her book again. Miss Grizzel said nothing more, but to herself she thought that Mr. Kneebreeches had not been recalled any too soon.

All day long it was much the same. Nothing seemed to come right to Griselda. It was a dull, cold day, what is called "a black frost;" not a bright, clear, *pretty*, cold day, but the sort of frost that really makes the world seem dead — makes it almost impossible to believe that there will ever be warmth and sound and "growing-ness" again.

Late in the afternoon Griselda crept up to the ante-room, and sat down by the window. Outside it was nearly dark, and inside it was not much more cheerful — for the fire was nearly out, and no lamps were lighted; only the cuckoo clock went on tick-ticking briskly as usual.

"I hate winter," said Griselda, pressing her cold little face against the colder window-pane, "I hate winter, and I hate lessons. I would give up being a *person* in a minute if I might be a — a — what would I best like to be? Oh yes, I know — a butterfly. Butterflies never see winter, and they *certainly* never have any lessons or any kind of work to do. I hate *must*-ing to do anything."

"Cuckoo," rang out suddenly above her head.

It was only four o'clock striking, and as soon as he had told it the cuckoo was back behind his doors again in an instant, just as usual. There was nothing for Griselda to feel offended at, but somehow she got quite angry.

"I don't care what you think, cuckoo!" she exclaimed defiantly. "I know you came out on purpose just now, but I don't care. I *do* hate winter, and I *do* hate lessons, and I *do* think it would be nicer to be a butterfly than a little girl."

In her secret heart I fancy she was half in hopes
that the cuckoo would come out again, and talk
things over with her. Even if he were to scold her,
she felt that it would be better than sitting there
alone with nobody to speak to, which was very dull
work indeed. At the bottom of her conscience there
lurked the knowledge that what she *should* be doing
was to be looking over her last lessons with Mr.
Kneebreeches, and refreshing her memory for the
next day; but, alas! knowing one's duty is by no
means the same thing as doing it, and Griselda sat
on by the window doing nothing but grumble and
work herself up into a belief that she was one of the
most-to-be-pitied little girls in all the world. So that
by the time Dorcas came to call her to tea, I doubt
if she had a single pleasant thought or feeling left in
her heart.

Things grew no better after tea, and before long
Griselda asked if she might go to bed. She was
"so tired," she said; and she certainly looked so,
for ill-humour and idleness are excellent "tirers,"
and will soon take the roses out of a child's cheeks,
and the brightness out of her eyes. She held up her
face to be kissed by her aunts in a meekly reproach-
ful way, which made the old ladies feel quite uncomfortable.

" I am by no means sure that I have done right in
recalling Mr. Kneebreeches so soon, Sister Tabitha,"
remarked Miss Grizzel, uneasily, when Griselda had

left the room. But Miss Tabitha was busy counting her stitches, and did not give full attention to Miss Grizzel's observation, so she just repeated placidly, " Oh yes, Sister Grizzel, you may be sure you have done right in recalling Mr. Kneebreeches."

" I am glad you think so," said Miss Tabitha, with again a little sigh of relief. " I was only distressed to see the child looking so white and tired."

Upstairs Griselda was hurry-scurrying into bed. There was a lovely fire in her room — fancy that! Was she not a poor neglected little creature ? But even this did not please her. She was too cross to be pleased with anything ; too cross to wash her face and hands, or let Dorcas brush her hair out nicely as usual; too cross, alas, to say her prayers ! She just huddled into bed, huddling up her mind in an untidy hurry and confusion, just as she left her clothes in an untidy heap on the floor. She would not look into herself, was the truth of it ; she shrank from doing so because she *knew* things had been going on in that silly little heart of hers in a most unsatisfactory way all day, and she wanted to go to sleep and forget all about it.

She did go to sleep, very quickly too. No doubt she really was tired ; tired with crossness and doing nothing, and she slept very soundly. When she woke up she felt so refreshed and rested that she fancied it must be morning. It was dark, of course, but that was to be expected in mid-winter, especially as the shutters were closed.

"I wonder," thought Griselda, "I wonder if it really *is* morning. I should like to get up early — I went so early to bed. I think I'll just jump out of bed and open a chink of the shutters. I'll see at once if it's nearly morning, by the look of the sky."

She was up in a minute, feeling her way across the room to the window, and without much difficulty she found the hook of the shutters, unfastened it, and threw one side open. Ah no, there was no sign of morning to be seen. There was moonlight, but nothing else, and not so very much of that, for the clouds were hurrying across the "orbèd maiden's" face at such a rate, one after the other, that the light was more like a number of pale flashes than the steady, cold shining of most frosty moonlight nights. There was going to be a change of weather, and the cloud armies were collecting together from all quarters; that was the real explanation of the hurrying and scurrying Griselda saw overhead, but this, of course, she did not understand. She only saw that it looked wild and stormy, and she shivered a little, partly with cold, partly with a half-frightened feeling that she could not have explained.

" I had better go back to bed," she said to herself; " but I am not a bit sleepy."

She was just drawing-to the shutter again, when something caught her eye, and she stopped short in surprise. A little bird was outside on the window-sill — a tiny bird crouching in close to the cold glass.

Griselda's kind heart was touched in an instant. Cold as she was, she pushed back the shutter again, and drawing a chair forward to the window, managed to unfasten it — it was not a very heavy one — and to open it wide enough to slip her hand gently along to the bird. It did not start or move.

"Can it be dead?" thought Griselda anxiously.

But no, it was not dead. It let her put her hand round it and draw it in, and to her delight she felt that it was soft and warm, and it even gave a gentle peck on her thumb.

"Poor little bird, how cold you must be," she said kindly. But, to her amazement, no sooner was the bird safely inside the room, than it managed cleverly to escape from her hand. It fluttered quietly up on to her shoulder, and sang out in a soft but cheery tone, "Cuckoo, cuckoo — cold, did you say, Griselda? Not so very, thank you."

Griselda stept back from the window.

"It's *you*, is it?" she said rather surlily, her tone seeming to infer that she had taken a great deal of trouble for nothing.

"Of course it is, and why shouldn't it be? You're not generally so sorry to see me. What's the matter?"

"Nothing's the matter," replied Griselda, feeling a little ashamed of her want of civility; "only, you see, if I had known it was *you* — " She hesitated.

"You wouldn't have clambered up and hurt your

poor fingers in opening the window if you had known it was me — is that it, eh?" said the cuckoo.

Somehow, when the cuckoo said "eh?" like that, Griselda was obliged to tell just what she was thinking.

"No, I wouldn't have *needed* to open the window," she said. "*You* can get in or out whenever you like; you're not like a real bird. Of course, you were just tricking me, sitting out there and pretending to be a starved robin."

There was a little indignation in her voice, and she gave her head a toss, which nearly upset the cuckoo.

"Dear me, dear me!" exclaimed the cuckoo. "You have a great deal to complain of, Griselda. Your time and strength must be very valuable for you to regret so much having wasted a little of them on me."

Griselda felt her face grow red. What did he mean? Did he know how yesterday had been spent? She said nothing, but she drooped her head, and one or two tears came slowly creeping up to her eyes.

"Child!" said the cuckoo, suddenly changing his tone, "you are very foolish. Is a kind thought or action *ever* wasted? Can your eyes see what such good seeds grow into? They have wings, Griselda — kindnesses have wings and roots, remember that — wings that never droop, and roots that never die. What do you think I came and sat outside your window for?"

"Cuckoo," said Griselda humbly, "I am very sorry."

"Very well," said the cuckoo, "we'll leave it for the present. I have something else to see about. Are you cold, Griselda?"

"*Very*," she replied. "I would very much like to go back to bed, cuckoo, if you please; and there's plenty of room for you too, if you'd like to come in and get warm."

"There are other ways of getting warm besides going to bed," said the cuckoo. "A nice brisk walk, for instance. I was going to ask you to come out into the garden with me."

Griselda almost screamed.

"Out into the garden! *Oh*, cuckoo!" she exclaimed, "how can you think of such a thing? Such a freezing cold night. Oh no, indeed, cuckoo, I couldn't possibly."

"Very well, Griselda," said the cuckoo; "if you haven't yet learnt to trust me, there's no more to be said. Good-night."

He flapped his wings, cried out "Cuckoo" once only, flew across the room, and almost before Griselda understood what he was doing, had disappeared.

She hurried after him, stumbling against the furniture in her haste, and by the uncertain light. The door was not open, but the cuckoo had got through it — "by the keyhole, I dare say," thought Griselda; "he can 'scrooge' himself up any way" — for a faint

"Cuckoo" was to be heard on its other side. In a moment Griselda had opened it, and was speeding down the long passage in the dark, guided only by the voice from time to time heard before her, "Cuckoo, cuckoo."

She forgot all about the cold, or rather, she did not feel it, though the floor was of uncarpeted old oak, whose hard, polished surface would have usually felt like ice to a child's soft, bare feet. It was a very long passage, and to-night, somehow, it seemed longer than ever. In fact, Griselda could have fancied she had been running along it for half a mile or more, when at last she was brought to a standstill by finding she could go no further. Where was she? She could not imagine! It must be a part of the house she had never explored in the daytime, she decided. In front of her was a little stair running downwards, and ending in a doorway. All this Griselda could see by a bright light that streamed in by the keyhole and through the chinks round the door — a light so brilliant that the little girl blinked her eyes, and for a moment felt quite dazzled and confused.

"It came so suddenly," she said to herself; "some one must have lighted a lamp in there all at once. But it can't be a lamp, it's too bright for a lamp. It's more like the sun; but how ever could the sun be shining in a room in the middle of the night? What shall I do? Shall I open the door and peep in?"

"Cuckoo, cuckoo," came the answer, soft but clear, from the other side.

"Can it be a trick of the cuckoo's to get me out into the garden?" thought Griselda; and for the first time since she had run out of her room a shiver of cold made her teeth chatter and her skin feel creepy.

"Cuckoo, cuckoo," sounded again, nearer this time, it seemed to Griselda.

"He's waiting for me. I *will* trust him," she said resolutely. "He has always been good and kind, and it's horrid of me to think he's going to trick me."

She ran down the little stair, she seized the handle of the door. It turned easily; the door opened — opened, and closed again noiselessly behind her, and what do you think she saw?

"Shut your eyes for a minute, Griselda," said the cuckoo's voice beside her; "the light will dazzle you at first. Shut them, and I will brush them with a little daisy dew, to strengthen them."

Griselda did as she was told. She felt the tip of the cuckoo's softest feather pass gently two or three times over her eyelids, and a delicious scent seemed immediately to float before her.

"I didn't know *daisies* had any scent," she remarked.

"Perhaps you didn't. You forget, Griselda, that you have a great —"

"Oh, please don't, cuckoo. Please, please don't, *dear* cuckoo," she exclaimed, dancing about with her hands clasped in entreaty, but her eyes still firmly closed. "Don't say that, and I'll promise to believe whatever you tell me. And how soon may I open my eyes, please, cuckoo?"

"Turn round slowly, three times. That will give the dew time to take effect," said the cuckoo. "Here goes — one — two — three. There, now."

Griselda opened her eyes.

CHAPTER VII.

BUTTERFLY-LAND.

"I'd be a butterfly."

GRISELDA opened her eyes.

What did she see?

The loveliest, loveliest garden that ever or never a little girl's eyes saw. As for describing it, I cannot. I must leave a good deal to your fancy. It was just a *delicious* garden. There was a charming mixture of all that is needed to make a garden perfect — grass, velvety lawn rather; water, for a little brook ran tinkling in and out, playing bo-peep among the bushes; trees, of course, and flowers, of course, flowers of every shade and shape. But all these beautiful things Griselda did not at first give as much attention to as they deserved; her eyes were so occupied with a quite unusual sight that met them.

This was butterflies! Not that butterflies are so very uncommon; but butterflies, as Griselda saw them, I am quite sure, children, none of you ever saw, or are likely to see. There were such enormous numbers of them, and the variety of their colours and sizes was so great. They were fluttering about everywhere; the garden seemed actually alive with them.

Griselda stood for a moment in silent delight, feasting her eyes on the lovely things before her, enjoying the delicious sunshine which kissed her poor little bare feet, and seemed to wrap her all up in its warm embrace. Then she turned to her little friend.

"Cuckoo," she said, "I thank you *so* much. This *is* fairyland, at last!"

The cuckoo smiled, I was going to say, but that would be a figure of speech only, would it not? He shook his head gently.

"No, Griselda," he said kindly; "this is only butterfly-land."

"*Butterfly*-land!" repeated Griselda, with a little disappointment in her tone.

"Well," said the cuckoo, "it's where you were wishing to be yesterday, isn't it?"

Griselda did not particularly like these allusions to "yesterday." She thought it would be as well to change the subject.

"It's a beautiful place, whatever it is," she said, "and I'm sure, cuckoo, I'm *very* much obliged to you for bringing me here. Now may I run about and look at everything? How delicious it is to feel the warm sunshine again! I didn't know how cold I was. Look, cuckoo, my toes and fingers are quite blue; they're only just beginning to come right again. I suppose the sun always shines here. How nice it must be to be a butterfly; don't you think so, cuckoo? Nothing to do but fly about."

She stopped at last, quite out of breath.

"Griselda," said the cuckoo, "if you want me to answer your questions, you must ask them one at a time. You may run about and look at everything if you like, but you had better not be in such a hurry. You will make a great many mistakes if you are — you have made some already."

"How?" said Griselda.

"*Have* the butterflies nothing to do but fly about? Watch them."

Griselda watched.

"They do seem to be doing something," she said, at last, "but I can't think what. They seem to be nibbling at the flowers, and then flying away something like bees gathering honey. *Butterflies* don't gather honey, cuckoo?"

"No," said the cuckoo. "They are filling their paint-boxes."

"What *do* you mean?" said Griselda.

"Come and see," said the cuckoo.

He flew quietly along in front of her, leading the way through the prettiest paths in all the pretty garden. The paths were arranged in different colours, as it were; that is to say, the flowers growing along their sides were not all "mixty-maxty," but one shade after another in regular order — from the

palest blush pink to the very deepest damask crimson;
then, again, from the soft greenish blue of the small
grass forget-me-not to the rich warm tinge of the
brilliant cornflower.   *Every* tint was there; shades,
to which, though not exactly strange to her, Griselda
could yet have given no name, for the daisy dew,
you see, had sharpened her eyes to observe delicate
variations of colour, as she had never done before.

" How beautifully the flowers are planned," she said
to the cuckoo.   " Is it just to look pretty, or why ? "

" It saves time," replied the cuckoo.   " The fetch-
and-carry butterflies know exactly where to go to for
the tint the world-flower-painters want."

" Who are the fetch-and-carry butterflies, and who
are the world-flower-painters ? " asked Griselda.

" Wait a bit and you'll see, and use your eyes,"
answered the cuckoo.   " It'll do your tongue no
harm to have a rest now and then."

Griselda thought it as well to take his advice,
though not particularly relishing the manner in
which it was given.   She did use her eyes, and as
she and the cuckoo made their way along the flower
alleys, she saw that the butterflies were never idle.
They came regularly, in little parties of twos and
threes, and nibbled away, as she called it, at flowers
of the same colour but different shades, till they had
got what they wanted.   Then off flew butterfly No. 1
with perhaps the palest tint of maize, or yellow, or
lavender, whichever he was in quest of, followed by

No. 2 with the next deeper shade of the same, and No. 3 bringing up the rear.

Griselda gave a little sigh.

"What's the matter?" said the cuckoo.

"They work very hard," she replied, in a melancholy tone.

"It's a busy time of year," observed the cuckoo, drily.

After a while they came to what seemed to be a sort of centre to the garden. It was a huge glass house, with numberless doors, in and out of which butterflies were incessantly flying — reminding Griselda again of bees and a beehive. But she made no remark till the cuckoo spoke again.

"Come in," he said.

Griselda had to stoop a good deal, but she did manage to get in without knocking her head or doing any damage. Inside was just a mass of butterflies. A confused mass it seemed at first, but after a while she saw that it was the very reverse of confused. The butterflies were all settled in rows on long, narrow, white tables, and before each was a tiny object about the size of a flattened-out pin's head, which he was most carefully painting with one of his tentacles, which, from time to time, he moistened by rubbing it on the head of a butterfly waiting patiently behind him. Behind this butterfly again stood another, who after a while took his place, while the first attendant flew away.

" To fill his paint-box again," remarked the cuckoo, who seemed to read Griselda's thoughts.

" But what *are* they painting, cuckoo ? " she inquired eagerly.

" All the flowers in the world," replied the cuckoo. "Autumn, winter, and spring, they're hard at work. It's only just for the three months of summer that the butterflies have any holiday, and then a few stray ones now and then wander up to the world, and people talk about ' idle butterflies ! ' And even then it isn't true that they are idle. They go up to take a look at the flowers, to see how their work has turned out, and many a damaged petal they repair, or touch up a faded tint, though no one ever knows it."

" *I* know it now," said Griselda. " I will never talk about idle butterflies again — never. But, cuckoo, do they paint all the flowers *here*, too? What a *fearful* lot they must have to do ! "

" No," said the cuckoo ; "the flowers down here are fairy flowers. They never fade or die, they are always just as you see them. But the colours of your flowers are all taken from them, as you have seen. Of course they don't look the same up there," he went on, with a slight contemptuous shrug of his cuckoo shoulders ; " the coarse air and the ugly things about must take the bloom off. The wild flowers do the best, to my thinking ; people don't meddle with them in their stupid, clumsy way."

"But how do they get the flowers sent up to the world, cuckoo?" asked Griselda.

"They're packed up, of course, and taken up at night when all of you are asleep," said the cuckoo. "They're painted on elastic stuff, you see, which fits itself as the plant grows. Why, if your eyes were as they are usually, Griselda, you couldn't even *see* the petals the butterflies are painting now."

"And the packing up," said Griselda; "do the butterflies do that too?"

"No," said the cuckoo, "the fairies look after that."

"How wonderful!" exclaimed Griselda. But before the cuckoo had time to say more a sudden tumult filled the air. It was butterfly dinner-time!

"Are you hungry, Griselda?" said the cuckoo.

"Not so very," replied Griselda.

"It's just as well perhaps that you're not," he remarked, "for I don't know that you'd be much the better for dinner here."

"Why not?" inquired Griselda curiously. "What do they have for dinner? Honey? I like that very well, spread on the top of bread-and-butter, of course —I don't think I should care to eat it alone."

"You won't get any honey," the cuckoo was beginning; but he was interrupted. Two handsome butterflies flew into the great glass hall, and making straight for the cuckoo, alighted on his shoulders. They fluttered about him for a minute or two, evi-

dently rather excited about something, then flew
away again, as suddenly as they had appeared.

"Those were royal messengers," said the cuckoo,
turning to Griselda. "They have come with a message from the king and queen to invite us to a banquet which is to be held in honour of your visit."

"What fun!" cried Griselda. "Do let's go at
once, cuckoo. But, oh dear me," she went on, with
a melancholy change of tone, "I was forgetting,
cuckoo. I can't go to the banquet. I have nothing
on but my night-gown. I never thought of it before,
for I'm not a bit cold."

"Never mind," said the cuckoo, "I'll soon have
that put to rights."

He flew off, and was back almost immediately,
followed by a whole flock of butterflies. They were
of a smaller kind than Griselda had hitherto seen,
and they were of two colours only; half were blue,
half yellow. They flew up to Griselda, who felt for
a moment as if she were really going to be suffocated
by them, but only for a moment. There seemed a
great buzz and flutter about her, and then the butterflies set to work to *dress* her. And how do you
think they dressed her? With *themselves!* They
arranged themselves all over her in the cleverest
way. One set of blue ones clustered round the
hem of her little white night-gown, making a thick
"*rûche*," as it were; and then there came two or
three thinner rows of yellow, and then blue again.

She looked like a Fairy Queen. — p. 99.

Round her waist they made the loveliest belt of mingled blue and yellow, and all over the upper part of her night-gown, in and out among the pretty white frills which Dorcas herself "goffered" so nicely, they made themselves into fantastic trimmings of every shape and kind; bows, rosettes — I cannot tell you what they did not imitate.

Perhaps the prettiest ornament of all was the coronet or wreath they made of themselves for her head, dotting over her curly brown hair too with butterfly spangles, which quivered like dew-drops as she moved about. No one would have known Griselda; she looked like a fairy queen, or princess, at least, for even her little white feet had what looked like butterfly shoes upon them, though these, you will understand, were only a sort of make-believe, as, of course, the shoes were soleless.

"Now," said the cuckoo, when at last all was quiet again, and every blue and every yellow butterfly seemed settled in his place, "now, Griselda, come and look at yourself."

He led the way to a marble basin, into which fell the waters of one of the tinkling brooks that were to be found everywhere about the garden, and bade Griselda look into the water mirror. It danced about rather; but still she was quite able to see herself. She peered in with great satisfaction, turning herself round, so as to see first over one shoulder then over the other.

"It *is* lovely," she said at last. "But, cuckoo, I'm just thinking — how shall I possibly be able to sit down without crushing ever so many?"

"Bless you, you needn't trouble about that," said the cuckoo; "the butterflies are quite able to take care of themselves. You don't suppose you are the first little girl they have ever made a dress for?"

Griselda said no more, but followed the cuckoo, walking rather "gingerly," notwithstanding his assurances that the butterflies could take care of themselves. At last the cuckoo stopped, in front of a sort of banked-up terrace, in the centre of which grew a strange-looking plant with large, smooth, spreading-out leaves, and on the two topmost leaves, their splendid wings glittering in the sunshine, sat two magnificent butterflies. They were many times larger than any Griselda had yet seen; in fact, the cuckoo himself looked rather small beside them, and they were *so* beautiful that Griselda felt quite over-awed. You could not have said what colour they were, for at the faintest movement they seemed to change into new colours, each more exquisite than the last. Perhaps I could best give you an idea of them by saying that they were like living rainbows.

"Are those the king and queen?" asked Griselda in a whisper.

"Yes," said the cuckoo. "Do you admire them?"

"I should rather think I did," said Griselda.

"But, cuckoo, do they never do anything but lie there in the sunshine?"

"Oh, you silly girl," exclaimed the cuckoo, "always jumping at conclusions. No, indeed, that is not how they manage things in butterfly-land. The king and queen have worked harder than any other butterflies. They are chosen every now and then, out of all the others, as being the most industrious and the cleverest of all the world-flower-painters, and then they are allowed to rest, and are fed on the finest essences, so that they grow as splendid as you see. But even now they are not idle; they superintend all the work that is done, and choose all the new colours."

"Dear me!" said Griselda, under her breath, "how clever they must be."

Just then the butterfly king and queen stretched out their magnificent wings, and rose upwards, soaring proudly into the air.

"Are they going away?" said Griselda in a disappointed tone.

"Oh no," said the cuckoo; "they are welcoming you. Hold out your hands."

Griselda held out her hands, and stood gazing up into the sky. In a minute or two the royal butterflies appeared again, slowly, majestically circling downwards, till at length they alighted on Griselda's little hands, the king on the right, the queen on the left, almost covering her fingers with their great dazzling wings.

"You *do* look nice now," said the cuckoo, hopping back a few steps and looking up at Griselda approvingly; "but it's time for the feast to begin, as it won't do for us to be late."

The king and queen appeared to understand. They floated away from Griselda's hands and settled themselves, this time, at one end of a beautiful little grass plot or lawn, just below the terrace where grew the large-leaved plant. This was evidently their dining-room, for no sooner were they in their place than butterflies of every kind and colour came pouring in, in masses, from all directions. Butterflies small and butterflies large; butterflies light and butterflies dark; butterflies blue, pink, crimson, green, gold-colour — *every* colour, and far, far more colours than you could possibly imagine.

They all settled down, round the sides of the grassy dining-table, and in another minute a number of small white butterflies appeared, carrying among them flower petals carefully rolled up, each containing a drop of liquid. One of these was presented to the king, and then one to the queen, who each sniffed at their petal for an instant, and then passed it on to the butterfly next them, whereupon fresh petals were handed to them, which they again passed on.

"What are they doing, cuckoo?" said Griselda; "that's not *eating*."

"It's their kind of eating," he replied. "They

don't require any other kind of food than a sniff of perfume ; and as there are perfumes extracted from every flower in butterfly-land, and there are far more flowers than you could count between now and Christmas, you must allow there is plenty of variety of dishes."

"Um-m," said Griselda ; " I suppose there is. But all the same, cuckoo, it's a very good thing I'm not hungry, isn't it? May I pour the scent on my pocket-handkerchief when it comes round to me? I have my handkerchief here, you see. Isn't it nice that I brought it? It was under my pillow, and I wrapped it round my hand to open the shutter, for the hook scratched it once."

" You may pour one drop on your handkerchief," said the cuckoo, " but not more. I shouldn't like the butterflies to think you greedy."

But Griselda grew very tired of the scent feast long before all the petals had been passed round. The perfumes were very nice, certainly, but there were such quantities of them — double quantities in honour of the guest, of course ! Griselda screwed up her handkerchief into a tight little ball, so that the one drop of scent should not escape from it, and then she kept sniffing at it impatiently, till at last the cuckoo asked her what was the matter.

" I am so tired of the feast," she said. " Do let us do something else, cuckoo."

" It is getting rather late," said the cuckoo. " But

see, Griselda, they are going to have an air-dance now."

"What's that?" said Griselda.

"Look, and you'll see," he replied.

Flocks and flocks of butterflies were rising a short way into the air, and there arranging themselves in bands according to their colours.

"Come up on to the bank," said the cuckoo to Griselda; "you'll see them better."

Griselda climbed up the bank, and as from there she could look down on the butterfly show, she saw it beautifully. The long strings of butterflies twisted in and out of each other in a most wonderful way, like ribbons of every hue plaiting themselves and then in an instant unplaiting themselves again. Then the king and queen placed themselves in the centre, and round and round in moving circles twisted and untwisted the brilliant bands of butterflies.

"It's like a kaleidoscope," said Griselda; "and now it's like those twisty-twirly dissolving views that papa took me to see once. It's *just* like them. Oh, how pretty! Cuckoo, are they doing it all on purpose to please me?"

"A good deal," said the cuckoo. "Stand up and clap your hands loud three times, to show them you're pleased."

Griselda obeyed. "Clap" number one — all the butterflies rose up into the air in a cloud; clap number two — they all fluttered and twirled and buzzed about, as if in the greatest excitement; clap number three — they all turned in Griselda's direction with a rush.

"They're going to kiss you, Griselda," cried the cuckoo.

Griselda felt her breath going. Up above her was the vast feathery cloud of butterflies, fluttering, *rushing* down upon her.

"Cuckoo, cuckoo," she screamed, "they'll suffocate me. Oh, cuckoo!"

"Shut your eyes, and clap your hands loud, very loud," called out the cuckoo.

And just as Griselda clapped her hands, holding her precious handkerchief between her teeth, she heard him give his usual cry, "Cuckoo, cuckoo."

Clap — where were they all?

Griselda opened her eyes — garden, butterflies, cuckoo, all had disappeared. She was in bed, and Dorcas was knocking at the door with the hot water.

"Miss Grizzel said I was to wake you at your usual time this morning, missie," she said. "I hope you don't feel too tired to get up."

"Tired! I should think not," replied Griselda. "I was awake this morning ages before you, I can tell you, my dear Dorcas. Come here for a minute, Dorcas, please," she went on. "There now, sniff my handkerchief. What do you think of that?"

"It's beautiful," said Dorcas. "It's out of the

big blue chinay bottle on your auntie's table, isn't it, missie?"

"Stuff and nonsense," replied Griselda; "it's scent of my own, Dorcas. Aunt Grizzel never had any like it in her life. There now! Please give me my slippers, I want to get up and look over my lessons for Mr. Kneebreeches before he comes. Dear me," she added to herself, as she was putting on her slippers, "how pretty my feet did look with the blue butterfly shoes! It was very good of the cuckoo to take me there, but I don't think I shall ever wish to be a butterfly again, now I know how hard they work! But I'd like to do my lessons well to-day. I fancy it'll please the dear old cuckoo."

CHAPTER VIII.

MASTER PHIL.

"Who comes from the world of flowers?
Daisy and crocus, and sea-blue bell,
And violet shrinking in dewy cell —
Sly cells that know the secrets of night,
When earth is bathed in fairy light —
    Scarlet, and blue, and golden flowers."

AND so Mr. Kneebreeches had no reason to complain of his pupil that day.

And Miss Grizzel congratulated herself more heartily than ever on her wise management of children.

And Miss Tabitha repeated that Sister Grizzel might indeed congratulate herself.

And Griselda became gradually more and more convinced that the only way as yet discovered of getting through hard tasks is to set to work and do them; also, that grumbling, as things are at present arranged in this world, does not *always*, nor I may say *often*, do good; furthermore, that an ill-tempered child is not, on the whole, likely to be as much loved as a good-tempered one; lastly, that if you wait long enough, winter will go and spring will come.

For this was the case this year, after all! Spring

had only been sleepy and lazy, and in such a case what could poor old winter do but fill the vacant post till she came? Why he should be so scolded and reviled for faithfully doing his best, as he often is, I really don't know. Not that all the ill words he gets have much effect on him — he comes again just as usual, whatever we say of, or to, him. I suppose his feelings have long ago been frozen up, or surely before this he would have taken offence — well for us that he has not done so!

But when the spring did come at last this year, it would be impossible for me to tell you how Griselda enjoyed it. It was like new life to her as well as to the plants, and flowers, and birds, and insects. Hitherto, you see, she had been able to see very little of the outside of her aunt's house; and charming as the inside was, the outside, I must say, was still "charminger." There seemed no end to the little up-and-down paths and alleys, leading to rustic seats and quaint arbours; no limits to the little pine-wood, down into which led the dearest little zig-zaggy path you ever saw, all bordered with snow-drops and primroses and violets, and later on with periwinkles, and wood anemones, and those bright, starry, white flowers, whose name no two people agree about.

This wood-path was the place, I think, which Griselda loved the best. The bowling-green was certainly very delightful, and so was the terrace where the famous roses grew; but lovely as the roses

were (I am speaking just now, of course, of later on
in the summer, when they were all in bloom), Griselda
could not enjoy them as much as the wild-flowers,
for she was forbidden to gather or touch them, except
with her funny round nose!

"You may *scent* them, my dear," said Miss Grizzel,
who was of opinion that smell was not a pretty word;
"but I cannot allow anything more."

And Griselda did "scent" them, I assure you.
She burrowed her whole rosy face in the big ones;
but gently, for she did not want to spoil them, both
for her aunt's sake, and because, too, she had a greater
regard for flowers now that she knew the secret of
how they were painted, and what a great deal of
trouble the butterflies take about them.

But after a while one grows tired of "scenting"
roses; and even the trying to walk straight across
the bowling-green with her eyes shut, from the arbour
at one side to the arbour exactly like it at the other,
grew stupid, though no doubt it would have been
capital fun with a companion to applaud or criticise.

So the wood-path became Griselda's favourite
haunt. As the summer grew on, she began to long
more than ever for a companion — not so much for
play, as for some one to play with. She had lessons,
of course, just as many as in the winter; but with
the long days, there seemed to come a quite unac-
countable increase of play-time, and Griselda sometimes found it hang heavy on her hands. She had

not seen or heard anything of the cuckoo either, save, of course, in his "official capacity" of time-teller, for a very long time.

"I suppose," she thought, "he thinks I don't need amusing, now that the fine days are come and I can play in the garden; and certainly, if I had *any one* to play with, the garden would be perfectly lovely."

But, failing companions, she did the best she could for herself, and this was why she loved the path down into the wood so much. There was a sort of mystery about it; it might have been the path leading to the cottage of Red-Ridinghood's grandmother, or a path leading to fairyland itself. There were all kinds of queer, nice, funny noises to be heard there — in one part of it especially, where Griselda made herself a seat of some moss-grown stones, and where she came so often that she got to know all the little flowers growing close round about, and even the particular birds whose nests were hard by.

She used to sit there and *fancy*—fancy that she heard the wood-elves chattering under their breath, or the little underground gnomes and kobolds hammering at their fairy forges. And the tinkling of the brook in the distance sounded like the enchanted bells round the necks of the fairy kine, who are sent out to pasture sometimes on the upper world hill-sides. For Griselda's head was crammed full, per. fectly full, of fairy lore; and the mandarins' country, and butterfly-land, were quite as real to her as the every-day world about her.

But all this time she was not forgotten by the cuckoo, as you will see.

One day she was sitting in her favourite nest, feeling, notwithstanding the sunshine, and the flowers, and the soft sweet air, and the pleasant sounds all about, rather dull and lonely. For though it was only May, it was really quite a hot day, and Griselda had been all the morning at her lessons, and had tried very hard, and done them very well, and now she felt as if she deserved some reward. Suddenly in the distance, she heard a well-known sound, "Cuckoo, cuckoo."

"Can that be the cuckoo?" she said to herself; and in a moment she felt sure that it must be. For, for some reason that I do not know enough about the habits of real "flesh and blood" cuckoos to explain, that bird was not known in the neighbourhood where Griselda's aunts lived. Some twenty miles or so further south it was heard regularly, but all this spring Griselda had never caught the sound of its familiar note, and she now remembered hearing it never came to these parts.

So, " it must be my cuckoo," she said to herself. " He must be coming out to speak to me. How funny! I have never seen him by daylight."

She listened. Yes, again there it was, " Cuckoo, cuckoo," as plain as possible, and nearer than before.

"Cuckoo," cried Griselda, "do come and talk to me. It's such a long time since I have seen you, and I have nobody to play with."

But there was no answer. Griselda held her breath to listen, but there was nothing to be heard.

"Unkind cuckoo!" she exclaimed. "He is tricking me, I do believe; and to-day too, just when I was so dull and lonely."

The tears came into her eyes, and she was beginning to think herself very badly used, when suddenly a rustling in the bushes beside her made her turn round, more than half expecting to see the cuckoo himself. But it was not he. The rustling went on for a minute or two without anything making its appearance, for the bushes were pretty thick just there, and any one scrambling up from the pinewood below would have had rather hard work to get through, and indeed for a very big person such a feat would have been altogether impossible.

It was not a very big person, however, who was causing all the rustling, and crunching of branches, and general commotion, which now absorbed Griselda's attention. She sat watching for another minute in perfect stillness, afraid of startling by the slightest movement the squirrel or rabbit or creature of some kind which she expected to see. At last — was that a squirrel or a rabbit — that rosy, round face, with shaggy, fair hair falling over the eager blue eyes, and a general look of breathlessness and over-heatedness and determination?

A squirrel or a rabbit! No, indeed, but a very sturdy, very merry, very ragged little boy.

"Where are that Cuckoo?"—p. 113.

"Where are that cuckoo? Does *you* know?" were the first words he uttered, as soon as he had fairly shaken himself, though not by any means all his clothes, free of the bushes (for ever so many pieces of jacket and knickerbockers, not to speak of one boot and half his hat, had been left behind on the way), and found breath to say something.

Griselda stared at him for a moment without speaking. She was so astonished. It was months since she had spoken to a child, almost since she had seen one, and about children younger than herself she knew very little at any time, being the baby of the family at home, you see, and having only big brothers older than herself for play-fellows.

"Who are you?" she said at last. "What's your name, and what do you want?"

"My name's Master Phil, and I want that cuckoo," answered the little boy. "He camed up this way. I'm sure he did, for he called me all the way."

"He's not here," said Griselda, shaking her head; "and this is my aunts' garden. No one is allowed to come here but friends of theirs. You had better go home; and you have torn your clothes so."

"This aren't a garden," replied the little fellow undauntedly, looking round him; "this are a wood. There are blue-bells and primroses here, and that shows it aren't a garden — not anybody's garden, I mean, with walls round, for nobody to come in."

"But it *is*," said Griselda, getting rather vexed.

" If it isn't a garden it's *grounds*, private grounds, and nobody should come without leave. This path leads down to the wood, and there's a door in the wall at the bottom to get into the lane. You may go down that way, little boy. No one comes scrambling up the way you did."

" But I want to find the cuckoo," said the little boy. " I do so want to find the cuckoo."

His voice sounded almost as if he were going to cry, and his pretty, hot, flushed face puckered up. Griselda's heart smote her; she looked at him more carefully. He was such a very little boy, after all; she did not like to be cross to him.

" How old are you ? " she asked.

" Five and a bit. I had a birthday after the summer, and if I'm good, nurse says perhaps I'll have one after next summer too. Do you ever have birthdays ? " he went on, peering up at Griselda. " Nurse says she used to when she was young, but she never has any now."

" *Have* you a nurse ? " asked Griselda, rather surprised ; for, to tell the truth, from " Master Phil's " appearance, she had not felt at all sure what *sort* of little boy he was, or rather what sort of people he belonged to.

" Of course I have a nurse, and a mother too," said the little boy, opening wide his eyes in surprise at the question. " Haven't you ? Perhaps you're too big, though. People leave off having nurses and mothers when they're big, don't they? Just like birthdays. But *I* won't. I won't never leave off having a mother, any way. I don't care so much about nurse and birthdays, not *kite* so much. Did you care when you had to leave off, when you got too big?"

"I hadn't to leave off because I got big," said Griselda sadly. "I left off when I was much littler than you," she went on, unconsciously speaking as Phil would best understand her. "My mother died."

"I'm werry sorry," said Phil; and the way in which he said it quite overcame Griselda's unfriend liness. "But perhaps you have a nice nurse. My nurse is rather nice; but she *will* 'cold me to-day, won't she?" he added, laughing, pointing to the terrible rents in his garments. "These are my very oldestest things; that's a good thing, isn't it? Nurse says I don't look like Master Phil in these, but when I have on my blue welpet, then I look like Master Phil. I shall have my blue welpet when mother comes."

"Is your mother away?" said Griselda.

"Oh yes, she's been away a long time; so nurse came here to take care of me at the farm-house, you know. Mother was ill, but she's better now, and some day she'll come too."

"Do you like being at the farm-house? Have you anybody to play with?" said Griselda.

Phil shook his curly head. "I never have any-body to play with," he said. "I'd like to play with you if you're not too big. And do you think you could help me to find the cuckoo?" he added insinuatingly.

"What do you know about the cuckoo?" said Griselda.

"He called me," said Phil, "he called me lots of times; and to-day nurse was busy, so I thought I'd come. And do you know," he added mysteriously, "I do believe the cuckoo's a fairy, and when I find him I'm going to ask him to show me the way to fairyland."

"He says we must all find the way ourselves," said Griselda, quite forgetting to whom she was speaking.

"*Does* he?" cried Phil, in great excitement. "Do you know him, then? and have you asked him? Oh, do tell me."

Griselda recollected herself. "You couldn't understand," she said. "Some day perhaps I'll tell you — I mean if ever I see you again."

"But I may see you again," said Phil, settling himself down comfortably beside Griselda on her mossy stone. "You'll let me come, won't you? I like to talk about fairies, and nurse doesn't understand. And if the cuckoo knows you, perhaps that's why he called me to come to play with you."

"How did he call you?" asked Griselda.

"First," said Phil gravely, "it was in the night. I was asleep, and I had been wishing I had somebody to play with, and then I d'eamed of the cuckoo — such a nice d'eam. And when I woke up I heard him calling me, and I wasn't d'eaming then. And then when I was in the field he called me, but I *couldn't* find him, and nurse said 'Nonsense.' And to-day he called me again, so I camed up through the bushes. And mayn't I come again? Perhaps if we both tried together we could find the way to fairyland. Do you think we could?"

"I don't know," said Griselda, dreamily. "There's a great deal to learn first, the cuckoo says."

"Have you learnt a great deal?" (he called it "a gate deal") asked Phil, looking up at Griselda with increased respect. "*I* don't know scarcely nothing. Mother was ill such a long time before she went away, but I know she wanted me to learn to read books. But nurse is too old to teach me."

"Shall I teach you?" said Griselda. "I can bring some of my old books and teach you here after I have done my own lessons."

"And then mother *would* be surprised when she comes back," said Master Phil, clapping his hands. "Oh, *do*. And when I've learnt to read a great deal, do you think the cuckoo would show us the way to fairyland?"

"I don't think it was that sort of learning he meant," said Griselda. "But I dare say that would help. I *think*," she went on, lowering her voice a little, and looking down gravely into Phil's earnest eyes, " I *think* he means mostly learning to be very good — very, *very* good, you know."

" Gooder than you ? " said Phil.

" Oh dear, yes ; lots and lots gooder than me," replied Griselda.

"*I* think you're very good," observed Phil, in a parenthesis. Then he went on with his cross-questioning.

" Gooder than mother ? "

" I don't know your mother, so how can I tell how good she is ? " said Griselda.

" *I* can tell you," said Phil, importantly. "She is just as good as — as good as — as good as *good*. That's what she is."

" You mean she couldn't be better," said Griselda, smiling.

" Yes, that'll do, if you like. Would that be good enough for us to be, do you think ? "

" We must ask the cuckoo," said Griselda. " But I'm sure it would be a good thing for you to learn to read. You must ask your nurse to let you come here every afternoon that it's fine, and I'll ask my aunt."

" I needn't ask nurse," said Phil composedly ; " she'll never know where I am, and I needn't tell her. She doesn't care what I do, except tearing my clothes ; and when she scolds me, *I* don't care."

"*That* isn't good, Phil," said Griselda gravely.
"You'll never be as good as good if you speak like
that."

"What should I say, then? Tell me," said the
little boy submissively.

"You should ask nurse to let you come to play
with me, and tell her I'm much bigger than you,
and I won't let you tear your clothes. And you
should tell her you're very sorry you've torn them
to-day."

"Very well," said Phil, "I'll say that. But, oh
see!" he exclaimed, darting off, "there's a field
mouse! If only I could catch him!"

Of course he couldn't catch him, nor could Griselda either; very ready, though, she was to do her
best. But it was great fun all the same, and the
children laughed heartily and enjoyed themselves
tremendously. And when they were tired they sat
down again and gathered flowers for nosegays, and
Griselda was surprised to find how clever Phil was
about it. He was much quicker than she at spying
out the prettiest blossoms, however hidden behind
tree, or stone, or shrub. And he told her of all the
best places for flowers near by, and where grew the
largest primroses and the sweetest violets, in a way
that astonished her.

"You're such a little boy," she said; "how do
you know so much about flowers?"

"I've had no one else to play with," he said

innocently. "And then, you know, the fairies are so fond of them."

When Griselda thought it was time to go home, she led little Phil down the wood-path, and through the door in the wall opening on to the lane.

"Now you can find your way home without scrambling through any more bushes, can't you, Master Phil?" she said.

"Yes, thank you, and I'll come again to that place to-morrow afternoon, shall I?" asked Phil. "I'll know when — after I've had my dinner and raced three times round the big field, then it'll be time. That's how it was to-day."

"I should think it would do if you *walked* three times — or twice if you like — round the field. It isn't a good thing to race just when you've had your dinner," observed Griselda sagely. "And you mustn't try to come if it isn't fine, for my aunts won't let me go out if it rains even the tiniest bit. And of course you must ask your nurse's leave."

"Very well," said little Phil as he trotted off. "I'll try to remember all those things. I'm so glad you'll play with me again; and if you see the cuckoo, please thank him."

CHAPTER IX.

UP AND DOWN THE CHIMNEY.

"*Helper.* Well, but if it was all dream, it would be the same as if it was all real, would it not?

"*Keeper.* Yes, I see. I mean, Sir, I do *not* see." — *A Liliput Revel.*

NOT having "just had her dinner," and feeling very much inclined for her tea, Griselda ran home at a great rate.

She felt, too, in such good spirits; it had been so delightful to have a companion in her play.

"What a good thing it was I didn't make Phil run away before I found out what a nice little boy he was," she said to herself. "I must look out my old reading books to-night. I shall so like teaching him, poor little boy, and the cuckoo will be pleased at my doing something useful, I'm sure."

Tea was quite ready, in fact waiting for her, when she came in. This was a meal she always had by herself, brought up on a tray to Dorcas's little sitting-room, where Dorcas waited upon her. And sometimes when Griselda was in a particularly good humour she would beg Dorcas to sit down and have a cup of tea with her — a liberty the old servant was far too dignified and respectful to have thought of taking, unless specially requested to do so.

This evening, as you know, Griselda was in a very particularly good humour, and besides this, so very full of her adventures, that she would have been glad of an even less sympathising listener than Dorcas was likely to be.

"Sit down, Dorcas, and have some more tea, do," she said coaxingly. "It looks ever so much more comfortable, and I'm sure you could eat a little more if you tried, whether you've had your tea in the kitchen or not. I'm *fearfully* hungry, I can tell you. You'll have to cut a whole lot more bread and butter, and not 'ladies' slices' either."

"How your tongue does go, to be sure, Miss Griselda," said Dorcas, smiling, as she seated herself on the chair Griselda had drawn in for her.

"And why shouldn't it?" said Griselda saucily. "It doesn't do it any harm. But oh, Dorcas, I've had such fun this afternoon — really, you couldn't guess what I've been doing."

"Very likely not, missie," said Dorcas.

"But you might try to guess. Oh no, I don't think you need — guessing takes such a time, and I want to tell you. Just fancy, Dorcas, I've been playing with a little boy in the wood."

"Playing with a little boy, Miss Griselda!" exclaimed Dorcas, aghast.

"Yes, and he's coming again to-morrow, and the day

after, and every day, I dare say," said Griselda. "He *is* such a nice little boy."

"But, missie," began Dorcas.

"Well? What's the matter? You needn't look like that — as if I had done something naughty," said Griselda sharply.

"But you'll tell your aunt, missie?"

"Of course," said Griselda, looking up fearlessly into Dorcas's face with her bright gray eyes. "Of course; why shouldn't I? I must ask her to give the little boy leave to come into *our* grounds; and I told the little boy to be sure to tell his nurse, who takes care of him, about his playing with me."

"His nurse," repeated Dorcas, in a tone of some relief. "Then he must be quite a little boy, perhaps Miss Grizzel would not object so much in that case."

"Why should she object at all? She might know I wouldn't want to play with a naughty rude boy," said Griselda.

"She thinks all boys rude and naughty, I'm afraid, missie," said Dorcas. "All, that is to say, excepting your dear papa. But then, of course, she had the bringing up of *him* in her own way from the beginning."

"Well, I'll ask her, anyway," said Griselda, "and if she says I'm not to play with him, I shall think — I know what I shall *think* of Aunt Grizzel, whether I *say* it or not."

And the old look of rebellion and discontent settled down again on her rosy face.

" Be careful, missie, now do, there's a dear good girl," said Dorcas anxiously, an hour later, when Griselda, dressed as usual in her little white muslin frock, was ready to join her aunts at dessert.

But Griselda would not condescend to make any reply.

" Aunt Grizzel," she said suddenly, when she had eaten an orange and three biscuits and drunk half a glass of home-made elder-berry wine, " Aunt Grizzel, when I was out in the garden to-day — down the wood-path, I mean — I met a little boy, and he played with me, and I want to know if he may come every day to play with me."

Griselda knew she was not making her request in a very amiable or becoming manner ; she knew, indeed, that she was making it in such a way as was almost certain to lead to its being refused ; and yet, though she was really so very, very anxious to get leave to play with little Phil, she took a sort of spiteful pleasure in injuring her own cause.

How *foolish* ill-temper makes us ! Griselda had allowed herself to get so angry at the *thought* of being thwarted that had her aunt looked up quietly and said at once, " Oh yes, you may have the little boy to play with you whenever you like," she would really, in a strange distorted sort of way, have been *disappointed*.

But, of course, Miss Grizzel made no such reply. Nothing less than a miracle could have made her answer Griselda otherwise than as she did. Like Dorcas, for an instant, she was utterly "flabbergasted," if you know what that means. For she was really quite an old lady, you know, and sensible as she was, things upset her much more easily than when she was younger.

Naughty Griselda saw her uneasiness, and enjoyed it.

"Playing with a boy!" exclaimed Miss Grizzel. "A boy in my grounds, and you, my niece, to have played with him!"

"Yes," said Griselda coolly, "and I want to play with him again."

"Griselda," said her aunt, "I am too astonished to say more at present. Go to bed."

"Why should I go to bed? It is not my bedtime," cried Griselda, blazing up. "What have I done to be sent to bed as if I were in disgrace?"

"Go to bed," repeated Miss Grizzel. "I will speak to you to-morrow."

"You are very unfair and unjust," said Griselda, starting up from her chair. "That's all the good of being honest and telling everything. I might have played with the little boy every day for a month and you would never have known, if I hadn't told you."

She banged across the room as she spoke, and out

at the door, slamming it behind her rudely. Then upstairs like a whirlwind; but when she got to her own room, she sat down on the floor and burst into tears, and when Dorcas came up, nearly half an hour later, she was still in the same place, crouched up in a little heap, sobbing bitterly.

"Oh, missie, missie," said Dorcas, "it's just what I was afraid of!"

As Griselda rushed out of the room Miss Grizzel leant back in her chair and sighed deeply.

"Already," she said faintly. "She was never so violent before. Can one afternoon's companionship with rudeness have already contaminated her? Already, Tabitha — can it be so?"

"Already," said Miss Tabitha, softly shaking her head, which somehow made her look wonderfully like an old cat, for she felt cold of an evening and usually wore a very fine woolly shawl of a delicate gray shade, and the borders of her cap and the ruffles round her throat and wrists were all of fluffy, downy white — "already," she said.

"Yet," said Miss Grizzel, recovering herself a little, "it is true what the child said. She might have deceived us. Have I been hard upon her, Sister Tabitha?"

"Hard upon her! Sister Grizzel," said Miss Tabitha with more energy than usual; "no, certainly not. For once, Sister Grizzel, I disagree with you. Hard upon her! Certainly not."

But Miss Grizzel did not feel happy.

When she went up to her own room at night she was surprised to find Dorcas waiting for her, instead of the younger maid.

"I thought you would not mind having me, instead of Martha, to-night, ma'am," she said, "for I did so want to speak to you about Miss Griselda. The poor, dear young lady has gone to bed so very unhappy."

"But do you know what she has done, Dorcas?" said Miss Grizzel. "Admitted a *boy*, a rude, common, impertinent *boy*, into my precincts, and played with him — with a *boy*, Dorcas."

"Yes, ma'am," said Dorcas. "I know all about it, ma'am. Miss Griselda has told me all. But if you would allow me to give an opinion, it isn't quite so bad. He's quite a little boy, ma'am — between five and six — only just about the age Miss Griselda's dear papa was when he first came to us, and, by all I can hear, quite a little gentleman.

"A little gentleman," repeated Miss Grizzel, "and not six years old! That is less objectionable than I expected. What is his name, as you know so much, Dorcas?"

"Master Phil," replied Dorcas. "That is what he told Miss Griselda, and she never thought to ask him more. But I'll tell you how we could get to hear more about him, I think, ma'am. From what Miss Griselda says, I believe he is staying at Mr. Crouch's

farm, and that, you know, ma'am, belongs to my Lady
Lavander, though it is a good way from Merrybrow
Hall. My lady is pretty sure to know about the
child, for she knows all that goes on among her
tenants, and I remember hearing that a little gentleman and his nurse had come to Mr. Crouch's to lodge
for six months."

Miss Grizzel listened attentively.

"Thank you, Dorcas," she said, when the old servant had left off speaking. "You have behaved with
your usual discretion. I shall drive over to Merrybrow to-morrow, and make inquiry. And you may
tell Miss Griselda in the morning what I purpose
doing; but tell her also that, as a punishment for her
rudeness and ill-temper, she must have breakfast in
her own room to-morrow, and not see me till I send
for her. Had she restrained her temper and explained
the matter, all this distress might have been saved."

Dorcas did not wait till "to-morrow morning;"
she could not bear to think of Griselda's unhappiness.
From her mistress's room she went straight to the
little girl's, going in very softly, so as not to disturb
her should she be sleeping.

"Are you awake, missie?" she said gently.

Griselda started up.

"Yes," she exclaimed. "Is it you, cuckoo? I'm
quite awake."

"Bless the child," said Dorcas to herself, "how
her head does run on Miss Sybilla's cuckoo. It's

really wonderful. There's more in such things than some people think."

But aloud she only replied —

"It's Dorcas, missie. No fairy, only old Dorcas come to comfort you a bit. Listen, missie. Your auntie is going over to Merrybrow Hall to-morrow to inquire about this little Master Phil from my Lady Lavander, for we think it's at one of her ladyship's farms that he and his nurse are staying, and if she hears that he's a nice-mannered little gentleman, and comes of good parents — why, missie, there's no saying but that you'll get leave to play with him as much as you like."

"But not to-morrow, Dorcas," said Griselda. "Aunt Grizzel never goes to Merrybrow till the afternoon. She won't be back in time for me to play with Phil to-morrow."

"No, but next day, perhaps," said Dorcas.

"Oh, but that won't do," said Griselda, beginning to cry again. "Poor little Phil will be coming up to the wood-path *to-morrow*, and if he doesn't find me, he'll be *so* unhappy — perhaps he'll never come again if I don't meet him to-morrow."

Dorcas saw that the little girl was worn out and excited, and not yet inclined to take a reasonable view of things.

"Go to sleep, missie," she said kindly, "and don't think anything more about it till to-morrow. It'll be all right, you'll see."

Her patience touched Griselda.

"You are very kind, Dorcas," she said. "I don't mean to be cross to *you;* but I can't bear to think of poor little Phil. Perhaps he'll sit down on my mossy stone and cry. Poor little Phil!"

But notwithstanding her distress, when Dorcas had left her she did feel her heart a little lighter, and somehow or other before long she fell asleep.

When she awoke it seemed to be suddenly, and she had the feeling that something had disturbed her. She lay for a minute or two perfectly still — listening. Yes; there it was — the soft, faint rustle in the air that she knew so well. It seemed as if something was moving away from her.

"Cuckoo," she said gently, "is that you?"

A moment's pause, then came the answer — the pretty greeting she expected.

"Cuckoo, cuckoo," soft and musical. Then the cuckoo spoke.

"Well, Griselda," he said, "and how are you? It's a good while since we have had any fun together."

"That's not *my* fault," said Griselda sharply. She was not yet feeling quite as amiable as might have been desired, you see. "That's *certainly* not my fault," she repeated.

"I never said it was," replied the cuckoo. "Why will you jump at conclusions so? It's a very bad habit, for very often you jump *over* them, you see, and go too far. One should always *walk* up to conclusions, very slowly and evenly, right foot first, then left, one with another — that's the way to get where you want to go, and feel sure of your ground. Do you see?"

"I don't know whether I do or not, and I'm not going to speak to you if you go on at me like that. You might see I don't want to be lectured when I am so unhappy."

"What are you unhappy about?"

"About Phil, of course. I won't tell you, for I believe you know," said Griselda. "Wasn't it you that sent him to play with me? I was so pleased, and I thought it was very kind of you; but it's all spoilt now."

"But I heard Dorcas saying that your aunt is going over to consult my Lady Lavander about it," said the cuckoo. "It'll be all right; you needn't be in such low spirits about nothing."

"Were you in the room *then?*" said Griselda. "How funny you are, cuckoo. But it isn't all right. Don't you see, poor little Phil will be coming up the wood-path to-morrow afternoon to meet me, and I won't be there! I can't bear to think of it."

"Is that all?" said the cuckoo. "It really is extraordinary how some people make troubles out of nothing! We can easily tell Phil not to come till the day after. Come along."

"Come along," repeated Griselda; "what do you mean?"

"Oh, I forgot," said the cuckoo. "You don't understand. Put out your hand. There, do you feel me?"

"Yes," said Griselda, stroking gently the soft feathers which seemed to be close under her hand. "Yes, I feel you."

"Well, then," said the cuckoo, "put your arms round my neck, and hold me firm. I'll lift you up."

"How *can* you talk such nonsense, cuckoo?" said Griselda. "Why, one of my little fingers would clasp your neck. How can I put my arms round it?"

"Try," said the cuckoo.

Somehow Griselda had to try.

She held out her arms in the cuckoo's direction, as if she expected his neck to be about the size of a Shetland pony's, or a large Newfoundland dog's; and, to her astonishment, so it was! A nice, comfortable, feathery neck it felt — so soft that she could not help laying her head down upon it, and nestling in the downy cushion.

"That's right," said the cuckoo.

Then he seemed to give a little spring, and Griselda felt herself altogether lifted on to his back. She lay there as comfortably as possible — it felt so firm as well as soft. Up he flew a little way — then stopped short.

"Are you all right?" he inquired. "You're not afraid of falling off?"

"Oh no," said Griselda; "not a bit."

"You needn't be," said the cuckoo, "for you couldn't if you tried. I'm going on, then."

"Where to?" said Griselda.

"Up the chimney first," said the cuckoo.

"But there'll never be room," said Griselda. "I might *perhaps* crawl up like a sweep, hands and knees, you know, like going up a ladder. But stretched out like this — it's just as if I were lying on a sofa — I *couldn't* go up the chimney."

"Couldn't you?" said the cuckoo. "We'll see. *I* intend to go, anyway, and to take you with me. Shut your eyes — one, two, three —here goes — we'll be up the chimney before you know."

It was quite true. Griselda shut her eyes tight. She felt nothing but a pleasant sort of rush. Then she heard the cuckoo's voice saying —

"Well, wasn't that well done? Open your eyes and look about you."

Griselda did so. Where were they?

They were floating about above the top of the house, which Griselda saw down below them, looking dark and vast. She felt confused and bewildered.

"Cuckoo," she said, "I don't understand. Is it I that have grown little, or you that have grown big?"

"Whichever you please," said the cuckoo. "You have forgotten. I told you long ago it is all a matter of fancy."

"Yes, if everything grew little *together*," persisted Griselda; "but it isn't everything. It's just you or me, or both of us. No, it can't be both of us. And I don't think it can be me, for if any of me had grown little all would, and my eyes haven't grown little, for everything looks as big as usual, only *you* a great deal bigger. My eyes can't have grown bigger without the rest of me, surely, for the moon looks just the same. And I must have grown little, or else we couldn't have get up the chimney. Oh, cuckoo, you have put all my thinking into such a muddle!"

"Never mind," said the cuckoo. "It'll show you how little consequence big and little are of. Make yourself comfortable all the same. Are you all right? Shut your eyes if you like. I'm going pretty fast."

"Where to?" said Griselda.

"To Phil, of course," said the cuckoo. "What a bad memory you have! Are you comfortable?"

"*Very*, thank you," replied Griselda, giving the cuckoo's neck an affectionate hug as she spoke.

"That'll do, thank you. Don't throttle me, if it's quite the same to you," said the cuckoo. "Here goes — one, two, three," and off he flew again.

Griselda shut her eyes and lay still. It was delicious — the gliding, yet darting motion, like nothing she had ever felt before. It did not make her the least giddy, either; but a slightly sleepy feeling came over her. She felt no inclination to open her eyes; and, indeed, at the rate they were going, she could have distinguished very little had she done so.

Suddenly the feeling in the air about her changed. For an instant it felt more *rushy* than before, and there was a queer, dull sound in her ears. Then she felt that the cuckoo had stopped.

"Where are we?" she asked.

"We've just come *down* a chimney again," said the cuckoo. "Open your eyes and clamber down off my back, but don't speak loud, or you'll waken him, and that wouldn't do. There you are — the moonlight's coming in nicely at the window — you can see your way."

Griselda found herself in a little bedroom, quite a tiny one, and by the look of the simple furniture and the latticed window, she saw that she was not in a grand house. But everything looked very neat and nice, and on a little bed in one corner lay a lovely sleeping child. It was Phil! He looked so pretty asleep — his shaggy curls all tumbling about, his rosy mouth half open as if smiling, one little hand tossed over his head, the other tight clasping a little basket which he had insisted on taking to bed with him, meaning as soon as he was dressed the next morning to run out and fill it with flowers for the little girl he had made friends with.

Griselda stepped up to the side of the bed on

tiptoe. The cuckoo had disappeared, but Griselda heard his voice. It seemed to come from a little way up the chimney.

"Don't wake him," said the cuckoo, "but whisper what you want to say into his ear, as soon as I have called him. He'll understand; he's accustomed to my ways."

Then came the old note, soft and musical as ever —

"Cuckoo, cuckoo, cuckoo. Listen, Phil," said the cuckoo, and without opening his eyes a change passed over the little boy's face. Griselda could see that he was listening to hear her message.

"He thinks he's dreaming, I suppose," she said to herself with a smile. Then she whispered softly —

"Phil, dear, don't come to play with me to-morrow, for I can't come. But come the day after. I'll be at the wood-path then."

"Welly well," murmured Phil. Then he put out his two arms towards Griselda, all without opening his eyes, and she, bending down, kissed him softly.

"Phil's so sleepy," he whispered, like a baby almost. Then he turned over and went to sleep more soundly than before.

"That'll do," said the cuckoo. "Come along, Griselda."

Griselda obediently made her way to the place whence the cuckoo's voice seemed to come.

"Shut your eyes and put your arms round my neck again," said the cuckoo.

She did not hesitate this time. It all happened just as before. There came the same sort of rushy sound; then the cuckoo stopped, and Griselda opened her eyes.

They were up in the air again — a good way up, too, for some grand old elms that stood beside the farmhouse were gently waving their topmost branches a yard or two from where the cuckoo was poising himself and Griselda.

"Where shall we go to now?" he said. "Or would you rather go home? Are you tired?"

"Tired!" exclaimed Griselda. "I should rather think not. How could I be tired, cuckoo?"

"Very well, don't excite yourself about nothing, whatever you do," said the cuckoo. "Say where you'd like to go."

"How can I?" said Griselda. "You know far more nice places than I do."

"You don't care to go back to the mandarins, or the butterflies, I suppose?" asked the cuckoo.

"No, thank you," said Griselda; "I'd like something new. And I'm not sure that I care for seeing any more countries of that kind, unless you could take me to the *real* fairyland."

"*I* can't do that, you know," said the cuckoo.

Just then a faint "soughing" sound among the branches suggested another idea to Griselda.

"Cuckoo," she exclaimed, "take me to the sea. It's *such* a time since I saw the sea. I can fancy I hear it; do take me to see it."

CHAPTER X.

THE OTHER SIDE OF THE MOON.

> " That after supper time has come,
>   And silver dews the meadows steep,
>   And all is silent in the home,
>   And even nurses are asleep,
> That be it late, or be it soon,
> Upon this lovely night in June
> They both will step into the moon."

" VERY well," said the cuckoo. " You would like to look about you a little on the way, perhaps, Griselda, as we shall not be going down chimneys, or anything of that kind just at present."

" Yes," said Griselda. " I think I should. I'm rather tired of shutting my eyes, and I'm getting quite accustomed to flying about with you, cuckoo."

" Turn on your side, then," said the cuckoo, " and you won't have to twist your neck to see over my shoulder. Are you comfortable now? And, by-the-by, as you may be cold, just feel under my left wing. You'll find the feather mantle there, that you had on once before. Wrap it round you. I tucked it in at the last moment, thinking you might want it."

" Oh, you dear, kind cuckoo!" cried Griselda. " Yes, I've found it. I'll tuck it all round me like a rug — that's it. I *am* so warm now, cuckoo."

"Here goes, then," said the cuckoo, and off they set. Had ever a little girl such a flight before? Floating, darting, gliding, sailing — no words can describe it. Griselda lay still in delight, gazing all about her.

"How lovely the stars are, cuckoo!" she said. "Is it true they're all great, big *suns?* I'd rather they weren't. I like to think of them as nice, funny little things."

"They're not all suns," said the cuckoo. "Not all those you're looking at now."

"I like the twinkling ones best," said Griselda. "They look so good-natured. Are they *all* twirling about always, cuckoo? Mr. Kneebreeches has just begun to teach me astronomy, and *he* says they are; but I'm not at all sure that he knows much about it."

"He's quite right all the same," replied the cuckoo.

"Oh dear me! How tired they must be, then!" said Griselda. "Do they never rest just for a minute?"

"Never."

"Why not?"

"Obeying orders," replied the cuckoo.

Griselda gave a little wriggle.

"What's the use of it?" she said. "It would be just as nice if they stood still now and then."

"Would it?" said the cuckoo. "I know somebody who would soon find fault if they did. What would you say to no summer; no day, or no night, whichever it happened not to be, you see : nothing growing, and nothing to eat before long? That's what it would be if they stood still, you see, because — "

" Thank you, cuckoo," interrupted Griselda. " It's very nice to hear you — I mean, very dreadful to think of, but I don't want you to explain. I'll ask Mr. Kneebreeches when I'm at my lessons. You might tell me one thing, however. What's at the other side of the moon ? "

" There's a variety of opinions," said the cuckoo.

" What are they ? Tell me the funniest."

" Some say all the unfinished work of the world is kept there," said the cuckoo.

" *That's* not funny," said Griselda. " What a messy place it must be ! Why, even *my* unfinished work makes quite a heap. I don't like that opinion at all, cuckoo. Tell me another."

" I *have* heard," said the cuckoo, " that among the places there you would find the country of the little black dogs. You know what sort of creatures those are ? "

" Yes, I suppose so," said Griselda, rather reluctantly.

" There are a good many of them in this world, as of course you know," continued the cuckoo. " But up there, they are much worse than here. When

a child has made a great pet of one down here, I've
heard tell the fairies take him up there when his
parents and nurses think he's sleeping quietly in his
bed, and make him work hard all night, with his own
particular little black dog on his back. And it's so
dreadfully heavy — for every time he takes it on his
back down here it grows a pound heavier up there —
that by morning the child is quite worn out. I dare
say you've noticed how haggard and miserable some
ill-tempered children get to look — now you'll know
the reason."

"Thank you, cuckoo," said Griselda again; "but
I can't say I like this opinion about the other side of
the moon any better than the first. If you please, I
would rather not talk about it any more."

"Oh, but it's not so bad an idea after all," said the
cuckoo. "Lots of children, they say, get quite cured
in the country of the little black dogs. It's this way
— for every time a child refuses to take the dog on
his back down here it grows a pound lighter up there,
so at last any sensible child learns how much better
it is to have nothing to say to it at all, and gets out
of the way of it, you see. Of course, there *are* children whom nothing would cure, I suppose. What
becomes of them I really can't say. Very likely
they get crushed into pancakes by the weight of the
dogs at last, and then nothing more is ever heard of
them."

"Horrid!" said Griselda, with a shudder. "Don't

let's talk about it any more, cuckoo; tell me your *own* opinion about what there really is on the other side of the moon."

The cuckoo was silent for a moment. Then suddenly he stopped short in the middle of his flight.

"Would you like to see for yourself, Griselda?" he said. "There would be about time to do it," he added to himself, "and it would fulfil her other wish, too."

"See the moon for myself, do you mean?" cried Griselda, clasping her hands. "I should rather think I would. Will you really take me there, cuckoo?"

"To the other side," said the cuckoo. "I couldn't take you to this side."

"Why not? Not that I'd care to go to this side as much as to the other; for, of course, we can *see* this side from here. But I'd like to know why you couldn't take me there."

"For *reasons*," said the cuckoo drily. "I'll give you one if you like. If I took you to this side of the moon you wouldn't be yourself when you got there."

"Who would I be, then?"

"Griselda," said the cuckoo, "I told you once that there are a great many things you don't know. Now, I'll tell you something more. There are a great many things you're not *intended* to know."

"Very well." said Griselda. "But do tell me

when you're going on again, and where you are going to take me to. There's no harm my asking that?"

"No," said the cuckoo. "I'm going on immediately, and I'm going to take you where you wanted to go to, only you must shut your eyes again, and lie perfectly still without talking, for I must put on steam — a good deal of steam — and I can't talk to you. Are you all right?"

"All right," said Griselda.

She had hardly said the words when she seemed to fall asleep. The rushing sound in the air all round her increased so greatly that she was conscious of nothing else. For a moment or two she tried to remember where she was, and where she was going, but it was useless. She forgot everything, and knew nothing more of what was passing till — till she heard the cuckoo again.

"Cuckoo, cuckoo; wake up, Griselda," he said.

Griselda sat up.

Where was she?

Not certainly where she had been when she went to sleep. Not on the cuckoo's back, for there he was standing beside her, as tiny as usual. Either he had grown little again, or she had grown big — which, she supposed, it did not much matter. Only it was very queer!

"Where am I, cuckoo?" she said.

"Where you wished to be," he replied. "Look about you and see."

Griselda looked about her. What did she see? Something that I can only give you a faint idea of, children; something so strange and unlike what she had ever seen before, that only in a dream could you see it as Griselda saw it. And yet *why* it seemed to her so strange and unnatural I cannot well explain; if I could, my words would be as good as pictures, which I know they are not.

After all, it was only the sea she saw; but such a great, strange, silent sea, for there were no waves. Griselda was seated on the shore, close beside the water's edge, but it did not come lapping up to her feet in the pretty, coaxing way that *our* sea does when it is in a good humour. There were here and there faint ripples on the surface, caused by the slight breezes which now and then came softly round Griselda's face, but that was all. King Canute might have sat "from then till now" by this still, lifeless ocean without the chance of reading his silly attendants a lesson — if, indeed, there ever were such silly people, which I very much doubt.

Griselda gazed with all her eyes. Then she suddenly gave a little shiver.

"What's the matter?" said the cuckoo. "You have the mantle on — you're not cold?"

"No," said Griselda, "I'm not cold; but somehow, cuckoo, I feel a little frightened. The sea is so strange, and so dreadfully big; and the light is so queer, too. What is the light, cuckoo? It isn't moonlight, is it?"

"Not exactly," said the cuckoo. "You can't both have your cake and eat it, Griselda. Look up at the sky. There's no moon there, is there?"

"No," said Griselda; "but what lots of stars, cuckoo. The light comes from them, I suppose? And where's the sun, cuckoo? Will it be rising soon? It isn't always like this up here, is it?"

"Bless you, no," said the cuckoo. "There's sun enough, and rather too much, sometimes. How would you like a day a fortnight long, and nights to match? If it had been daytime here just now, I couldn't have brought you. It's just about the very middle of the night now, and in about a week of *your* days the sun will begin to rise, because, you see — "

"Oh, *dear* cuckoo, please don't explain!" cried Griselda. "I'll promise to ask Mr. Kneebreeches, I will indeed. In fact, he was telling me something just like it to-day or yesterday — which should I say? — at my astronomy lesson. And that makes it so strange that you should have brought me up here to-night to see for myself, doesn't it, cuckoo?"

"An odd coincidence," said the cuckoo.

"What *would* Mr. Kneebreeches think if I told him where I had been?" continued Griselda. "Only, you see, cuckoo, I never tell anybody about what I see when I am with you."

"No," replied the cuckoo; "better not. ('Not

that you could if you tried,' he added to himself.)
You're not frightened now, Griselda, are you?"

"No, I don't think I am," she replied. "But,
cuckoo, isn't this sea *awfully* big?"

"Pretty well," said the cuckoo. "Just half, or
nearly half, the size of the moon; and, no doubt,
Mr. Kneebreeches has told you that the moon's
diameter and circumference are respec—"

"Oh *don't*, cuckoo!" interrupted Griselda, be-
seechingly. "I want to enjoy myself, and not to
have lessons. Tell me something funny, cuckoo.
Are there any mermaids in the moon-sea?"

"Not exactly," said the cuckoo.

"What a stupid way to answer," said Griselda.
"There's no sense in that; there either must be or
must not be. There couldn't be half mermaids."

"I don't know about that," replied the cuckoo.
"They might have been here once and have left
their tails behind them, like Bopeep's sheep, you
know; and some day they might be coming to find
them again, you know. That would do for 'not
exactly,' wouldn't it?"

"Cuckoo, you're laughing at me," said Griselda.
"Tell me, are there any mermaids, or fairies, or
water-sprites, or any of those sort of creatures here?"

"I must still say 'not exactly,'" said the cuckoo.
"There are beings here, or rather there have been,
and there may be again; but you, Griselda, can
know no more than this."

His tone was rather solemn, and again Griselda felt a little "eerie."

"It's a dreadfully long way from home, anyway," she said. "I feel as if, when I go back, I shall perhaps find I have been away fifty years or so, like the little boy in the fairy story. Cuckoo, I think I would like to go home. Mayn't I get on your back again?"

"Presently," said the cuckoo. "Don't be uneasy, Griselda. Perhaps I'll take you home by a short cut."

"Was ever any child here before?" asked Griselda, after a little pause.

"Yes," said the cuckoo.

"And did they get safe home again?"

"Quite," said the cuckoo. "It's so silly of you, Griselda, to have all these ideas still about far and near, and big and little, and long and short, after all I've taught you and all you've seen."

"I'm very sorry," said Griselda humbly; "but you see, cuckoo, I can't help it. I suppose I'm made so."

"Perhaps," said the cuckoo, meditatively.

He was silent for a minute. Then he spoke again. "Look over there, Griselda," he said. "There's the short cut."

Griselda looked. Far, far over the sea, in the silent distance, she saw a tiny speck of light. It was very tiny; but yet the strange thing was that, far away as it appeared, and minute as it was, it seemed to throw off a thread of light to Griselda's very feet

— right across the great sheet of faintly gleaming water. And as Griselda looked, the thread seemed to widen and grow, becoming at the same time brighter and clearer, till at last it lay before her like a path of glowing light.

"Am I to walk along there?" she said softly to the cuckoo.

"No," he replied; "wait."

Griselda waited, looking still, and presently in the middle of the shining streak she saw something slowly moving — something from which the light came, for the nearer it got to her the shorter grew the glowing path, and behind the moving object the sea looked no brighter than before it had appeared.

At last — at last, it came quite near — near enough for Griselda to distinguish clearly what it was.

It was a little boat — the prettiest, the loveliest little boat that ever was seen; and it was rowed by a little figure that at first sight Griselda felt certain was a fairy. For it was a child with bright hair and silvery wings, which with every movement sparkled and shone like a thousand diamonds.

Griselda sprang up and clapped her hands with delight. At the sound, the child in the boat turned and looked at her. For one instant she could not remember where she had seen him before; then she exclaimed, joyfully —

"It is Phil! Oh, cuckoo, it is Phil. Have you turned into a fairy, Phil?"

But, alas, as she spoke the light faded away, the boy's figure disappeared, the sea and the shore and the sky were all as they had been before, lighted only by the faint, strange gleaming of the stars. Only the boat remained. Griselda saw it close to her, in the shallow water, a few feet from where she stood.

"Cuckoo," she exclaimed in a tone of reproach and disappointment, "where is Phil gone? Why did you send him away?"

"I didn't send him away," said the cuckoo. "You don't understand. Never mind, but get into the boat. It'll be all right, you'll see."

"But are we to go away and leave Phil here, all alone at the other side of the moon?" said Griselda, feeling ready to cry.

"Oh, you silly girl!" said the cuckoo. "Phil's all right, and in some ways he has a great deal more sense than you, I can tell you. Get into the boat and make yourself comfortable; lie down at the bottom and cover yourself up with the mantle. You needn't be afraid of wetting your feet a little, moon water never gives cold. There, now."

Griselda did as she was told. She was beginning to feel rather tired, and it certainly was very comfortable at the bottom of the boat, with the nice warm feather-mantle well tucked round her.

"Who will row?" she said sleepily. "*You* can't, cuckoo, with your tiny little claws, you could never hold the oars, I'm—"

" Hush ! " said the cuckoo ; and whether he rowed or not Griselda never knew.

Off they glided somehow, but it seemed to Griselda that *somebody* rowed, for she heard the soft dip, dip of the oars as they went along, so regularly that she couldn't help beginning to count in time — one, two, three, four — on, on — she thought she had got nearly to a hundred, when —

CHAPTER XI.

"CUCKOO, CUCKOO, GOOD-BYE!"

"Children, try to be good!
  That is the end of all teaching;
Easily understood,
  And very easy in preaching.
And if you find it hard,
  Your efforts you need but double;
Nothing deserves reward
  Unless it has given us trouble."

— WHEN she forgot everything, and fell fast, fast asleep, to wake, of course, in her own little bed as usual!

"One of your tricks again, Mr. Cuckoo," she said to herself with a smile. "However, I don't mind. It *was* a short cut home, and it was very comfortable in the boat, and I certainly saw a great deal last night, and I'm very much obliged to you — particularly for making it all right with Phil about not coming to play with me to-day. Ah! that reminds me, I'm in disgrace. I wonder if Aunt Grizzel will really make me stay in my room all day. How tired I shall be, and what will Mr. Kneebreeches think! But it serves me right. I *was* very cross and rude."

There came a tap at the door. It was Dorcas with the hot water.

151

"Good morning, missie," she said gently, not feeling, to tell the truth, very sure as to what sort of a humour "missie" was likely to be found in this morning. "I hope you've slept well."

"Exceedingly well, thank you, Dorcas. I've had a delightful night," replied Griselda amiably, smiling to herself at the thought of what Dorcas would say if she knew where she had been, and what she had been doing since last she saw her.

"That's good news," said Dorcas in a tone of relief; "and I've good news for you, too, missie. At least, I hope you'll think it so. Your aunt has ordered the carriage for quite early this morning — so you see she really wants to please you, missie, about playing with little Master Phil; and if to-morrow's a fine day, we'll be sure to find some way of letting him know to come."

"Thank you, Dorcas. I hope it will be all right, and that Lady Lavander won't say anything against it. I dare say she won't. I feel ever so much happier this morning, Dorcas; and I'm very sorry I was so rude to Aunt Grizzel, for of course I know I *should* obey her."

"That's right, missie," said Dorcas approvingly.

"It seems to me, Dorcas," said Griselda dreamily, when, a few minutes later, she was standing by the window while the old servant brushed out her thick, wavy hair, "it seems to me, Dorcas, that it's *all* 'obeying orders' together. There's the sun now,

just getting up, and the moon just going to bed —
they are always obeying, aren't they? I wonder why
it should be so hard for people — for children, at
least."

"To be sure, missie, you do put it a way of your
own," replied Dorcas, somewhat mystified; "but I
see how you mean, I think, and it's quite true. And
it *is* a hard lesson to learn."

"I want to learn it *well*, Dorcas," said Griselda,
resolutely. "So will you please tell Aunt Grizzel
that I'm very sorry about last night, and I'll do
just as she likes about staying in my room or anything. But, if she *would* let me, I'd far rather go
down and do my lessons as usual for Mr. Kneebreeches. I won't ask to go out in the garden;
but I would like to please Aunt Grizzel by doing
my lessons *very* well."

Dorcas was both delighted and astonished. Never
had she known her little "missie" so altogether submissive and reasonable.

"I only hope the child's not going to be ill," she
said to herself. But she proved a skilful ambas-
sadress, notwithstanding her misgivings; and Griselda's imprisonment confined her only to the bounds
of the house and terrace walk, instead of within the
four walls of her own little room, as she had feared.

Lessons *were* very well done that day, and Mr.
Kneebreeches' report was all that could be wished.

"I am particularly gratified," he remarked to Miss

Grizzel, "by the intelligence and interest Miss Griselda displays with regard to the study of astronomy,
which I have recently begun to give her some ele-
mentary instruction in. And, indeed, I have no
fault to find with the way in which any of the young
lady's tasks are performed."

"I am extremely glad to hear it," replied Miss
Grizzel graciously, and the kiss with which she
answered Griselda's request for forgiveness was a
very hearty one.

And it was "all right" about Phil.

Lady Lavander knew all about him; his father
and mother were friends of hers, for whom she
had a great regard, and for some time she had
been intending to ask the little boy to spend the
day at Merrybrow Hall, to be introduced to her god-
daughter Griselda. So, *of course*, as Lady Lavander
knew all about him, there could be no objection
to his playing in Miss Grizzel's garden!

And "to-morrow" turned out a fine day. So
altogether you can imagine that Griselda felt very
happy and light-hearted as she ran down the wood-
path to meet her little friend, whose rosy face soon
appeared among the bushes.

"What did you do yesterday, Phil?" asked Griselda. "Were you sorry not to come to play with
me?"

"No," said Phil mysteriously, "I didn't mind.
I was looking for the way to fairyland to show you,

and I do believe I've found it. Oh, it *is* such a pretty way."

Griselda smiled.

"I'm afraid the way to fairyland isn't so easily found," she said. "But I'd like to hear about where you went. Was it far?"

"A good way," said Phil. "Won't you come with me? It's in the wood. I can show you quite well, and we can be back by tea-time."

"Very well," said Griselda; and off they set.

Whether it was the way to fairyland or not, it was not to be wondered at that little Phil thought so. He led Griselda right across the wood to a part where she had never been before. It was pretty rough work part of the way. The children had to fight with brambles and bushes, and here and there to creep through on hands and knees, and Griselda had to remind Phil several times of her promise to his nurse that his clothes should not be the worse for his playing with her, to prevent his scrambling through "anyhow" and leaving bits of his knickerbockers behind him.

But when at last they reached Phil's favourite spot all their troubles were forgotten. Oh, how pretty it was! It was a sort of tiny glade in the very middle of the wood — a little green nest enclosed all round by trees, and right through it the merry brook came rippling along as if rejoicing at getting out into the sunlight again for a while. And all the choicest and sweetest of the early summer flowers seemed to be collected here in greater variety and profusion than in any other part of the wood.

"*Isn't* it nice?" said Phil, as he nestled down beside Griselda on the soft, mossy grass. "It must have been a fairies' garden some time, I'm sure, and I shouldn't wonder if one of the doors into fairyland is hidden somewhere here, if only we could find it."

"If only!" said Griselda. "I don't think we shall find it, Phil; but, any way, this is a lovely place you've found, and I'd like to come here very often."

Then at Phil's suggestion they set to work to make themselves a house in the centre of this fairies' garden, as he called it. They managed it very much to their own satisfaction, by dragging some logs of wood and big stones from among the brushwood hard by, and filling the holes up with bracken and furze.

"And if the fairies *do* come here," said Phil, "they'll be very pleased to find a house all ready, won't they?"

Then they had to gather flowers to ornament the house inside, and dry leaves and twigs all ready for a fire in one corner. Altogether it was quite a business, I can assure you, and when it was finished they were very hot and very tired and *rather* dirty. Suddenly a thought struck Griselda.

"Phil," she said, "it must be getting late."

"Past tea-time?" he said coolly.

"I dare say it is. Look how low down the sun has got. Come, Phil, we must be quick. Where is the place we came out of the wood at?"

"Here," said Phil, diving at a little opening among the bushes.

Griselda followed him. He had been a good guide hitherto, and she certainly could not have found her way alone. They scrambled on for some way, then the bushes suddenly seemed to grow less thick, and in a minute they came out upon a little path.

"Phil," said Griselda, "this isn't the way we came."

"Isn't it?" said Phil, looking about him. "Then we must have comed the wrong way."

"I'm afraid so," said Griselda, "and it seems to be so late already. I'm so sorry, for Aunt Grizzel will be vexed, and I did so want to please her. Will your nurse be vexed, Phil?"

"I don't care if she are," replied Phil valiantly.

"You shouldn't say that, Phil. You know we *shouldn't* have stayed so long playing."

"Nebber mind," said Phil. "If it was mother I would mind. Mother's so good, you don't know. And she never 'colds me, except when I *am* naughty —so I *do* mind."

"She wouldn't like you to be out so late, I'm sure," said Griselda in distress, "and it's most my fault, for I'm the biggest. Now, which way *shall* we go?"

They had followed the little path till it came to a point where two roads, rough cart-ruts only, met; or, rather, where the path ran across the road. Right, or left, or straight on, which should it be? Griselda stood still in perplexity. Already it was growing dusk; already the moon's soft light was beginning faintly to glimmer through the branches. Griselda looked up to the sky.

"To think," she said to herself — "to think that I should not know my way in a little bit of a wood like this — I that was up at the other side of the moon last night."

The remembrance put another thought into her mind.

"Cuckoo, cuckoo," she said softly, "couldn't you help us?"

Then she stood still and listened, holding Phil's cold little hands in her own.

She was not disappointed. Presently, in the distance, came the well-known cry, "cuckoo, cuckoo," so soft and far away, but yet so clear.

Phil clapped his hands.

"He's calling us," he cried joyfully. "He's going to show us the way. That's how he calls me always. Good cuckoo, we're coming;" and, pulling Griselda along, he darted down the road to the right — the direction from whence came the cry.

They had some way to go, for they had wandered far in a wrong direction, but the cuckoo never failed them. Whenever they were at a loss — whenever the path turned or divided, they heard his clear, sweet call; and, without the least misgiving, they followed it, till at last it brought them out upon the high-road, a stone's throw from Farmer Crouch's gate.

"I know the way now, good cuckoo," exclaimed Phil. "I can go home alone now, if your aunt will be vexed with you."

"No," said Griselda, "I must take you quite all the way home, Phil dear. I promised to take care of you, and if nurse scolds any one it must be me, not you."

There was a little bustle about the door of the farmhouse as the children wearily came up to it. Two or three men were standing together receiving directions from Mr. Crouch himself, and Phil's nurse was talking eagerly. Suddenly she caught sight of the truants.

"Here he is, Mr. Crouch!" she exclaimed. "No need now to send to look for him. Oh, Master Phil, how could you stay out so late? And to-night of all nights, just when your — I forgot, I mustn't say. Come in to the parlour at once — and this little girl, who is she?"

"She isn't a little girl, she's a young lady," said Master Phil, putting on his lordly air, "And she's to come into the parlour and have some supper with me, and then some one must take her home to her auntie's house — that's what I say."

More to please Phil than from any wish for "supper," for she was really in a fidget to get home, Griselda let the little boy lead her into the parlour. But she was for a moment perfectly startled by the cry that broke from him when he opened the door and looked into the room. A lady was standing there, gazing out of the window, though in the quickly growing darkness she could hardly have distinguished the little figure she was watching for so anxiously.

The noise of the door opening made her look round.

"Phil," she cried, "my own little Phil; where have you been to? You didn't know I was waiting here for you, did you?"

"Mother, mother!" shouted Phil, darting into his mother's arms.

But Griselda drew back into the shadow of the doorway, and tears filled her eyes as for a minute or two she listened to the cooings and caressings of the mother and son.

Only for a minute, however. Then Phil called to her.

"Mother, mother," he cried again, "you must kiss Griselda, too! She's the little girl that is so kind, and plays with me; and she has no mother," he added in a lower tone.

The lady put her arm round Griselda, and kissed her, too. She did not seem surprised.

"I think I know about Griselda," she said very kindly, looking into her face with her gentle eyes, blue and clear like Phil's.

And then Griselda found courage to say how uneasy she was about the anxiety her aunts would be feeling, and a messenger was sent off at once to tell of her being safe at the farm.

But Griselda herself the kind lady would not let go till she had had some nice supper with Phil, and was both warmed and rested.

"And what were you about, children, to lose your way?" she asked presently.

"I took Griselda to see a place that I thought was the way to fairyland, and then we stayed to build a house for the fairies, in case they come, and then we came out at the wrong side, and it got dark," explained Phil.

"And *was* it the way to fairyland?" asked his mother, smiling.

Griselda shook her head as she replied —

"Phil doesn't understand yet," she said gently. "He isn't old enough. The way to the true fairyland is hard to find, and we must each find it for ourselves, mustn't we?"

She looked up in the lady's face as she spoke, and saw that *she* understood.

"Yes, dear child," she answered softly, and perhaps a very little sadly. "But Phil and you may help each other, and I perhaps may help you both."

Griselda slid her hand into the lady's. "You're not going to take Phil away, are you?" she whispered.

"No, I have come to stay here," she answered, "and Phil's father is coming too, soon. We are going to live at the White House — the house on the other side of the wood, on the way to Merry-brow. Are you glad, children?"

*　　*　　*　　*　　*

Griselda had a curious dream that night — merely a dream, nothing else. She dreamt that the cuckoo came once more; this time, he told her, to say "good-bye."

"For you will not need me now," he said. "I leave you in good hands, Griselda. You have friends now who will understand you — friends who will help you both to work and to play. Better friends than the mandarins, or the butterflies, or even than your faithful old cuckoo."

And when Griselda tried to speak to him, to thank him for his goodness, to beg him still sometimes to come to see her, he gently fluttered away. "Cuckoo, cuckoo, cuckoo," he warbled; but somehow the last "cuckoo" sounded like "good-bye."

In the morning, when Griselda awoke, her pillow was wet with tears. Thus many stories end. She was happy, very happy in the thought of her kind new friends; but there were tears for the one she felt she had said farewell to, even though he was only a cuckoo in a clock.

THE TAPESTRY ROOM

A CHILD'S ROMANCE

"What tale did Iseult to the children say,
Under the hollies, that bright winter's day?"

MATTHEW ARNOLD

BY

MRS. MOLESWORTH

TO

H.R.H. VITTORIO EMANUELE

PRINCE OF NAPLES

CROWN PRINCE OF ITALY

ONE OF THE KINDLIEST OF MY

YOUNG READERS

MAISON DU CHANOINE
October, 1879

THE TAPESTRY ROOM.

CHAPTER I.

MADEMOISELLE JEANNE.

"Maitre Corbeau, sur un arbre perché."
LA FONTAINE.

IT was so cold. Ah, so very cold! So thought
the old raven as he hobbled up and down the terrace
walk at the back of the house — the walk that was so
pleasant in summer, with its pretty view of the lower
garden, gay with the bright, stiffly-arranged flower-
beds, so pleasantly warm and yet shady with the old
trees overhead, where the raven's second cousins, the
rooks, managed their affairs, not without a good deal
of chatter about it, it must be confessed. "Silly
creatures," the raven was in the habit of calling them
with contempt — all to himself, of course, for no one
understood the different tones of his croaking, even
though he was a French raven and had received the
best of educations. But to-day he was too depressed
in spirit by the cold to think of his relations or their
behaviour at all. He just hopped or hobbled — I
hardly know which you would call it — slowly and
solemnly up and down the long walk, where the snow

lay so thick that at each hop it came ever so far up his black claws, which annoyed him very much, I assure you, and made him wish more than ever that summer was back again.

Poor old fellow! he was not usually of a discontented disposition; but to-day, it must be allowed, he was in the right about the cold. It was *very* cold.

Several others beside the raven were thinking so — the three chickens who lived in a queer little house in one corner of the yard thought so, and huddled the closer together, as they settled themselves for the night. For though it was only half-past three in the afternoon, they thought it was no use sitting up any longer on such a make-believe of a day, when not the least little ray of sunshine had succeeded in creeping through the leaden-gray sky. And the tortoise *would* have thought so too if he could, but he was too sleepy to think at all, as he "cruddled" himself into his shell in the corner of the laurel hedge, and dreamt of the nice hot days that were past.

And upstairs, inside the old house, somebody else was thinking so too — a little somebody who seemed to be doing her best to make herself, particularly her nose, colder still, for she was pressing it hard on to the icy window-pane and staring out on to the deserted, snow-covered garden, and thinking how cold it was, and wishing it was summer time again, and fancying how it would feel to be a raven like old "Dudu," all at once, in the mixed-up, dancing-about

"Dudu"

way that "thinking" was generally done in the funny little brain of Mademoiselle Jeanne.

Inside the room it was getting dark, and the white snow outside seemed to make it darker.

"Mademoiselle Jeanne," said a voice belonging to a servant who just then opened the door; "Mademoiselle Jeanne, what are you doing at the window? You will catch cold."

Jeanne gave a little start when she heard herself spoken to. She had been all alone in the room for some time, with not a sound about her. She turned slowly from the window and came near the fire.

"If I did catch cold, it would not be bad," she said. "I would stay in bed, and you, Marcelline, would make me nice things to eat, and nobody would say, 'Don't do that, Mademoiselle.' It would be charming."

Marcelline was Jeanne's old nurse, and she had been her mother's nurse too. She was really rather old, how old nobody seemed exactly to know, but Jeanne thought her *very* old, and asked her once if she had not been her grandmother's nurse too. Any one else but Marcelline would have been offended at such a question; but Marcelline was not like any one else, and she never was offended at anything. She was so old that for many years no one had seen much difference in her — she had reached a sort of settled oldness, like an arm-chair which may once have been covered with bright-coloured silk, but which, with time and wear, has got to have an all-over-old look which never seems to get any worse. Not that Marcelline was dull or gray to look at — she was bright and cheery, and when she had a new clean cap on, all beautifully frilled and crimped round her face, Jeanne used to tell her that she was beautiful, quite beautiful, and that if she was *very* good and always did exactly what Jeanne asked her, she — Jeanne — would have her to be nurse to her children when she had grown up to be a lady, married to some very nice gentleman.

And when Jeanne chattered like that, Marcelline used to smile; she never said anything, she just smiled. Sometimes Jeanne liked to see her smile; sometimes it would make her impatient, and she would say, "Why do you smile like that, Marcelline? *Speak!* When I speak I like you to speak too."

But all she could get Marcelline to answer would be, "Well, Mademoiselle, it is very well what you say."

This evening — or perhaps I should say afternoon, for whatever hour the chickens' timepiece made it, it was only half-past three by the great big clock that stood at the end of the long passage by Jeanne's room door; — this afternoon Jeanne was not quite as lively as she sometimes was. She sat down on the floor in front of the fire and stared into it. It was pretty to look at just then, for the wood was burning redly, and at the tiniest touch a whole bevy of

lovely sparks would fly out like bees from a hive, or
a covey of birds, or better still, like a thousand im-
prisoned fairies escaping at some magic touch. Of
all things, Jeanne loved to give this magic touch.
There was no poker, but she managed just as well
with a stick of unburnt wood, or sometimes, when
she was *quite* sure Marcelline was not looking, with
the toe of her little shoe. Just now it was Marcelline who set the fairy sparks free by moving the logs
a little and putting on a fresh one behind.

"How pretty they are, are they not, Marcelline?"
said Jeanne.

Marcelline did not speak, and when Jeanne looked
up at her, she saw by the light of the fire that she
was smiling. Jeanne held up her forefinger.

"Naughty Marcelline," she said; "you are not to
smile. You are to *speak*. I want you to speak very
much, for it is so dull, and I have nothing to do. I
want you to tell me stories, Marcelline. Do you
hear, you naughty little thing?"

"And what am I to tell you stories about then,
Mademoiselle? You have got all out of my old
head long ago; and when the grain is all ground
what can the miller do?"

"Get some more, of course," said Jeanne. "Why,
I could make stories if I tried, I daresay, and I am
only seven, and you who are a hundred — are you
quite a hundred, Marcelline?"

Marcelline shook her head.

"Not *quite*, Mademoiselle," she said.

"Well, never mind, you are old enough to make stories, anyway. Tell me more about the country where you lived when you were little as I; the country you will never tell me the name of. Oh, I do like that one about the Golden Princess shut up in the castle by the sea! I like stories about princesses best of all. I do wish I were a princess; next my best wish of all, I wish to be a princess. Marcelline, do you hear? I want you to tell me a story."

Still Marcelline did not reply. She in her turn was looking into the fire. Suddenly she spoke.

"One, two, three," she said. "Quick, now, Mademoiselle, quick, quick. Wish a wish before that last spark is gone. Quick, Mademoiselle."

"Oh dear, what shall I wish?" exclaimed Jeanne. "When you tell me to be quick it all goes out of my head; but I know now. I wish — "

"Hush, Mademoiselle," said Marcelline, quickly again. "You must not say it aloud. Never mind, it is all right. You have wished it before the spark is gone. It will come true, Mademoiselle."

Jeanne's bright dark eyes glanced up at Marcelline with an expression of mingled curiosity and respect.

"How do you know it will come true?" she said.

Marcelline's old eyes, nearly as bright and dark still as Jeanne's own, had a half-mischievous look in them as she replied, solemnly shaking her head,

"I know, Mademoiselle, and that is all I can say.

And when the time comes for your wish to be granted, you will see if I am not right."

"Shall I?" said Jeanne, half impressed, half rebellious. "Do the fairies tell you things, Marcelline? Not that I believe there are any fairies — not now, anyway."

"Don't say that, Mademoiselle," said Marcelline. "In that country I have told you of no one ever said such a thing as that."

"Why didn't they? Did they really *see* fairies there?" asked Jeanne, lowering her voice a little.

"Perhaps," said Marcelline; but that was all she *would* say, and Jeanne couldn't get her to tell her any fairy stories, and had to content herself with making them for herself instead out of the queer shapes of the burning wood of the fire.

She was so busy with these fancies that she did not hear the stopping of the click-click of Marcelline's knitting needles, nor did she hear the old nurse get up from her chair and go out of the room. A few minutes before, the *facteur* had rung at the great wooden gates of the courtyard — a rather rare event, for in those days letters came only twice a week — but this, too, little Jeanne had not heard. She must have grown drowsy with the quiet and the heat of the fire, for she quite started when the door again opened, and Marcelline's voice told her that her mother wanted her to go down to the salon, she had something to say to her.

"O Marcelline," said Jeanne, rubbing her eyes, "I didn't know you had gone away. What does mamma want? O Marcelline, I am so sleepy, I would like to go to bed."

"To go to bed, Mademoiselle, and not yet five o'clock! Oh no, you will wake up nicely by the time you get down to the salon."

"I am so tired, Marcelline," persisted Jeanne. "These winter days it is so dull. I don't mind in summer, for then I can play in the garden with Dudu and the tortoise, and all the creatures. But in winter it is so dull. I would not be tired if I had a little friend to play with me."

"Keep up your heart, Madamoiselle. Stranger things have happened than that you should have some one to play with."

"What do you mean, Marcelline?" said Jeanne, curiously. "Do you know something, Marcelline? Tell me, do. Did you know what my wish was?" she added, eagerly.

"I know, Mademoiselle, that Madame will be waiting for you in the salon. We can talk about your wish later; when I am putting you to bed."

She would say no more, but smoothed Jeanne's soft dark hair, never very untidy it must be owned, for it was always neatly plaited in two tails that hung down her back, as was then the fashion for little girls of Jeanne's age and country, and bade her again not to delay going downstairs.

Jeanne set off. In that great rambling old house it was really quite a journey from her room to her mother's salon. There was the long corridor to pass, at one end of which were Jeanne's quarters, at the other a room which had had for her since her baby-hood a mingled fascination and awe. It was hung with tapestry, very old, and in some parts faded, but still distinct. As Jeanne passed by the door of this room, she noticed that it was open, and the gleam of the faint moonlight on the snow-covered garden outside attracted her.

"I can see the terrace ever so much better from the tapestry room window," she said to herself. "I wonder what Dudu is doing, poor old fellow. Oh, how cold he must be! I suppose Grignan is asleep in a hole in the hedge, and the chickens will be all right anyway. I have not seen Houpet all day."

"Houpet" was Jeanne's favourite of the three chickens. He had come by his name on account of a wonderful tuft of feathers on the top of his head, which stuck straight up and then waved down again, something like a little umbrella. No doubt he was a very rare and wonderful chicken, and if I were clever about chickens I would be able to tell you all his re-markable points. But that I cannot do. I can only say he was the queerest-looking creature that ever pecked about a poultry-yard, and how it came to pass that Jeanne admired him so, I cannot tell you either.

"Poor Houpet!" she repeated, as she ran across

the tapestry room to the uncurtained window; "I am sure he must have been very sad without me all day. He has such a loving heart. The others are nice too, but not half so loving. And Grignan has no heart at all; I suppose tortoises never have; only he is very comical, which is nearly as nice. As for Dudu, I really cannot say, he is so stuck up, as if he knew better than any one else. Ah, there he is, the old fellow! Well, Dudu," she called out, as if the raven could have heard her so far off and through the closely shut window; "well, Dudu, how are you to-day, my dear sir? How do you like the snow and the cold?"

Dudu calmly continued his promenade up and down the terrace. Jeanne could clearly distinguish his black shape against the white ground.

"I am going downstairs to see mamma, Dudu," she went on. "I love mamma very much, but I wish she wasn't my mother at all, but my sister. I wish she was turned into a little girl to play with me, and that papa was turned into a little boy. How funny he would look with his white hair, wouldn't he, Dudu? Oh, you stupid Dudu, why won't you speak to me? I wish you would come up here; there's a beautiful castle and garden in the tapestry, where you would have two peacocks to play with;" for just at that moment the moon, passing from under a cloud, lighted up one side of the tapestry, which, as Jeanne said, represented a garden with various curious occupants. And as the wavering brightness caught the grotesque figures in turn, it really seemed to the little girl as if they moved. Half pleased, half startled at the fancy, she clapped her hands.

" Dudu, Dudu," she cried, " the peacocks want you to come; they're beginning to jump about; " and almost as she said the words a loud croak from the raven sounded in her ears, and turning round, there, to her amazement, she saw Dudu standing on the ledge of the window outside, his bright eyes shining, his black wings flapping, just as if he would say,

" Let me in, Mademoiselle, let me in. Why do you mock me by calling me if you won't let me in ? "

Completely startled by this time, Jeanne turned and fled.

" He must be a fairy," she said by herself; " I'll never make fun of Dudu any more — *never*. He must be a fairy, or how else could he have got up from the terrace on to the window-sill all in a minute? And I don't think a raven fairy would be nice at all; he'd be a sort of an imp, I expect. I wouldn't mind now if Houpet was a fairy, he's so gentle and loving ; but Dudu would be a sort of ogre fairy, he's so black and solemn. Oh dear, how he startled me ! How did he get up there? I'm very glad *I* don't sleep in the tapestry room."

But when she got down to the brightly-lighted salon, her cheeks were so pale and her eyes so

startled-looking that her mother was quite concerned, and eagerly asked what was the matter.

"Nothing," said Jeanne at first, after the manner
of little girls, and boys too, when they do not want to
be cross-questioned; but after a while she confessed
that she had run into the tapestry room on her way
down, and that the moonlight made the figures look
as if they were moving — and — and — that Dudu
came and stood on the window-sill and croaked at
her.

"Dudu stood on the window-sill outside the tapestry room!" repeated her father; "impossible, my
child! Why, Dudu could not by any conceivable
means get up there; you might as well say you saw
the tortoise there too."

"If I had called him perhaps he *would* have come
too; I believe Dudu and he are great friends,"
thought Jeanne to herself, for her mind was in a
queer state of confusion, and she would not have
felt very much astounded at anything. But aloud
she only repeated, "I'm sure he was there, dear
papa."

And to satisfy her, her kind father, though he was
not so young as he had been, and the bad weather
made him very rheumatic, mounted upstairs to the
tapestry room, and carefully examined the window
inside and out.

"Nothing of the kind to be seen, my little girl,"
was his report. "Master Dudu was hobbling about

in the snow on his favourite terrace walk as usual.
I hope the servants give him a little meat in this
cold weather, by the by. I must speak to Eugène
about it. What you fancied was Dudu, my little
Jeanne," he continued, "must have been a branch of
the ivy blown across the window. In the moonlight,
and with the reflections of the snow, things take
queer shapes."

"But there is no wind, and the ivy doesn't grow
so high up, and the ivy could not have *croaked*,"
thought Jeanne to herself again, though she was far
too well brought up a little French girl to contradict
her father by saying so.

"Perhaps so, dear papa," was all she said.

But her parents still looked a little uneasy.

"She cannot be quite well," said her mother.
"She must be feverish. I must tell Marcelline to
make her a little tisane when she goes to bed."

"Ah, bah!" said Jeanne's white-headed papa.
"What we were speaking of will be a much better
cure than tisane. She needs companionship of her
own age."

Jeanne pricked up her ears at this, and glanced at
her mother inquiringly. Instantly there started into
her mind Marcelline's prophecy about her wish.

"The naughty little Marcelline!" she thought to
herself. "She has been tricking me. I believe she
knew something was going to happen. Mamma,
my dear mamma!" she cried, eagerly but respect-

fully, "have you something to tell me? Have you had letters, mamma, from the country, where the little cousin lives?"

Jeanne's mother softly stroked the cheeks, red enough now, of her excited little daughter.

"Yes, my child," she replied. "I have had a letter. It was for that I sent for you — to tell you about it. I have a letter from the grandfather of Hugh, with whom he has lived since his parents died, and he accepts my invitation. Hugh is to come to live with us, as his mother would have wished. His grandfather can spare him, for he has other grandchildren, and we need him, do we not, my Jeanne? My little girl needs a little brother — and I loved his mother so much," she added in a lower voice.

Jeanne could not speak. Her face was glowing with excitement, her breath came quick and short, almost, it seemed, as if she were going to cry. "O, mamma!" was all she could say — "O mamma!" but her mother understood her.

"And when will he come?" asked Jeanne next.

"Soon, I hope. In a few days; but it depends on the weather greatly. The snow has stopped the diligences in several places, they say; but his grandfather writes that he would like Hugh to come soon, as he himself has to leave home."

"And will he be always with us? Will he do lessons with me, mamma, and go to the château with us in summer, and always be with us?"

"I hope so. For a long time at least. And he will do lessons with you at first — though when he gets big he will need more teachers, of course."

"He is a year older than I, mamma."

"Yes, he is eight."

"And, mamma," added Jeanne, after some consideration, "what room will he have?"

"The tapestry room," said her mother. "It is the warmest, and Hugh is rather delicate, and may feel it cold here. And the tapestry room is not far from yours, my little Jeanne, so you can keep your toys and books together. There is only one thing I do not quite understand in the letter," went on Jeanne's mother, turning to her husband as she always did in any difficulty — he was so much older and wiser than she, she used to say. "Hugh's grandfather says Hugh has begged leave to bring a pet with him, and he hopes I will not mind. What can it be? I cannot read the other word."

"A little dog probably," said Jeanne's father, putting on his spectacles as he took the letter from his wife, "a pet — gu — ga — and then comes another word beginning with 'p.' It almost looks like 'pig,' but it could not be a pet pig. No, I cannot read it either; we must wait to see till he comes."

As Marcelline was preparing to put Jeanne to bed that night, the little girl suddenly put her arms round her nurse's neck, and drew down her old face till it was on a level with her own.

" Look in my face, Marcelline," she said. " Now look in my face and confess. Now, didn't you know that mamma had got a letter to-night and what it said, and was not that how you knew my wish would come true ? "

Marcelline smiled.

" That was one way I knew, Mademoiselle," she said.

" Well, it shows I'm right not to believe in fairies anyway. I really did think at first that the fairies had told you something, but—" suddenly she stopped as the remembrance of her adventure in the tapestry room returned to her mind. " Dudu may be a fairy, whether Marcelline has anything to do with fairies or not," she reflected. It was better certainly to approach such subjects respectfully. " Marcelline," she added, after a little silence, " there is only one thing I don't like. I wish the little cousin were not going to sleep in the tapestry room."

" Not in the tapestry room, Mademoiselle ? " exclaimed Marcelline, " why, it is the best room in the house ! You, who are so fond of stories, Mademoiselle — why there are stories without end on the walls of the tapestry room ; particularly on a moonlight night."

" *Are* there ? " said Jeanne. " I wonder then if the little cousin will be able to find them out. If he does, he must tell them to me. Are they fairy stories, Marcelline ? "

But old Marcelline only smiled.

CHAPTER II.

PRINCE CHÉRI.

"I'll take my guinea-pig always to church."
CHILD WORLD.

IF it were cold just then in the thick-walled, well-warmed old house, which was Jeanne's home, you may fancy *how* cold it was in the rumbling diligence, which in those days was the only way of travelling in France. And for a little boy whose experience of long journeys was small, this one was really rather trying. But Jeanne's cousin Hugh was a very patient little boy. His life, since his parents' death, had not been a *very* happy one, and he had learnt to bear troubles without complaining. And now that he was on his way to the kind cousins his mother had so often told him of, the cousins who had been so kind to *her*, before she had any home of her own, his heart was so full of happiness that, even if the journey had been twice as cold and uncomfortable, he would not have thought himself to be pitied.

It was a pale little face, however, which looked out of the diligence window at the different places where it stopped, and a rather timid voice which asked in the pretty broken French he had not quite

17

forgotten since the days that his mother taught him her own language, for a little milk for his "pet." The pet, which had travelled on his knees all the way from England — comfortably nestled up in hay and cotton wool in its cage, which looked something like a big mouse-trap — much better off in its way certainly than its poor little master. But it was a great comfort to him: the sight of its funny little nose poking out between the bars of its cage made Hugh feel ever so much less lonely, and when he had secured a little milk for his guinea-pig he did not seem to mind half so much about anything for himself.

Still it was a long and weary journey, and poor Hugh felt very glad when he was wakened up from the uncomfortable doze, which was all in the way of sleep he could manage, to be told that at last they had arrived. This was the town where his friends lived, and a "monsieur," the conductor added, was inquiring for him — Jeanne's father's valet it was, who had been sent to meet him and take him safe to the old house, where an eager little heart was counting the minutes till he came.

They looked at each other curiously when at last they met. Jeanne's eyes were sparkling and her cheeks burning, and her whole little person in a flutter of joyful excitement, and yet she couldn't speak. Now that the little cousin was there, actually standing before her, she could not speak. How was it? He was not *quite* what she had expected; he looked paler and quieter than any boys she had seen, and — was he not glad to see her? — glad to have come? — she asked herself with a little misgiving. She looked at him again — his blue eyes were very sweet and gentle, and, tired though he was, Jeanne could see that he was trying to smile and look pleased. But he was *very* tired and very shy. That was all that was the matter. And his shyness made Jeanne feel shy too.

"Are you very tired, my cousin?" she said at last.

"Not very, thank you," said Hugh. "I am rather tired, but I am not very hungry," he added, glancing at a side-table where a little supper had been laid out for him. "I am not very hungry, but I think Nibble is. Might I have a little milk for Nibble, please?"

As he spoke he held up for Jeanne to see the small box he was carrying, and she gave a little scream of pleasure when, through the bars, she caught sight of the guinea-pig's soft nose, poking out, saying as plainly almost as if he had spoken, "I want my supper; please to see at once about my supper, little girl."

"Neeble," cried Jeanne, "O my cousin, is Neeble your pet? Why, he is a 'cochon de Barbarie!' O the dear little fellow! We could not — at least papa and mamma could not — read what he was. And have you brought him all the way, my cousin, and do you love him very much? Marcelline, Marcelline, oh, do give us some milk for the cochon de Barbarie — oh, see, Marcelline, how sweet he is!"

Once set free, her tongue ran on so fast that sometimes Hugh had difficulty to understand her. But the ice was broken anyway, and when, an hour or two later, Jeanne's mother told her she might take Hugh up to show him his room, the two trotted off, hand-in-hand, as if they had been close companions for years.

"I hope you will like your room, chéri," said Jeanne, with a tiny tone of patronising. "It is not very far from mine, and mamma says we can keep all our toys and books together in my big cupboard in the passage."

Hugh looked at Jeanne for a moment without speaking. "What was that name you called me just now, Jeanne?" he asked, after a little pause.

Jeanne thought for a minute.

"'Mon cousin,' was it that?" she said. "Oh no, I remember, it was 'chéri.' I *cannot* say your name — I have tried all these days. I cannot say it better than 'Ee-ou,' which is not pretty."

She screwed her rosy little mouth into the funniest shape as she tried to manage "Hugh." Hugh could hardly help laughing.

"Never mind," he said. "I like 'chéri' ever so much better. I like it better than 'mon cousin' or

"Isn't it a Funny Room, Chéri?"—p. 21.

any name, because, do you know," he added, dropping his voice a little, "I remember now, though I had forgotten till you said it — that was the name mamma called me by."

"Chéri!" repeated Jeanne, stopping half-way up the staircase to throw her arms round Hugh's neck at the greatest risk to the equilibrium of the whole party, including the guinea-pig — "*Chéri!* I shall always call you so, then. You shall be my Prince Chéri. Don't you love fairy stories, mon cousin?"

"*Awfully,*" said Hugh, from the bottom of his soul.

"I knew you would," said Jeanne triumphantly. "And oh, so do I! Marcelline says, Chéri, that the tapestry room — that's the room you're going to have — is full of fairy stories. I wonder if you'll find out any of them. You must tell me if you do."

"The tapestry room?" repeated Hugh; "I don't think I ever saw a tapestry room. Oh," he added, as a sudden recollection struck him, "is it like what that queen long ago worked about the battles and all that? I mean all about William the Conqueror."

"No," said Jeanne, "it's quite different from that work. I've seen that, so I know. It isn't pretty at all. It's just long strips of linen with queer-shaped horses and things worked on. Not *at all* pretty. And I think the pictures on the walls of your room *are* pretty. Here it is. Isn't it a funny room, Chéri?"

She opened the door of the tapestry room as she spoke, for while chattering they had mounted the staircase and made their way along the corridor. Hugh followed his little cousin into the room, and stood gazing round him with curious surprise and pleasure. The walls were well lighted up, for Marcelline had carried a lamp upstairs and set it down on the table, and a bright fire was burning in the wide old-fashioned hearth.

"Jeanne," said Hugh, after a minute's silence, "Jeanne, it is very funny, but, do you know, I am *sure* I have seen this room before. I seem to know the pictures on the walls. Oh, *how* nice they are! I didn't think that was what tapestry meant. Oh, how glad I am this is to be my room — is yours like this too, Jeanne?"

Jeanne shook her head.

"Oh no, Chéri," she said. "My room has a nice paper — roses and things like that running up and down. I am very glad my room is not like this. I don't think I should like to see all these funny creatures in the night. You don't know how queer they look in the moonlight. They quite frightened me once."

Hugh opened his blue eyes very wide.

"*Frightened* you?" he said. "I should never be frightened at them. They are so nice and funny. Just look at those peacocks, Jeanne. They are lovely."

Jeanne still shook her head.

"I don't think so," she said. "I can't bear those peacocks. But I'm very glad *you* like them, Chéri."

"I wish it was moonlight to-night," continued Hugh. "I don't think I should go to sleep at all. I would lie awake watching all the pictures. I daresay they look rather nice in the firelight too, but still not *so* nice as in the moonlight."

"No, Monsieur," said Marcelline, who had followed the children into the room. "A moonlight night is the time to see them best. It makes the colours look quite fresh again. Mademoiselle Jeanne has never looked at the tapestry properly by moonlight, or she would like it better."

"I shouldn't mind with Chéri," said Jeanne. "You must call me some night when it's very pretty, Chéri, and we'll look at it together."

Marcelline smiled and seemed pleased, which was rather funny. Most nurses would have begun scolding Jeanne for dreaming of such a thing as running about the house in the middle of the night to admire the moonlight on tapestry or on anything else. But then Marcelline certainly was rather a funny person.

"And the cochon de Barbarie, where is he to sleep, Monsieur?" she said to Hugh.

Hugh looked rather distressed.

"I don't know," he said. "At home he slept in his little house on a sort of balcony there was outside my window. But there isn't any balcony here — besides, it's so *very* cold, and he's quite strange, you know."

He looked at Marcelline, appealingly.

" I daresay, while it is so cold, Madame would not mind if we put him in the cupboard in the passage," she said; but Jeanne interrupted her.

" Oh no," she said. " He would be far better in the chickens' house. It's nice and warm, I know, and his cage can be in one corner. He wouldn't be nearly so lonely, and to-morrow I'll tell Houpet and the others that they must be very kind to him. Houpet always does what I tell him."

" Who is Houpet?" said Hugh.

" He's my pet chicken," replied Jeanne. " They're all pets, of course, but he's the most of a pet of all. He lives in the chicken-house with the two other little chickens. O Chéri," she added, glancing round, and seeing that Marcelline had left the room, " do let us run out and peep at Houpet for a minute. We can go through the tonnelle, and the chickens' house is close by."

She darted off as she spoke, and Hugh, nothing loth, his precious Nibble still in his arms, followed her. They ran down the long corridor, on to which opened both the tapestry room and Jeanne's room at the other end, through a small sort of ante-room, and then — for though they were *upstairs*, the garden being built in terraces was at this part of the house on a level with the first floor — then straight out into what little Jeanne called " the tonnelle."

Hugh stood still and gazed about him with delight and astonishment.

"O Jeanne," he exclaimed, "how pretty it is! oh, how very pretty!"

Jeanne stopped short in her progress along the tonnelle.

"What's pretty?" she said in a matter-of-fact tone. "Do you mean the garden with the snow?"

"No, no, that's pretty too, but I mean the trees. Look up, Jeanne, do."

There was no moonlight, but the light from the windows streamed out to where the children stood, and shone upon the beautiful icicles on the branches above their heads. For the tonnelle was a kind of arbour — a long covered passage made by trees at each side, whose boughs had been trained to meet and interlace overhead. And now, with their fairy tracery of snow and frost, the effect of the numberless little branches forming a sparkling roof was pretty and fanciful in the extreme. Jeanne looked up as she was told.

"Yes," she said, "it's pretty. If it was moonlight it would be prettier still, for then we could see right along the tonnelle to the end."

"I don't think that *would* be prettier," said Hugh; "the dark at the end makes it look so nice — like as if it was a fairy door into some queer place — a magic cavern, or some place like that."

"So it does," said Jeanne. "What nice fancies you have, Chéri! But I wish you could see the tonnelle in summer. It *is* pretty then, with all the leaves on. But we must run quick, or else Marcelline will be calling us before we have got to the chicken-house."

Off she set again, with Hugh after her, though not so fast, for Jeanne knew every step of the way, and poor Hugh had never been in the garden before. It was not very far to go, however — the chickens' house was in a little courtyard just a few steps from the tonnelle, and guided by Jeanne's voice in front as much as by the faint glimpses of her figure, dark against the snow, Hugh soon found himself safe beside her at the door of the chickens' house. Jeanne felt about till she got hold of the latch, which she lifted, and was going to push open the door and enter when Hugh stopped her.

"Jeanne," he said, "it's *quite* dark. We can't possibly see the chickens. Hadn't we better wait till to-morrow, and put Nibble in the cupboard, as Marcelline said, for to-night?"

"Oh no," said Jeanne. "It doesn't matter a bit that it's dark." She opened the door as she spoke, and gently pulled Hugh in after her. "Look," she went on, "there is a very, very little light from the kitchen window after all, when the door is opened. Look, Chéri, up in that corner sleep Houpet and the others. Put the cochon de Barbarie down here — so — that will do. He will be quite safe here, and you feel it is not cold."

"And are there no rats, or naughty dogs about — nothing like that?" asked Hugh rather anxiously.

"Of course not," replied Jeanne. "Do you think I'd leave Houpet here if there were? I'll call to Houpet now, and tell him to be kind to the little cochon."

"But Houpet's asleep, and, besides, how would he know what you say?" objected Hugh.

For all answer Jeanne gave a sort of little whistle — half whistle, half coo it was. "Houpet, Houpet," she called softly, "we've brought a little cochon de Barbarie to sleep in your house. You must be very kind to him — do you hear, Houpet dear? and in the morning you must fly down and peep in at his cage and tell him you're very glad to see him."

A faint, a very faint little rustle was heard up above in the corner where Jeanne had tried to persuade her cousin that the chickens were to be *seen*, and delighted at this evidence that anyway they were to be *heard*, she turned to him triumphantly.

"That's Houpet," she said. "Dear little fellow, he's too sleepy to crow — he just gives a little wriggle to show that he's heard me. Now put down the cage, Chéri — oh, you have put it down — and let's run in again. Your pet will be quite safe, you see, but if we're not quick, Marcelline will be running out to look for us."

She felt about for Hugh's hand, and having got it, turned to go. But she stopped to put her head in again for a moment at the door.

"Houpet, dear," she said, "don't let Dudu come

into your house. If he tries to, you must fly at him and scold him and peck him."

"Who is Dudu?" said Hugh, as they were running back to the house together along the snowy garden path.

"He is — " began Jeanne. "Hush," she went on, in a lower voice, "there he is! I do believe he heard what I said, and he's angry." For right before them on the path stood the old raven, on one leg as usual, though this it was too dark to see clearly. And, as Jeanne spoke, he gave a sharp, sudden croak, which made both the children jump, and then deliberately hopped away.

"He's a raven!" said Hugh with surprise. "Why, what funny pets you have, Jeanne!"

Jeanne laughed.

"Dudu isn't my pet," she said. "I don't like him. To tell you the truth, Chéri, I'm rather frightened of him. I think he's a sort of a fairy."

Hugh looked much impressed, but not at all surprised.

"Do you really, Jeanne?" he said.

"Yes," she said, "I do. And I'm not *sure* but that Grignan is too. At least I think Grignan is enchanted, and that Dudu is the spiteful fairy that did it. Grignan is the tortoise, you know."

"Yes," said Hugh, "you told me about him. I do wonder if what you think is true," he added reflectively. "We must try to find out, Jeanne."

"But we mustn't offend Dudu," said Jeanne. "He might, you know, turn *us* into something — two little mice, perhaps — that wouldn't be very nice, would it, Chéri?"

"I don't know," Hugh replied. "I wouldn't mind for a little, if he would turn us back again. We could get into such funny places and see such funny things — couldn't we, Jeanne?"

They both laughed merrily at the idea, and were still laughing when they ran against Marcelline at the door which they had left open at the end of the tonnelle.

"My children!" she exclaimed. "Monsieur Chéri and Mademoiselle Jeanne! Where have you been? And in the snow too! Who would have thought it?"

Her tone was anxious, but not cross. She hurried them in to the warm fire, however, and carefully examined their feet to make sure that their shoes and stockings were not wet.

"Marcelline is very kind," said Hugh, fixing his soft blue eyes on the old nurse in surprise. "At home, grandmamma's maid would have scolded me dreadfully if I had run out in the snow."

"Yes," said Jeanne, flinging her arms round the old nurse's neck, and giving her a kiss first on one cheek then on the other; "she is very kind. Nice little old Marcelline."

"Perhaps," said Hugh, meditatively, "she remem-

bers that when she was a little girl she liked to do
things like that herself."

"I don't believe you ever were a little girl, were
you, Marcelline?" said Jeanne. "I believe you
were always a little old woman like what you are
now."

Marcelline laughed, but did not speak.

"Ask Dudu," she said at last. "If he is a fairy,
he should know."

Jeanne pricked up her ears at this.

"Marcelline," she said solemnly, "I believe you
do know something about Dudu. Oh, *do* tell us,
dear Marcelline."

But nothing more was to be got out of the old
nurse.

When the children were undressed, Jeanne begged
leave to run into Hugh's room with him to tuck him
into bed, and make him feel at home the first night.
There was no lamp in the room, but the firelight
danced curiously on the quaint figures on the walls.

"You're sure you're not frightened, Chéri?" said
little Jeanne in a motherly way, as she was leaving
the room.

"Frightened! what is there to be frightened at?"
said Hugh.

"The funny figures," said Jeanne. "Those peacocks look just as if they were going to jump out at
you."

"I think they look very nice," said Hugh. "I am

sure I shall have nice dreams. I shall make the peacocks give a party some night, Jeanne, and we'll invite Dudu and Grignan, and Houpet and the two little hens, and Nibble, of course, and we'll make them all tell stories."

Jeanne clapped her hands.

"Oh, what fun!" she exclaimed. "And you'll ask me and let me hear the stories, won't you, Chéri?"

"*Of course*," said Hugh. So Jeanne skipped off in the highest spirits.

CHAPTER III.

> " O moon! in the night I have seen you sailing,
> And shining so round and low."
>
> CHILD NATURE.

" AND what did you dream, Chéri?" inquired Jeanne the next morning in a confidential and mysterious tone.

Hugh hesitated.

"I don't know," he said at last. "At least —" he stopped and hesitated again.

The two children were having their "little breakfast," consisting of two great big cups of nice hot milky coffee and two big slices of bread, with the sweet fresh butter for which the country where Jeanne's home was is famed. They were alone in Jeanne's room, and Marcelline had drawn a little table close to the fire for them, for this morning it seemed colder than ever; fresh snow had fallen during the night, and out in the garden nothing was to be seen but smoothly-rounded white mounds of varying sizes and heights, and up in the sky the dull blue-gray curtain of snow-cloud made one draw back shivering from the window, feeling as if the sun had

32

gone off in a sulky fit and would *never* come back again.

But inside, close by the brightly-blazing wood fire, Jeanne and Hugh found themselves "very well," as the little girl called it, very well indeed. And the hot coffee was very nice, much nicer, Hugh thought, than the very weak tea which his grandmother's maid used to give him for breakfast at home. He stirred it round and round slowly with his spoon, staring into his cup, while he repeated, in answer to little Jeanne's question about what he had dreamt, "No, I don't know."

"But you did dream *something*," said Jeanne rather impatiently. "Can't you tell me about it? I thought you were going to have all sorts of funny things to tell me. You said you would have a party of the peacocks and all the pets, and make them tell stories."

"Yes," said Hugh slowly. "But I couldn't make them — I must wait till they come. I think I did dream some funny things last night, but I can't remember. There seemed to be a lot of chattering, and once I thought I saw the raven standing at the end of the bed, but that time I wasn't dreaming. I'm sure I wasn't; but I was very sleepy, and I couldn't hear what he said. He seemed to want me to do something or other, and then he nodded his head to where the peacocks are, and do you know, Jeanne, I thought they nodded too. Wasn't that funny? But

I daresay it was only the firelight — the fire had burnt low, and then it bobbed up again all of a sudden."

"And what more?" asked Jeanne eagerly. "O Chéri, I think that's wonderful! Do tell me some more."

"I don't think I remember any more," said Hugh. "After that I went to sleep, and then it was all a muddle. There were the chickens and Nibble and the tortoise all running about, and Dudu seemed to be talking to me all the time. But it was just a muddle; you know how dreams go sometimes. And when I woke up the fire was quite out and it was all dark. And then I saw the light of Marcelline's candle through the hinge of the door, and she came to tell me it was time to get up."

"Oh dear," said Jeanne, "I do hope you'll dream some more to-night."

"I daresay I shan't dream at all," said Hugh. "Some nights I go to sleep, and it's morning in one minute. I don't like that much, because it's nice to wake up and feel how cosy it is in bed."

"But, Chéri," pursued Jeanne after a few moments' silence, and a few more bites at her bread and butter, "there's one thing I don't understand. It's about Dudu. You said it wasn't a dream, you were sure. Do you think he was really there, at the foot of the bed? It might have been the firelight that made you think you saw the peacocks nodding, but it couldn't have been the firelight that made you think you saw Dudu."

"No," said Hugh, "I can't understand it either. If it was a dream it was a very queer one, for I never felt more awake in my life. I'll tell you what, Jeanne, the next time I think I see Dudu like that I'll run and tell you."

"Yes, do," said Jeanne, "though I don't know that it would be much good. Dudu's dreadfully tricky."

She had not told Hugh of the trick the raven had played her, though why she had not done so she could hardly have explained. Perhaps she was a little ashamed of having been so frightened; perhaps she was still a little afraid of Dudu; and most of all, I think, she had a great curiosity to find out more about the mysterious bird, and thought it best to leave Hugh to face his own adventures.

"If Dudu thinks I've told Chéri all about his funny ways," she thought, "perhaps he'll be angry and not do any more queer things."

The snow was still, as I said, thick on the ground, thicker, indeed, than the day before. But the children managed to amuse themselves very well. Marcelline would not hear of their going out, not even as far as the chickens' house, but she fetched Nibble to pay them a visit in the afternoon, and they had great fun with him.

"He looks very happy, doesn't he, Chéri?" said Jeanne. "I am sure Houpet has been kind to him. What a pity pets can't speak, isn't it? they could tell us such nice funny things."

"Yes," said Hugh, "I've often thought that, and I often have thought Nibble could speak if he liked."

"*Houpet* could, I'm quite sure," said Jeanne, "and I believe Dudu and he do speak to each other. You should just see them sometimes. Why, there they are!" she added, going close up to the window near which she had been standing. "Do come here, Chéri, quick, but come very quietly."

Hugh came forward and looked out. There were the four birds, making the quaintest group you could fancy. Houpet with his waving tuft of feathers was perched on the top rung of a short garden ladder, his two little hens as usual close beside him. And down below on the path stood the raven, on one leg of course, his queer black head very much on one side, as he surveyed the little group above him.

"Silly young people," he seemed to be saying to himself; but Houpet was not to be put down so. With a shrill, clear crow he descended from his perch, stepped close up to Dudu, looked him in the face, and then quietly marched off, followed by his two companions. The children watched this little scene with the greatest interest.

"They *do* look as if they were talking to each other," said Hugh. "I wonder what it's about."

"Perhaps it's about the party," said Jeanne; "the party you said you'd give to the peacocks on the wall, and all the pets."

"Perhaps," said Hugh. "I am sure there must

be beautiful big rooms in that castle with the lots of
steps up to it, where the peacocks stand. Don't you
think it would be nice to get inside that castle and
see what it's like?"

"Oh, wouldn't it!" said Jeanne, clapping her
hands. "How I do wish we could! You might tell
Dudu to take us, Chéri. Perhaps it's a fairy palace
really, though it only looks like a picture, and if
Dudu's a fairy, he might know about it."

"I'll ask him if I get a chance," said Hugh.
"Good morning, Monsieur Dudu," he went on, bowing politely from the window to the raven, who had
cocked his head in another direction, and seemed
now to be looking up at the two children with the
same supercilious stare he had bestowed upon the
cock and hens. "Good morning, Monsieur Dudu;
I hope you won't catch cold with this snowy weather.
It's best to be very polite to him, you see," added
Hugh, turning to Jeanne; "for if he took offence
we should get no fun out of him."

"Oh yes," said Jeanne, "it is much best to be
very polite to him. Look at him now, Chéri; *doesn't*
he look as if he knew what we were saying?"

For Dudu was eyeing them unmistakably by this
time, his head more on one side than ever, and his
lame leg stuck out in the air like a walking-stick.

"That's *just* how he stood at the foot of the bed,
on the wood part, you know," said Hugh, in a
whisper.

"And weren't you frightened, Chéri?" said Jeanne. "I always think Dudu looks not at all like a good fairy, when he cocks his head on one side and sticks his claw out like that. I quite believe then that he's a wicked enchanter. O Chéri," she went on, catching hold of Hugh, "what *should* we do if he was to turn us into two little frogs or toads?"

"We should have to live in the water, and eat nasty little worms and flies, I suppose," said Hugh gravely.

"And that sort of thick green stuff that grows at the top of dirty ponds; fancy having that for soup," said Jeanne pathetically. "O Chéri, we must indeed be very polite to Dudu, and take *great* pains not to offend him; and if he comes to you in the night, you must be sure to call me at once."

But the following night and several nights after that went by, and nothing was heard or seen of Monsieur Dudu. The weather got a little milder; that is to say, the snow gradually melted away, and the children were allowed to go out into the garden and visit their pets. Nibble seemed quite at home in his new quarters, and was now permitted to run about the chicken-house at his own sweet will; and Jeanne greatly commended Houpet for his kindness to the little stranger, which commendation the chicken received in very good part, particularly when it took the shape of all the tit-bits left on the children's plates.

"See how tame he is," said Jeanne one day when she had persuaded the little cock to peck some crumbs out of her hand; "isn't he a darling, Chéri, with his *dear* little tuft of feathers on the top of his head?"

"He's awfully funny-looking," said Hugh, consideringly; "do you really think he's very pretty, Jeanne?"

"Of course I do," said Jeanne, indignantly; "all my pets are pretty, but Houpet's the prettiest of all."

"He's prettier than Grignan, certainly," said Hugh, giving an amiable little push to the tortoise, who happened to be lying at his feet; "but I like Grignan, he's so comical."

"I think Grignan must know a great deal," said Jeanne, "he's so solemn."

"So is Dudu," said Hugh. "By the by, Jeanne," he went on, but stopped suddenly.

"What?" said Jeanne.

"It just came into my head while we were talking that I must have dreamt of Dudu again last night; but now I try to remember it, it has all gone out of my head."

"*What* a pity," said Jeanne; "do try to remember. Was it that he came and stood at the foot of the bed again, like the last time? You promised to call me if he did."

"No, I don't think he did. I have more a sort of

feeling that he and the peacocks on the wall were whispering to each other — something about us — you and me, Jeanne — it was, I think."

"Perhaps they were going to give a party, and were planning about inviting us," suggested Jeanne.

"I don't know," said Hugh; "it's no good my trying to think. It's just a sleepy feeling of having heard something. I can't remember anything else, and the more I think, the less I remember."

"Well, you must be sure to tell me if you do hear anything more. I was awake ever so long in the night, ever so long; but I didn't mind, there was such nice moonlight."

"Moonlight, was there?" said Hugh; "I didn't know that. I'll try to keep awake to-night, because Marcelline says the figures on the walls are so pretty when it's moonlight."

"And if Dudu comes, or you see anything funny, you'll promise to call me?" said Jeanne.

Hugh nodded his head. There was not much fear of his forgetting his promise. Jeanne reminded him of it at intervals all that day, and when the children kissed each other for good-night she whispered again, "Remember to call me, Chéri."

Chéri went to sleep with the best possible intentions as to "remembering." He had, first of all, intended not to go to sleep at all, for his last glance out of the window before going to bed showed him Monsieur Dudu on the terrace path, enjoying the moonlight apparently, but, Hugh strongly suspected, bent on mischief, for his head was very much on one side and his claw very much stuck out, in the way which Jeanne declared made him look like a very impish raven indeed.

"I wonder what Marcelline meant about the moonlight," thought Hugh to himself as he lay down. "I hardly see the figures on the wall at all. The moon must be going behind a cloud. I wonder if it will be brighter in the middle of the night. I don't see that I need stay awake all the night to see. I can easily wake again. I'll just take a little sleep first."

And the little sleep turned out such a long one, that when poor Hugh opened his eyes, lo and behold! it was to-morrow morning — there was Marcelline standing beside the bed, telling him it was time to get up, he would be late for his tutor if he did not dress himself at once.

"Oh dear," exclaimed Hugh, "what a pity! I meant to stay awake all night to watch the moonlight."

Marcelline smiled what Jeanne called her funny smile.

"You would find it very difficult to do that, I think, my little Monsieur," she said. "However, you did not miss much last night. The clouds came over so that the moon had no chance. Perhaps it will be clearer to-night."

With this hope Hugh had to be satisfied, and to satisfy also his little cousin, who was at first quite disappointed that he had nothing wonderful to tell her.

"To-night," she said, "*I* shall stay awake all night, and if the moonlight is very nice and bright I shall come and wake *you*, you sleepy Chéri. I do *so* want to go up those steps and into the castle where the peacocks are standing at the door."

"So do I," said Hugh, rather mortified; "but if one goes to sleep, whose fault is it? I am sure you will go to sleep too, if you try to keep awake. There's *nothing* makes people go to sleep so fast as trying to keep awake."

"Well, don't try then," said Jeanne, "and see what comes then."

And when night came, Hugh, partly perhaps because he was particularly sleepy — the day had been so much finer that the children had had some splendid runs up and down the long terrace walk in the garden, and the unusual exercise had made both of them very ready for bed when the time came — took Jeanne's advice, tucked himself up snugly and went off to sleep without thinking of the moonlight, or the peacocks, or Dudu, or anything. He slept so soundly, that when he awoke he thought it was morning, and brighter morning than had hitherto greeted him since he came to Jeanne's home.

"Dear me!" he said to himself, rubbing his eyes,

"it must be very late; it looks just as if summer had come," for the whole room was flooded with light — such beautiful light — bright and clear, and yet soft. No wonder that Hugh rubbed his eyes in bewilderment — it was not till he sat up in bed and looked well about him, quite awake now, that he saw that after all it was moonlight, not sunshine, which was illumining the old tapestry room and everything which it contained in this wonderful way.

"Oh, how pretty it is!" thought Hugh. "No wonder Marcelline told us that we should see the tapestry in the moonlight. I never could have thought it would have looked so pretty. Why, even the peacocks' tails seem to have got all sorts of new colours."

He leant forward to examine them better. They were standing — just as usual — one on each side of the flight of steps leading up to the castle. But as Hugh gazed at them it certainly seemed to him — could it be his fancy only? — no, it *must* be true — that their long tails grew longer and swept the ground more majestically — then that suddenly — fluff! a sort of little wind seemed to rustle for an instant, and fluff! again, the two peacocks had spread their tails, and now stood with them proudly reared fan-like, at their backs, just like the real living birds that Hugh had often admired in his grandfather's garden. Hugh was too much amazed to rub his eyes again — he could do nothing but stare, and stare he did with all his might, but for a moment or two there was nothing else to be seen. The peacocks stood still — so still that Hugh now began to doubt whether they had not always stood, tails spread, just as he saw them now, and whether these same tails having ever drooped on the ground was not altogether his fancy. A good deal puzzled, and a little disappointed, he was turning away to look at another part of the pictured walls, when again a slight flutter of movement caught his eyes. What was about to happen this time?

"Perhaps they are going to furl their tails again," thought Hugh; but no. One on each side of the castle door, the peacocks solemnly advanced a few steps, then stood still — quite still — but yet with a certain waiting look about them as if they were expecting some one or something. They were not kept waiting long. The door of the castle opened slowly, very slowly, the peacocks stepped still a little farther forward, and out of the door of the castle — the castle into which little Jeanne had so longed to enter — who, what, who *do* you think came forth? It was Dudu!

A small black figure, black from head to foot, head very much cocked on one side, foot — claw I should say — stuck out like a walking-stick; he stood between the peacocks, right in Hugh's view, just in front of the door which had closed behind him, at the top of the high flight of steps. He stood

It was Dudu!—p. 44.

still with an air of great dignity, which seemed to say,
" Here you see me for the first time in my rightful
character — monarch of all I survey." And somehow
Hugh felt that this unspoken address was directed
to *him*. Then, quietly and dignifiedly still, the
raven turned, first to the right, then to the left, and
gravely bowed to the two attendant peacocks, who
each in turn saluted him respectfully and withdrew
a little farther back, on which Dudu began a very
slow and imposing progress down the steps. How
he succeeded in making it so imposing was the puzzle, for after all, his descent was undoubtedly a series
of hops, but all the same it was very majestic, and
Hugh felt greatly impressed, and watched him with
bated breath.

" One, two, three, four," said Hugh to himself,
half unconsciously counting each step as the raven
advanced, "what a lot of steps! Five, six, seven,"
up to twenty-three Hugh counted on. And " what
is he going to do now?" he added, as Dudu, arrived
at the foot of the stairs, looked calmly about him for
a minute or two, as if considering his next move-
ments. Then — how he managed it Hugh could not
tell — he suddenly stepped out of the tapestry land-
scape, and in another moment was perched in his old
place at the foot of Hugh's bed.

He looked at Hugh for an instant or two, gravely
and scrutinisingly, then bowed politely. Hugh, who
was half sitting up in bed, bowed too, but without

speaking. He remembered Jeanne's charges to be very polite to the raven, and thought it better to take no liberties with him, but to wait patiently till he heard what Monsieur Dudu had to say. For somehow it seemed to him a matter of course that the raven *could* speak — he was not the very least surprised when at last Dudu cleared his throat pompously and began —

"You have been expecting me, have you not?"

Hugh hesitated.

"I don't know exactly. I'm not quite sure. Yes, I think I thought perhaps you'd come. But oh! if you please, Monsieur Dudu," he exclaimed, suddenly starting up, "do let me go and call Jeanne. I promised her I would if you came, or if I saw anything funny. Do let me go. I won't be a minute."

But the raven cocked his head on one side and looked at Hugh rather sternly.

"No," he said. "You cannot go for Jeanne. I do not wish it at present."

Hugh felt rather angry. Why should Dudu lay down the law to him in this way?

"But I promised," he began.

"People should not promise what they are not sure of being able to perform," he said sententiously. "Besides, even if you did go to get Jeanne, she couldn't come. She is ever so far away."

"Away!" repeated Hugh in amazement, "away! Little Jeanne gone away. Oh no, you must be joking Du—, I beg your pardon, Monsieur Dudu."

"Not at all," said Dudu. "She *is* away, and farther away than you or she has any notion of, even though if you went into her room you would see her little rosy face lying on the pillow. *She* is away."

Hugh still looked puzzled, though rather less so.

"You mean that her thinking is away, I suppose," he said. "But I could wake her."

Again the raven cocked his head on one side.

"No," he said. "You must be content to do my way at present. Now, tell me what it is you want. Why did you wish me to come to see you?"

"I wanted — at least I thought, and Jeanne said so," began Hugh. "We thought perhaps you were a fairy, Monsieur Dudu, and that you could take us into the castle in the tapestry. It looked so bright and real a few minutes ago," he added, turning to the wall, which was now only faintly illumined by the moonlight, and looked no different from what Hugh had often seen it in the daytime. "What has become of the beautiful light, Monsieur Dudu? And the peacocks? They have shut up their tails again — "

"Never mind," said the raven. "So you want to see the castle, do you?" he added.

"Yes," said Hugh; "but not so much as Jeanne. It was she wanted it most. She wants dreadfully to see it. *I* thought," he added, rather timidly, "*I* thought we might play at giving a party in the castle, and inviting Houpet, you know, and Nibble."

"*Only*," observed the raven, drily, "there is one little objection to that. *Generally* — I may be mistaken, of course, my notions are very old-fashioned, I daresay — but, *generally*, people give parties in their own houses, don't they?"

And as he spoke he looked straight at Hugh, cocking his head on one side more than ever.

CHAPTER IV.

THE FOREST OF THE RAINBOWS.

" Rose and amethyst, gold and grey."
" ONCE."

HUGH felt rather offended. It was natural that he should do so, I think. At least I am sure that in his place I too should have felt hurt. He had said nothing to make the raven speak in that disagreeably sarcastic way.

"I wish Jeanne were here," he said to himself; "she would think of something to put him down a little."

But aloud he said nothing, so, great was his surprise, when the raven coolly remarked in answer to his unspoken thoughts,

"So Jeanne could put me down, you think? I confess, I don't agree with you. However, never mind about that. We shall be very good friends in time. And now, how about visiting the castle?"

"I should like to go," replied Hugh, thinking it wiser, all things considered, to get over his offended feelings. "I should like to see the castle very much, though I should have liked Jeanne to be with me; but still," he went on, reflecting that Jeanne would

49

be extremely disappointed if he did not make the most of his present opportunity, such as it was, "if you will be so kind as to show me the way, Monsieur Dudu, I'd like to go, and then, anyway, I can tell Jeanne all about it."

"I cannot exactly show you the way," said the raven, "I am only the guardian on this side. But if you will attend to what I say, you will get on very well. Here, in the first place, is a pair of wall-climbers to put on your feet."

He held out his claw, on the end of which hung, by a narrow ribbon, two round little cushions about the size of a macaroon biscuit. Hugh took them and examined them curiously. They were soft and elastic, what Hugh in his own words would have described as "blobby." They seemed to be made of some stuff like india-rubber, and were just the colour of his skin.

"What funny things!" said Hugh.

"They are made after the pattern of the fly's wall-climbers," remarked the raven. "Put them on —tie them on, that is to say, so that they will be just in the middle of your foot, underneath of course. That's right; now jump out of bed and follow me," and before Hugh knew what he was doing he found himself walking with the greatest ease straight up the wall to where the long flight of steps to the tapestry castle began. On the lowest steps the raven stopped a moment.

"Shall I take them off now?" asked Hugh. "I don't need them to walk up steps with."

"Take them off?" said the raven; "oh dear no. When you don't need them they won't incommode you, and they'll be all ready for the next time. Besides, though it mayn't seem so to you, these steps are not so easy to get up as you think. At least they wouldn't be without the wall-climbers."

With them, however, nothing could have been easier. Hugh found himself in no time at the top of the flight of steps in front of the door from which the raven had come out. The peacocks, now he was close to them, seemed to him larger than ordinary peacocks, but the brilliant colours of their feathers, which he had noticed in the bright moonlight, had disappeared. It was light enough for him to distinguish their figures, but that was all.

"I must leave you now," said the raven; "but you will get on very well. Only remember these two things — don't be impatient, and don't take off your wall-climbers; and if you are very much at a loss about anything, call me."

"How shall I call you?" asked Hugh.

"Whistle softly three times. Now, I think it is time to light up. Peacocks."

The peacocks, one on each side of the door, came forward solemnly, saluting the raven with the greatest respect.

"Ring," said the raven, and to Hugh's surprise

each peacock lifted up a claw, and taking hold of a bell-rope, of which there were two, one on each side of the door, pulled them vigorously. No sound ensued, but at the instant there burst forth the same soft yet brilliant light which had so delighted Hugh when he first awoke, and which he now discovered to come not from the moon, still shining in gently at the window of the tapestry room down below, but from those of the castle at whose door he was standing. He had never before noticed how many windows it had. Jeanne and he had only remarked the door at the top of the steps, but now the light which flowed out from above him was so clear and brilliant that it seemed as if the whole castle must be transparent. Hugh stood in eager expectation of what was to happen next, and was on the point of speaking to the raven, standing, as he thought, beside him, when a sudden sound made him turn round. It was that of the castle door opening, and at the same moment the two peacocks, coming forward, pushed him gently, one at each side, so that Hugh found himself obliged to enter. He was by no means unwilling to do so, but he gave one last look round for his conductor. He was gone.

For about half a second Hugh felt a little frightened and bewildered.

"I wish Dudu had come with me," he said. But almost before he had time to think the wish, what he saw before him so absorbed his attention that he forgot everything else.

It was a long, long passage, high in the roof, though narrow of course in comparison with its length, but wide enough for Hugh — for Hugh and Jeanne hand-in-hand even — to walk along with perfect comfort and great satisfaction, for oh, it was so prettily lighted up! You have, I daresay, children, often admired in London or Paris, or some great town, the rows of gas lamps lighting up at night miles of some very long street. Fancy those lights infinitely brighter and clearer, and yet softer than any lamps you ever saw, and each one of a different colour, from the richest crimson to the softest pale blue, and you will have some idea how pretty the long corridor before him looked to Hugh. He stepped along delightedly, as well he might. "Why, this of itself is worth staying awake ever so many nights to see," he said to himself; "only I do wish Jeanne were with me."

Where did the corridor lead to? He ran on and on for some time without thinking much about this, so interested was he in observing the lamps and the pretty way in which the tints were arranged; but after a while he began to find it a little monotonous, especially when he noticed that at long intervals the colours repeated themselves, the succession of shades beginning again from time to time.

"I shall learn them by heart if I go on here much longer," thought Hugh. "I think I'll sit down a little to rest. Not that I feel tired of walking, but I may as well sit down a little."

He did so — on the ground, there was nothing else to sit on — and then a very queer thing happened. The lamps took to moving instead of him, so that when he looked up at them the impression was just the same as when he himself had been running along. The colours succeeded each other in the same order, and Hugh began to wonder whether his eyes were not deceiving him in some queer way.

"Anyhow, I'll run on a little farther," he said to himself, "and if I don't come to the end of this passage soon, I'll run back again to the other end. It feels just as if I had got inside a kaleidoscope."

He hastened on, and was beginning really to think of turning back again and running the other way, when, all of a sudden — everything in this queer tapestry world he had got into seemed to happen all of a sudden — a little bell was heard to ring, clear and silvery, but not very loud, and in another instant — oh dear! — all the pretty coloured lamps were extinguished, and poor Hugh was left standing all in the dark. Where he was he did not know, what to do he did not know; had he not been eight years old on his last birthday I almost think he would have begun to cry. He felt, too, all of a sudden so cold, even though before he had got out of bed he had taken the precaution to put on his red flannel dressing-gown, and till now had felt quite pleasantly warm. It was only for half a moment, however, that the idea of crying came over him.

"I'm very glad poor little Jeanne isn't here," he said to himself by way of keeping up his own courage; "she *would* have been afraid. But as I'm a boy it doesn't matter. I'll just try to find my way all the same. I suppose it's some trick of that Dudu's."

He felt his way along bravely for a few minutes, and more bravely still was forcing back his tears, when a sound caught his ears. It was a cock's crow, sharp and shrill, but yet sounding as if outside the place where he was. Still it greatly encouraged Hugh, who continued to make his way on in the dark, much pleased to find that the farther he got the nearer and clearer sounded the crow, repeated every few seconds. And at last he found himself at the end of the passage — he knew it must be so, for in front of him the way was barred, and *quite* close to him now apparently, sounded the cock's shrill call. He pushed and pulled — for some time in vain. If there were a door at this end of the passage, as surely there must be — who would make a passage and hang it so beautifully with lamps if it were to lead to nowhere? — it was a door of which the handle was very difficult to find.

"Oh dear!" exclaimed Hugh, half in despair, "what shall I do?"

"Kurroo — kurroorulloo," sounded the cock's crow. "Try again," it seemed to say, encouragingly. And at last Hugh's hand came in contact with a little

round knob, and as he touched it, all at once everything about him was lighted up again with the same
clear, lovely light coming from the thousands of
lamps down the long corridor behind him. But
Hugh never turned to look at them — what he saw
in front of him was so delightful and surprising.

The door had opened, Hugh found himself standing at the top of two or three steps, which apparently
were the back approach to the strange long passage
which he had entered from the tapestry room. Outside it was light too, but not with the wonderful
bright radiance that had streamed out from the castle
at the other side. Here it was just very soft, very
clear moonlight. There were trees before him —
almost it seemed as if he were standing at the entrance of a forest. But, strange to say, they were
not winter trees, such as he had left behind him in
the garden of Jeanne's house — bare and leafless, or
if covered at all, covered only with their Christmas
dress of snow and icicles — these trees were clothed
with the loveliest foliage, fresh and green and feathery, which no winter's storms or nipping frosts had
ever come near to blight. And in the little space
between the door where Hugh stood and these wonderful trees was drawn up, as if awaiting him, the
prettiest, queerest, most delicious little carriage that
ever was seen. It was open; the cushions with
which it was lined were of rose-coloured plush — not
velvet, I think; at least if they *were* velvet, it was of

some marvellous kind that couldn't be rubbed the
wrong way, that felt exquisitely smooth and soft
whichever way you stroked it; the body of the carriage was shaped something like a cockle-shell; you
could lie back in it so beautifully without cricking
or straining your neck or shoulders in the least; and
there was just room for two. One of these two was
already comfortably settled — shall I tell you who
it was now, or shall I keep it for a tit-bit at the end
when I have quite finished about the carriage? Yes,
that will be better. For the funniest things about
the carriage have to be told yet. Up on the box, in
the coachman's place, you understand, holding with
an air of the utmost importance in one claw a pair of
yellow silk reins, his tufted head surmounted by a
gold-laced livery hat, which, however, must have had
a hole in the middle to let the tuft through, for there
it was in all its glory waving over the hat like a
dragoon's plume, sat, or stood rather, Houpet; while,
standing behind, holding on each with one claw to
the back of the carriage, like real footmen, were the
two other chickens. They, too, had gold-laced hats
and an air of solemn propriety, not *quite* so majestic
as Houpet's, for in their case the imposing tuft was
wanting, but still very fine of its kind. And who do
think were the horses? for there were two — or, to
speak more correctly, there were no horses at all,
but in the place where they should have been were
harnessed, tandem-fashion, not abreast, Nibble the

guinea-pig and Grignan the tortoise! Nibble next
the carriage, Grignan, of all creatures in the world,
as leader.

On sight of them Hugh began to laugh, so that he
forgot to look more closely at the person in the carriage, whose face he had not yet seen, as it was turned
the other way. But the sound of his laughing was
too infectious to be resisted — the small figure began
to shake all over, and at last could contain itself no
longer. With a shout of merriment little Jeanne,
for it was she, sprang out of the carriage and threw
her arms round Hugh's neck.

"O Chéri," she said, "I *couldn't* keep quiet any
longer, though I wanted to hide my face till you had
got into the carriage, and then surprise you. But it
was so nice to hear you laugh — I *couldn't* keep
still."

Hugh felt too utterly astonished to reply. He
just stared as Jeanne as if he could not believe his
own eyes. And Jeanne did not look surprised at
all! That, to Hugh, was the most surprising part
of the whole.

"Jeanne!" he exclaimed, "you here! Why,
Dudu told me you were ever so far away."

"And so I am," replied Jeanne, laughing again,
"and so are you, Chéri. You have no idea how far
away you are — miles, and miles, and miles, only in
this country they don't have milestones. It's all
quite different."

"How do you mean?" asked Hugh. "How do you know all about it? You have never been here before, have you? I couldn't quite understand Dudu — *he* meant, I think, that it was only your thinking part, or your fancying part, that was away."

Jeanne laughed again. Hugh felt a little impatient.

"*Jeanne*," he said, "do leave off laughing and speak to me. What is this place? and how did you come here? and have you ever been here before?"

"Yes," said Jeanne, "I think so; but I don't know how I came. And I don't want to do anything but laugh and have fun. Never mind how we came. It's a beautiful country, anyway, and did you *ever* see anything so sweet as the little carriage they've sent for us, and wasn't it nice to see Houpet and all the others?"

"Yes," said Hugh, "very. But whom do you mean by 'they,' Jeanne?"

"Oh dear, dear!" exclaimed Jeanne, "what a terrible boy you are. Do leave off asking questions, and let us have fun. Look, there are Grignan and the little cochon quite eager to be off. Now, do jump in — we shall have such fun."

Hugh got in, willingly enough, though still he would have preferred to have some explanation from Jeanne of all the strange things that were happening.

"*Isn't* it nice?" said Jeanne, when they had both nestled down among the delicious soft cushions of the carriage.

"Yes," said Hugh, "it's very nice *now*, but it wasn't very nice when I was all alone in the dark in that long passage. As you seem to know all about everything, Jeanne, I suppose you know about that."

He spoke rather, just a very little, grumpily, but Jeanne, rather to his surprise, did not laugh at him this time. Instead, she looked up in his face earnestly, with a strange deep look in her eyes.

"I think very often we have to find our way in the dark," she said dreamily. "I think I remember about that. But," she went on, with a complete change of voice, her eyes dancing merrily as if they had never looked grave in their life, "it's not dark now, Chéri, and it's going to be ever so bright. Just look at the lovely moon through the trees. Do let us go now. Gee-up, gee-up, crack your whip, Houpet, and make them gallop as fast as you can."

Off they set — they went nice and fast certainly, but not so fast but that the children could admire the beautiful feathery foliage as they passed. They drove through the forest — for the trees that Hugh had so admired were those of a forest — on and on, swiftly but yet smoothly; never in his life had Hugh felt any motion so delightful.

"*What* a good coachman Houpet is!" exclaimed

Hugh. "I never should have thought he could drive so well. How does he know the road, Jeanne?"

"There isn't any road, so he doesn't need to know it," said Jeanne. "Look before you, Chéri. You see there is no road. It makes itself as we go, so we can't go wrong."

Hugh looked straight before him. It was as Jeanne had said. The trees grew thick and close in front, only dividing — melting away like a mist — as the quaint little carriage approached them.

Hugh looked at them with fresh surprise.

"Are they not real trees?" he said.

"Of course they are," said Jeanne. "Now they're beginning to change; that shows we are getting to the middle of the forest. Look, look, Chéri!"

Hugh "looked" with all his eyes. What Jeanne called "changing" was a very wonderful process. The trees, which hitherto had been of a very bright, delicate green, began gradually to pale in colour, becoming first greenish-yellow, then canary colour, then down to the purest white. And from white they grew into silver, sparkling like innumerable diamonds, and then slowly altered into a sort of silver-gray, gradually rising into gray-blue, then into a more purple-blue, till they reached the richest corn-flower shade. Then began another series of lessening shades, which again, passing through a boundary line of gold, rose by indescribable degrees to deep yet brilliant crimson. It would be impossible to

name all the variations through which they passed
I use the names of the colours and shades which are
familiar to you, children, but the very naming any
shade gives an unfair idea of the marvellous delicacy
with which one tint melted into another, — as well
try to divide and mark off the hues of a dove's breast,
or of the sky at sunset. And all the time the trees
themselves were of the same form and foliage as at
first, the leaves — or fronds I feel inclined to call
them, for they were more like very, very delicate
ferns or ferny grass than leaves — with which each
branch was luxuriantly clothed, seeming to bathe
themselves in each new colour as the petals of a
flower welcome a flood of brilliant sunshine.

" Oh, how pretty ! " said Hugh, with a deep sigh
of pleasure. " It is like the lamps, only much
prettier. I think, Jeanne, this must be the country
of pretty colours."

" This forest is called the Forest of the Rainbows.
I know *that*," said Jeanne. " But I don't think they
call this the country of pretty colours, Chéri. You
see it is the country of so many pretty things. If
we lived in it always, we should never see the end
of the beautiful things there are. Only — "

" Only what ? " asked Hugh.

" I don't think it would be a good plan to live in
it *always*. Just sometimes is best, I think. Either
the things wouldn't be so pretty, or our eyes wouldn't
see them so well after a while. But see, Chéri, the

trees are growing common-coloured again, and Houpet is stopping. We must have got to the end of the Forest of the Rainbows."

"And where shall we be going to now?" asked Hugh. "Must we get out, do you think, Jeanne? Oh, listen, I hear the sound of water! Do you hear it, Jeanne? There must be a river near here. I wish the moonlight was a little brighter. Now that the trees don't shine, it seems quite dull. But oh, how plainly I hear the water. Listen, Jeanne, don't you hear it too?"

"Yes," said Jeanne. "It must be — " but before she had time to say more they suddenly came out of the enchanted forest; in an instant every trace of the feathery trees had disappeared. Houpet pulled up his steeds, the two chickens got down from behind, and stood one on each side of the carriage door, waiting apparently for their master and mistress to descend. And plainer and nearer than before came the sound of fast-rushing water.

"You see we are to get down," said Hugh.

"Yes," said Jeanne again, looking round her a little timidly. "Chéri, do you know, I feel just a very, very little bit frightened. It is such a queer place, and I don't know what we should do. Don't you think we'd better ask Houpet to take us back again?"

"Oh no," said Hugh. "I'm sure we'll be all right. You said you wanted to have some fun, Jeanne, and you seemed to know all about it. You needn't be frightened with *me*, Jeanne."

"No, of course not," said Jeanne, quite brightly again; "but let us stand up a minute, Hugh, before we get out of the carriage, and look all about us. *Isn't* it a queer place?"

"It" was a wide, far-stretching plain, over which the moonlight shone softly. Far or near not a shrub or tree was to be seen, yet it was not like a desert, for the ground was entirely covered with most beautiful moss, so fresh and green, even by the moonlight, that it was difficult to believe the hot sunshine had ever glared upon it. And here and there, all over this great plain — all over it, at least, as far as the children could see — rose suddenly from the ground innumerable jets of water, not so much like fountains as like little waterfalls turned the wrong way; they rushed upwards with such surprising force and noise, and fell to the earth again in numberless tiny threads much more gently and softly than they left it.

"It seems as if somebody must be shooting them up with a gun, doesn't it?" said Hugh. "I never saw such queer fountains."

"Let's go and look at them close," said Jeanne, preparing to get down. But before she could do so, Houpet gave a shrill, rather peremptory crow, and Jeanne stopped short in surprise.

"What do you want, Houpet?" she said.

By way of reply, Houpet hopped down from his box, and in some wonderfully clever way of his own, before the children could see what he was about, had unharnessed Nibble and Grignan. Then the three arranged themselves in a little procession, and drew up a few steps from the side of the carriage where still stood the chicken-footmen. Though they could not speak, there was no mistaking their meaning.

"They're going to show us the way," said Hugh; and as he spoke he jumped out of the carriage, and Jeanne after him.

CHAPTER V.

FROG-LAND.

"They have a pretty island,
    Whereon at night they rest;
They have a sparkling lakelet,
    And float upon its breast."

THE TWO SWANS.

ONWARDS quietly stepped the little procession, Houpet first, his tuft waving as usual, with a comfortable air of importance and satisfaction; then Nibble and Grignan abreast — hand-in-hand, I was going to have said; next Hugh and Jeanne; with the two attendant chickens behind bringing up the rear.

"I wonder where they are going to take us to," said Hugh in a low voice. Somehow the soft light; the strange loneliness of the great plain, where, now that they were accustomed to it, the rushing of the numberless water-springs seemed to be but one single, steady sound; the solemn behaviour of their curious guides, altogether, had subdued the children's spirits. Jeanne said no more about "having fun," yet she did not seem the least frightened or depressed; she was only quiet and serious.

"Where *do* you think they are going to take us to?" repeated Hugh.

"I don't know — at least I'm not sure," said
Jeanne; "but, Chéri, isn't it a good thing that
Houpet and the others are with us to show us the
way, for though the ground looks so pretty it is
quite boggy here and there. I notice that Houpet
never goes quite close to the fountains, and just
when I went the least bit near one a minute ago my
feet began to slip down."

"I haven't felt it like that at all," said Hugh.
"Perhaps it's because of my wall-climbers. Dudu
gave me a pair of wall-climbers like the flies', you
know, Jeanne."

"Did he?" said Jeanne, not at all surprised, and
as if wall-climbers were no more uncommon than
goloshes. "He didn't give me any, but then I came
a different way from you. I think every one comes
a different way to this country, do you know,
Chéri?"

"And very likely Dudu thought I could carry you
if there was anywhere you couldn't climb," said
Hugh, importantly. "I'm sure I —" he stopped
abruptly, for a sudden crow from Houpet had
brought all the party to a standstill. At first the
children could not make out why their guide had
stopped here — there was nothing to be seen. But
pressing forward a few steps to where Houpet stood,
Hugh saw, imbedded in the moss at his feet, a stone
with a ring in it, just like those which one reads of
in the *Arabian Nights*. Houpet stood at the edge of

the stone eyeing it gravely, and somehow he managed to make Hugh understand that he was to lift
it. Nothing loth, but rather doubtful as to whether
he would be strong enough, the boy leant forward
to reach the ring, first whispering, however, to
Jeanne,

" It's getting like a quite real fairy tale, isn't it,
Jeanne ? "

Jeanne nodded, but looked rather anxious.

" I'm *afraid* you can't lift it, Chéri," she said. " I
think I'd better stand behind and pull *you* — the ring
isn't big enough for us both to put our hands in it."

Hugh made no objection to her proposal, so Jeanne
put her arms round his waist, and when he gave a
great pug to the ring she gave a great pug to him.
The first time it was no use, the stone did not move
in the least.

" Try again," said Hugh, and try again they did.
But no — the second try succeeded no better than the
first — and the children looked at each other in perplexity. Suddenly there was a movement among the
animals, who had all been standing round watching
the children's attempts ; Jeanne felt a sort of little
pecking tug at her skirts — how it came about I cannot say, but I think I forgot to tell you that, unlike
Hugh in his red flannel dressing-gown, *she* was
arrayed for their adventures in her best Sunday
pelisse, trimmed with fur — and, looking round, lo
and behold ! there was Houpet holding on to her

with his beak, then came Nibble, his two front paws embracing Houpet's feathered body, Grignan behind him again, clutching with his mouth at Nibble's fur, and the two chickens at the end holding on to Grignan and each other in some indescribable and marvellous way. It was, for all the world, as if they were preparing for the finish-up part of the game of "oranges and lemons," or for that of "fox and geese!"

The sight was so comical that it was all the children could do to keep their gravity; they succeeded in doing so, however, fearing that it might hurt the animals' feelings to seem to make fun of their well-meant efforts.

"Not that *they* can be any use," whispered Hugh, "but it's very good-natured of them all the same."

"I am not so sure that they can't be of any use," returned Jeanne. "Think of how well Houpet drave."

"Here goes, then," said Hugh. "One, two, *three;*" and with "three" he gave a tremendous tug — a much more tremendous tug than was required, for, to his surprise, the stone yielded at once without the slightest resistance, and back they all fell, one on the top of the other, Hugh, Jeanne, Houpet, Nibble, Grignan, and the two chickens! But none of them were any the worse, and with the greatest eagerness to see what was to be seen where the stone had been, up jumped Hugh and Jeanne and ran forward to the spot.

" There should be," said Jeanne, half out of breath —" there *should* be a little staircase for us to go down, if it is like the stories in the *Arabian Nights*."

And, wonderful to relate, so there was! The children could hardly believe their eyes, when below them they saw the most tempting little spiral staircase of white stone or marble steps, with a neat little brass balustrade at one side. It looked quite light all the way down, though of course they could distinguish nothing at the bottom, as the corkscrew twists of the staircase entirely filled up the space.

Houpet hopped forward and stood at the top of the steps crowing softly.

" He means that we're to go down," said Hugh " Shall we ? "

" Of course," said Jeanne. " I'm not a bit afraid. We won't have any fun if we don't go on."

" Well then," said Hugh, " I'll go first as I'm a boy, just *in case*, you know, Jeanne, of our meeting anything disagreeable."

So down he went, Jeanne following close after.

" I suppose Houpet and the others will come after us," said Jeanne, rather anxiously. But just as she uttered the words a rather shrill crow made both Hugh and her stop short and look up to the top. They saw Houpet and the others standing round the edge of the hole. Houpet gave another crow, in which the two chickens joined him, and then suddenly the stone was shut down — the two children found themselves alone in this strange place, leading to they knew not where! Jeanne gave a little cry — Hugh, too, for a moment was rather startled, but he soon recovered himself.

" Jeanne," he said, "it must be all right. I don't think we need be frightened. See, it is quite light! The light comes up from below — down there it must be quite bright and cheerful. Give me your hand — if we go down sideways — so — we can hold each other's hands all the way."

So, in a rather queer fashion, they clambered down the long staircase. By the time they got to its end they were really quite tired of turning round and round so many times. But now the view before them was so pleasant that they forgot all their troubles.

They had found a little door at the foot of the stair, which opened easily. They passed through it, and there lay before them a beautiful expanse of water surrounded by hills : the door which had closed behind them seemed on this side to have been cut out of the turf of the hill, and was all but invisible. It was light, as Hugh had said, but not with the light of either sun or moon ; a soft radiance was over everything, but whence it came they could not tell. The hills on each side of the water, which was more like a calmly flowing river than a lake, prevented their seeing very far, but close to the shore by which they stood a little boat was moored — a little boat with seats for two. and one light pair of oars.

"Oh, how lovely!" said Jeanne. "It is even nicer than the carriage. Get in, Hugh, and let us row down the river. The boat must be on purpose for us."

They were soon settled in it, and Hugh, though he had only rowed once or twice before in his life, found it very easy and pleasant, and they went over the water swiftly and smoothly. After a while the hills approached more nearly, gradually the broad river dwindled to a mere stream, so narrow and small at last, that even their tiny boat could go no farther. Hugh was forced to leave off rowing.

"I suppose we are meant to go on shore here," he said. "The boat won't go any farther, anyway."

Jeanne was peering forward: just before them the brook, or what still remained of it, almost disappeared in a narrow little gorge between the hills.

"Chéri," said she, "I shouldn't wonder if the stream gets wider again on the other side of this little narrow place. Don't you think we'd better try to pull the boat through, and then we might get into it again?"

"Perhaps," said Hugh. "We may try." So out the children got — Jeanne pulled in front, Hugh pushed behind. It was so very light that there was no difficulty as to its weight; only the gorge was so narrow that at last the boat stuck fast.

"We'd better leave it and clamber through ourselves," said Hugh.

"But, O Chéri, we can't!" cried Jeanne. "From where I am I can see that the water gets wider again a little farther on. And the rocks come quite sharp down to the side. There is nowhere we could clamber on to, and I dare say the water is very deep. There are lots of little streams trickling into it from the rocks, and the boat could go quite well if we could but get it a little farther."

"But we can't," said Hugh; "it just won't go."

"Oh dear," said Jeanne, "we'll have to go back. But how should we find the door in the hillside to go up the stair; or if we did get up, how should we push away the stone? And even then, there would be the forest to go through, and perhaps we couldn't find our way among the trees as Houpet did. O Chéri, what shall we do?"

Hugh stood still and considered.

"I think," he said at last, "I think the time's come for whistling."

And before Jeanne could ask him what he meant, he gave three clear, short whistles, and then waited to see the effect.

It was a most unexpected one. Hugh had antici pated nothing else than the sudden appearance, some· how and somewhere, of Monsieur Dudu himself, as large as life — possibly, in this queer country of sur- prises, where they found themselves, a little larger! When and how he would appear Hugh was perfectly at a loss to imagine — he might fly down from the sky; he might spring up from the water; he might just suddenly stand before them without their having any idea how he had come. Hugh laughed to himself at the thought of Jeanne's astonishment, and after all it was Jeanne who first drew his attention to what was really happening.

"Hark, Chéri, hark!" she cried, "what a queer noise! What can it be?"

Hugh's attention had been so taken up in staring about in every direction for the raven that he had not noticed the sound which Jeanne had heard, and which now increased every moment.

It was a soft, swishy sound — as if innumerable little boats were making their way through water, or as if innumerable little fairies were bathing themselves, only every instant it came nearer and nearer, till at last, on every side of the boat in which the children were still standing, came creeping up from below lots and lots and *lots* of small, bright green frogs, who clambered over the sides and arranged themselves in lines along the edges in the most methodical and orderly manner. Jeanne gave a scream of horror, and darted across the boat to where Hugh was standing.

"O Chéri," she cried, "why did you whistle? It's all that naughty Dudu. He's going to turn us into frogs too, I do believe, because he thinks I laughed at him. Oh dear, oh dear, what shall we do?"

Chéri himself, though not quite so frightened as Jeanne, was not much pleased with the result of his summons to the raven.

" It does look like a shabby trick," he said; " but still I do not think the creatures mean to do us any harm. And I don't feel myself being turned into a frog yet; do you, Jeanne?"

"I don't know," said Jeanne, a very little comforted; " I don't know what it would feel like to be turned into a frog; I've always been a little girl, and so I can't tell. I feel rather creepy and chilly, but perhaps it's only with seeing the frogs. What funny red eyes they've got. What can they be going to do?"

She forgot her fears in the interest of watching them; Hugh, too, stared with all his eyes at the frogs, who, arranged in regular lines round the edge of the boat, began working away industriously at something which, for a minute or two, the children could not make out. At last Jeanne called out eagerly,

" They are throwing over little lines, Chéri — lots and lots of little lines. There must be frogs down below waiting to catch them."

So it was; each frog threw over several threads which he seemed to unwind from his body; these threads were caught by something invisible down below, and twisted round and round several times, till at last they became as firm and strong as a fine twine. And when, apparently, the frogs considered that they had made cables enough, they settled themselves down, each firmly on his two hind legs, still holding by the rope with their front ones, and then — in another moment — to the children's great delight, they felt the boat beginning to move. It moved on smoothly — almost as smoothly as when on the water — there were no jogs or tugs, as might have been the case if it had been pulled by two or three coarse, strong ropes, for all the hundreds of tiny cables puliing together made one even force.

" Why, how clever they are!" cried Jeanne. " We go as smoothly as if we were on wheels. Nice little frogs. I am sure we are very much obliged to them — aren't we, Chéri?"

" And to Dudu," observed Hugh.

Jeanne shrugged her shoulders. She was not over and above sure of Dudu even now.

The boat moved along for some time; the pass between the hills was dark and gloomy, and though the water got wider, as Jeanne had seen, it would not for some distance have been possible for the children to row. After a time it suddenly grew much lighter; they came out from the narrow pass and found themselves but a few yards from a sheet of still water, with trees all round it — a sort of mountain lake it seemed, silent and solitary, and reflecting back from its calm bosom the soft, silvery, even radiance which since they came out from the door on the hillside had been the children's only light.

And in the middle of this lake lay a little island —a perfect nest of trees, whose long drooping branches hung down into the water.

"Oh, do let us row on to the island," said Jeanne eagerly, for by this time the frogs had drawn them to the edge of the lake; there could no longer be any difficulty in rowing for themselves.

"First, anyway, we must thank the frogs," said Hugh, standing up. He would have taken off his cap if he had had one on; as it was, he could only bow politely.

As he did so, each frog turned round so as to face him, and each gave a little bob of the head, which, though not very graceful, was evidently meant as an acknowledgment of Hugh's courtesy.

"They are very polite frogs," whispered Hugh. "Jeanne, do stand up and bow to them too."

Jeanne, who all this time had been sitting with her feet tucked up under her, showed no inclination to move.

"I don't like to stand up," she said, "for fear the frogs should run up my legs. But I can thank them just as well sitting down. Frogs," she added, "frogs, I am very much obliged to you, and I hope you will excuse my not standing up."

The frogs bowed again, which was very considerate of them; then suddenly there seemed a movement among them, those at the end of the boat drew back a little, and a frog, whom the children had not hitherto specially observed, came forward and stood in front of the others. He was bigger, his colour was a brighter green, and his eyes more brilliantly red. He stood up on his hind legs and bowed politely. Then, after clearing his throat, of which there is much need, for even with this precaution it sounded very croaky, he addressed the children.

"Monsieur and Mademoiselle," he began, "are very welcome to what we have done for them — the small service we have rendered. Monsieur and Mademoiselle, I and my companions," — "He should say, 'My companions and I,'" whispered Jeanne — "are well brought up frogs. We know our place in society. We disapprove of newfangled notions. We are frogs — we desire to be nothing else, and we are deeply sensible of the honour Monsieur and Mademoiselle have done us by this visit."

"He really speaks very nicely," said Jeanne in a whisper.

"Before Monsieur and Mademoiselle bid us farewell — before they leave our shores," continued the frog with a wave of his "top legs," as Jeanne afterwards called them, "we should desire to give them what, without presumption, I may call a treat. Monsieur and Mademoiselle are, doubtless, aware that in our humble way we are artists. Our weakness — our strength I should rather say — is music. Our croaking concerts are renowned far and wide, and by a most fortunate coincidence one is about to

take place, to celebrate the farewell — the departure
to other regions — of a songster whose family fame
for many ages has been renowned. Monsieur and
Mademoiselle, to-night is to be heard for the first
time in this century the 'Song of the Swan.'"

"The song of the swan," repeated Hugh, rather
puzzled; "I didn't know swans ever sang. I thought
it was just an old saying that they sing once only —
when they are dying."

The frog bowed.

"Just so," he said; "it is the truth. And, therefore, the extreme difficulty of assisting at so unique
a performance. It is but seldom — not above half-a-
dozen times in the recollection of the oldest of my
venerated cousins, the toads, that such an opportunity
has occurred — and as to whether human ears have
ever before been regaled with what you are about to
enjoy, you must allow me, Monsieur and Mademoiselle, with all deference to your race, for whom naturally we cherish the highest respect, to express a
doubt."

"It's a little difficult to understand quite what he
means, isn't it, Chéri?" whispered Jeanne. "But, of
course, we mustn't say so. It might hurt his feelings."

"Yes," agreed Hugh, "it might. But we must
say something polite."

"You say it," said Jeanne. "I really daren't
stand up, and it's not so easy to make a speech sitting down."

"Monsieur Frog, we are very much obliged to you," began Hugh. "Please tell all the other frogs so too. We would like very much to hear the concert. When does it begin, and where will it be ? "

"All round the lake the performers will be stationed," replied the frog pompously. "The chief artist occupies the island which you see from here. If you move forward a little — to about half-way between the shore and the island — you will, I think, be excellently placed. But first," seeing that Hugh was preparing to take up the oars, "first, you will allow us, Monsieur and Mademoiselle, to offer you a little collation — some slight refreshment after all the fatigues of your journey to our shores."

"Oh dear! oh dear!" whispered Jeanne in a terrible fright; "please say 'No, thank you,' Chéri. I *know* they'll be bringing us that horrid green stuff for soup."

"Thank you very much," said Hugh; "you are very kind indeed, Monsieur Frog, only, really, we're not hungry."

"A little refreshment — a mere nothing," said the frog, waving his hands in an elegantly persuasive manner. "Tadpoles " — in a brisk, authoritative tone — "tadpoles, refreshments for our guests."

Jeanne shivered, but nevertheless could not help watching with curiosity. Scores of little tadpoles came hopping up the sides of the boat, each dozen or so of them carrying among them large water-lily leaves, on each of which curious and dainty-looking little cakes and bonbons were arranged. The first that was presented to Jeanne contained neat little biscuits about the size of a half-crown piece, of a tempting rich brown colour.

" Flag-flour cakes," said the frog. " We roast and grind the flour in our own mills. You will find them good."

Jeanne took one and found it very good. She would have taken another, but already a second tray-ful or leaf-ful was before her, with pinky-looking balls.

" Those are made from the sugar of water-brambles," remarked the frog, with a self-satisfied smile. " No doubt you are surprised at the delicacy and refinement of our tastes. Many human beings are under the deplorable mistake of supposing we live on slimy water and dirty insects — ha, ha, ha ! whereas our cuisine is astounding in variety and delicacy of material and flavour. If it were not too late in the season, I wish you could have tasted our mushroom pâtés and minnows' eggs vols-au-vent."

" Thank you," said Hugh, " what we have had is very nice indeed."

" I *couldn't* eat minnows' eggs," whispered Jeanne, looking rather doubtfully at the succession of leaf trays that continued to appear. She nibbled away at some of the least extraordinary-looking cakes, which the frog informed her were made from the pith of rushes roasted and ground down, and then flavoured with essence of marsh marigold, and found them nearly as nice as macaroons. Then, having eaten quite as much as they wanted, the tadpoles handed to each a leaf of the purest water, which they drank with great satisfaction.

"Now," said Hugh, "we're quite ready for the concert. Shall I row out to the middle of the lake, Monsieur Frog?"

"Midway between the shore and the island," said the frog; "that will be the best position;" and, as by this time all the frogs that had been sitting round the edge of the boat had disappeared, Hugh took the oars and paddled away.

CHAPTER VI.

THE SONG OF THE SWAN.

"—— If I were on that shore,
I should live there and not die, but sing evermore."
JEAN INGELOW.

"ABOUT here will do, I should think — eh, Monsieur Frog?" said Hugh, resting on his oars half-way to the island. But there was no answer. The frog had disappeared.

"What a queer way all these creatures behave, don't they, Jeanne?" he said. "First Dudu, then Houpet and the others. They go off all of a sudden in the oddest way."

"I suppose they have to go when we don't need them any more," said Jeanne. "I daresay they are obliged to."

"Who obliges them?" said Hugh.

"Oh, I don't know! The fairies, I suppose," said Jeanne.

"Was it the fairies you meant when you kept saying 'they'?" asked Hugh.

"I don't know — perhaps — it's no use asking me," said Jeanne. "Fairies, or dream-spirits, or something like that. Never mind who they are if they

83

give us nice things. I am sure the frogs have been *very* kind, haven't they?"

"Yes; you won't be so afraid of them now, will you, Jeanne?"

"Oh, I don't know. I daresay I shall be, for they're quite different from *our* frogs. Ours aren't so bright green, and their eyes aren't red, and they can't *talk*. Oh no, our frogs are quite different from *theirs*, Chéri," she added with profound conviction.

"Just like our trees and everything else, I suppose," said Hugh. "Certainly this is a funny country. But hush, Jeanne! I believe the concert's going to begin."

They sat perfectly still to listen, but for a minute or two the sound which had caught Hugh's attention was not repeated. Everything about them was silent, except that now and then a soft faint breeze seemed to flutter across the water, slightly rippling its surface as it passed. The strange, even light which had shone over all the scene ever since the children had stepped out at the hillside door had now grown paler: it was not now bright enough to distinguish more than can be seen by an autumn twilight. The air was fresh and clear, though not the least cold; the drooping forms of the low-hanging branches of the island trees gave the children a melancholy feeling when they glanced in that direction.

"I don't like this very much," said Jeanne. "It makes me sad, and I wanted to have fun."

"It must be sad for the poor swan if it's going to die," said Hugh. "But I don't mind this sort of sad feeling. I think it's rather nice. Ah! Jeanne, listen, there it is again. They must be going to begin."

"It" was a low sort of "call" which seemed to run round the shores of the lake like a preliminary note, and then completely died away. Instantly began from all sides the most curious music that Hugh and Jeanne had ever heard. It was croaking, but croaking in unison and regular time, and harsh as it was, there was a very strange charm about it — quite impossible to describe. It sounded pathetic at times, and at times monotonous, and yet inspiriting, like the beating of a drum; and the children listened to it with actual enjoyment. It went on for a good while, and then stopped as suddenly as it had begun; and then again, after some minutes of perfect silence, it recommenced in a low and regular chant — if such a word can be used for croaking — a steady, regular croak, croak, as if an immense number of harsh-sounding instruments were giving forth one note in such precise tune and measure that the harshness was softened and lost by the union of sound. It grew lower and lower, seeming almost to be about to die altogether away, when, from another direction — from the tree-shaded island in the centre of the lake — rose, low and faint at first, gathering strange strength as it mounted ever higher and higher, the song of the swan.

The children listened breathlessly and in perfect silence to the wonderful notes which fell on their ears — notes which no words of mine could describe, for in themselves they were words, telling of suffering and sorrow, of beautiful things and sad things, of strange fantastic dreams, of sunshine and flowers and summer days, of icy winds from the snow-clad hills, and days of dreariness and solitude. Each and all came in their turn; but, at the last, all melted, all grew rather, into one magnificent song of bliss and triumph, of joyful tenderness and brilliant hope, too pure and perfect to be imagined but in a dream. And as the last clear mellow notes fell on the children's ears, a sound of wings seemed to come with them, and gazing ever more intently towards the island they saw rising upwards the pure white snow-like bird — upwards and upwards, ever higher, till at last, with the sound of its own joyous song, it faded and melted into the opal radiance of the calm sky above.

For long the children gazed after it — a spot of light seemed to linger for some time in the sky just where it had disappeared — almost, to their fancy, as if the white swan was resting there, again to return to earth. But it was not so. Slowly, like the light of a dying star, the brightness faded; there was no longer a trace of the swan's radiant flight; again a soft low breeze, like a farewell sigh, fluttered across the lake, and the children withdrew their eyes from the sky and looked at each other.

" Jeanne! " said Hugh.

" Chéri! " said Jeanne.

" What was it? Was it not an angel, and not a swan? "

Jeanne shook her little head in perplexity.

" I don't know," she said. " It was wonderful. Did you hear all it told, Chéri? "

" Yes," said Hugh. " But no one could ever tell it again, Jeanne. It is a secret for us."

" And for the frogs," added Jeanne.

" And for the frogs," said Hugh.

"But," said Jeanne, "I thought the swan was going to die. *That* was not dying."

" Yes," said the queer croaking voice of the frog, suddenly reappearing on the edge of the boat; "yes, my children," he repeated, with a strange solemnity, "for such as the swan that *is* dying. And now once more — for you will never see me again, nor revisit this country — once again, my children, I bid you farewell."

He waved his hands in adieu, and hopped away.

" Chéri," said Jeanne, after a short silence, "I feel rather sad, and a very little sleepy. Do you think I might lie down a little — it is not the least cold — and take a tiny sleep? You might go to sleep too, if you like. I should think there will be time before we row back to the shore, only I do not know how we shall get the boat through the narrow part if the frogs have all gone. And no doubt Houpet and the others will be wondering why we are so long."

"We can whistle for Dudu again if we need," said Hugh. "He helped us very well the last time. I too am rather sleepy, Jeanne, but still I think I had better not go *quite* asleep. You lie down, and I'll just paddle on very slowly and softly for a little, and when you wake up we'll fix whether we should whistle or not."

Jeanne seemed to fall asleep in a moment when she lay down. Hugh paddled on quietly, as he had said, thinking dreamily of the queer things they had seen and heard in this nameless country inside the tapestry door. He did not feel troubled as to how they were to get back again; he had great faith in Dudu, and felt sure it would all come right. But gradually he too began to feel very sleepy; the dip of the oars and the sound of little Jeanne's regular breathing seemed to keep time together in a curious way. And at last the oars slipped from Hugh's hold; he lay down beside Jeanne, letting the boat drift; he was so *very* sleepy, he could keep up no more.

But after a minute or two when, not *quite* asleep, he lay listening to the soft breathing of the little girl, it seemed to him he heard still the gentle dip of the oars. The more he listened, the more sure he became that it was so, and at last his curiosity grew so great that it half overcame his drowsiness. He opened his eyes just enough to look up. Yes, he was right, the boat was gliding steadily along, the oars were doing their work, and who do you think were the rowers?

Dudu on one side, Houpet on the other, rowing away as cleverly as if they had never done anything else in their lives, steadying themselves on one claw, rowing with the other. Hugh did not feel the least surprised; he smiled sleepily, and turned over quite satisfied.

"They'll take us safe back," he said to himself; and that was all he thought about it.

"Good-night, Chéri, good-night," was the next thing he heard, or remembered hearing.

Hugh half sat up and rubbed his eyes.

Where was he?

Not in the boat, there was no sound of oars, the light that met his gaze was not that of the strange country where Jeanne and he had had all these adventures, it was just clear ordinary moonlight; and as for where he was, he was lying on the floor of the tapestry room close to the part of the wall where stood, or hung, the castle with the long flight of steps, which Jeanne and he had so wished to enter. And from the other side of the tapestry — from inside the castle one might almost say — came the voice he had heard in his sleep, the voice which seemed to have awakened him.

"Good-night, Chéri," it said, "good-night. I have gone home the other way."

"Jeanne, Jeanne, where are you? Wait!" cried Hugh, starting to his feet. But there was no reply.

Hugh looked all round. The moon seemed just

the same as usual, and if he had looked out of the
window, though this he did not know, he would have
seen the old raven on the terrace marching about,
and, in his usual philosophical way, failing the sunshine, enjoying the moonlight; while down in the
chickens' house, in the corner of the yard, Houpet
and his friends were calmly roosting; fat little Nibble
soundly sleeping in his cage, cuddled up in the hay;
poor, placid Grignan reposing in his usual corner
under the laurel bush. All these things Hugh would
have seen, and would no doubt have wondered much
at them. But though neither tired nor cold, he was
still sleepy, very sleepy, so, after another stare all
round, he decided that he would defer further inquiry
till the morning, and in the meantime follow the advice
of Jeanne's farewell " good-night."

And " after all," he said to himself, as he climbed
up into his comfortable bed, "after all, bed is very
nice, even though that little carriage was awfully
jolly, and the boat almost better. What fun it will
be to talk about it all to-morrow morning with
Jeanne."

It was rather queer when to-morrow morning came
— when he woke to find it had come, at least; it was
rather queer to see everything looking just the same
as on other to-morrow mornings. Hugh had not time
to think very much about it, for it had been Marcelline's knock at the door that had wakened him, and
she told him it was rather later than usual. Hugh,

however, was so eager to see Jeanne and talk over with her their wonderful adventures that he needed no hurrying. But, to his surprise, when he got to Jeanne's room, where as usual their "little breakfast" was prepared for them on the table by the fire, Jeanne was seated on her low chair, drinking her coffee in her every-day manner, not the least different from what she always was, not in any particular hurry to see him, nor, apparently, with anything particular to say.

"Well, Chéri," she said, merrily, "you are rather late this morning. Have you slept well?"

Hugh looked at her; there was no mischief in her face; she simply meant what she said. In his astonishment, Hugh rubbed his eyes and then stared at her again.

"Jeanne," he said, quite bewildered.

"Well, Chéri," she repeated, "what is the matter? How funny you look!" and in her turn Jeanne seemed surprised.

Hugh looked round; old Marcelline had left the room.

"Jeanne," he said, "it is so queer to see you just the same as usual, with nothing to say about it all."

"About all what?" said Jeanne, seemingly more and more puzzled.

"About our adventures — the drive in the carriage, with Houpet as coachman, and the stair down to the frog's country, and the frogs and the boat, and the concert, and O Jeanne! the song of the swan."

Jeanne opened wide her eyes.

"Chéri!" she said, "you've been dreaming all these funny things."

Hugh was so hurt and disappointed that he nearly began to cry.

"O Jeanne," he said, "it is very unkind to say that," and he turned away quite chilled and perplexed.

Jeanne ran after him and threw her arms round his neck.

"Chéri, Chéri," she said, "I didn't mean to vex you, but I *don't* understand."

Hugh looked into her dark eyes with his earnest blue ones.

"Jeanne," he said, "don't you remember *any* of it — don't you remember the trees changing their colours so prettily? — don't you remember the frogs' banquet?"

Jeanne stared at him so earnestly that she quite frowned.

"I think — I think," she said, and then she stopped. "When you say that of the trees, I think I did see rainbow colours all turning into each other. I think, Chéri, part of me was there and part not; can there be two of me, I wonder? But please, Chéri, don't ask me any more. It puzzles me so, and then perhaps I may say something to vex you. Let us play at our day games now, Chéri, and never mind about the other things. But if you go anywhere else like that, ask the fairies to take me too, for I always like to be with you, you know, Chéri."

So they kissed and made friends. But still it seemed very queer to Hugh. Till now Jeanne had always been eager to talk about the tapestry castle, and full of fancies about Dudu and Houpet and the rest of the animals, and anxious to hear Hugh's dreams. Now she seemed perfectly content with her every-day world, delighted with a new and beautiful china dinner-service which her godmother had sent her, and absorbed in cooking all manner of wonderful dishes for a grand dolls' feast, for which she was sending invitations to all her dolls, young and old, ugly and pretty, armless, footless, as were some, in the perfection of Parisian toilettes as were others. For she had, like most only daughters, an immense collection of dolls, though she was not as fond of them as many little girls.

"I thought you didn't much care for dolls. It was one of the things I liked you for at the first," said Hugh, in a slightly aggrieved tone of voice. Lessons were over, and the children were busy at the important business of cooking the feast. Hugh didn't mind the cooking; he had even submitted to a paper cap which Jeanne had constructed for him on the model of that of the "chef" downstairs; he found great consolation in the beating up an egg which Marcelline had got for them as a great treat, and immense satisfaction in watching the stewing, in one

of Jeanne's toy pans on the nursery fire, of a prepa-
ration of squashed prunes, powdered chocolate, and
bread crumbs, which was to represent a "ragout à la "
— I really do not remember what.

" I thought you didn't care for dolls, Jeanne,"
Hugh repeated. " It would be ever so much nicer to
have all the animals at our feast. We could put
them on chairs all round the table. That *would* be
some fun."

" They wouldn't sit still one minute," said Jeanne.
" How funny you are to think of such a thing, Chéri !
Of course it would be fun if they *would*, but fancy
Dudu and Grignan helping themselves with knives
and forks like people."

Jeanne burst out laughing at the idea, and laughed
so heartily that Hugh could not help laughing too.
But all the same he said to himself,

" I'm sure Dudu and the others *could* sit at the
table and behave like ladies and gentlemen if they
chose. How *very* funny of Jeanne to forget about all
the clever things they did ! But it is no use saying
any more to her. It would only make us quarrel.
There must be two Jeanne's, or else ' they,' whoever
they are, make her forget on purpose."

And as Hugh, for all his fancifulness, was a good
deal of a philosopher, he made up his mind to amuse
himself happily with little Jeanne as she was. The
feast was a great success. The dolls behaved irre-
proachably, with which their owner was rather in·

clined to twit Hugh, when, just at the end of the
banquet, greatly to his satisfaction, a certain Mademoiselle Zéphyrine, a blonde with flaxen ringlets and
turquoise blue eyes, suddenly toppled over, something having no doubt upset her equilibrium, and
fell flat on her nose on the table.

"Ah!" cried Jeanne, greatly concerned, "my poor
Zéphyrine has fainted," and, rushing forward to her
assistance, worse results followed. Mesdames Lili
and Joséphine, two middle-aged ladies somewhat the
worse for wear, overcome by the distressing spectacle,
or by the sleeve of Jeanne's dress as she leant across
them, fell off their chairs too — one, like Zéphyrine, on
to the table, the other on to the floor, dragging down
with her the plateful of ragout in front of her, while
her friend's sudden descent upon the table completed
the general knockings over and spillings which
Zéphyrine had begun.

"Oh dear! oh dear!" cried Jeanne; "all the
chocolate ragout is spilt, and the whipped-up egg is
mixed with the orange-juice soup. Oh dear! oh
dear! and I thought we should have had the whole
feast to eat up ourselves after the dolls had had
enough."

"Yes," said Hugh, "that's what comes of having
stupid sticks of dolls at your feasts. The *animals*
wouldn't have behaved like that."

But, seeing that poor Jeanne was really in tears
at this unfortunate termination of her entertainment,

he left off teasing her, and having succeeded in rescuing some remains of the good things, they sat down on the floor together and ate them up very amicably.

"I don't think I *do* care much for dolls," said Jeanne meditatively, when she had munched the last crumbs of the snipped-up almonds, which were supposed to represent some very marvellous dish. ("I like almonds terribly — don't you, Chéri?") she added, as a parenthesis. "No, I don't care for dolls. You are quite right about them; they *are* stupid, and you can't make fancies about them, because their faces always have the same silly look. I don't know what I like playing at best. O Marcelline!" she exclaimed, as the old nurse just then came into the room, "O Marcelline! *do* tell us a story; we are tired of playing."

"Does Monsieur Chéri, too, wish me tell him a story?" asked Marcelline, looking curiously at Hugh.

"Yes, of course," said Hugh. "Why do you look at me that funny way, Marcelline?"

"Why," said Marcelline, smiling, "I was thinking only that perhaps Monsieur finds so many stories in the tapestry that he would no longer care for my stupid little old tales."

Hugh did not answer. He was wondering to himself what Marcelline really meant; whether she knew of the wonders concealed behind the tapestry, or was only teasing him a little in the kind but queer way she sometimes did.

"Marcelline," he said suddenly at last, "I don't understand you."

"Do you understand yourself, my little Monsieur?" said Marcelline. "Do any of us understand ourselves? all the different selves that each of us is?"

"No," said Hugh, "I daresay we don't. It is very puzzling; it's all very puzzling."

"In the country where I lived when I was a little girl," began Marcelline, but Jeanne interrupted her.

"Have you never been there since, Marcelline?" she asked.

Marcelline smiled again her funny smile.

"Oh dear, yes," she said; "often, very often. I should not have been near so happy as I am if I had not often visited that country."

"Dear me," exclaimed Jeanne, "how very queer! I had no idea of that. You haven't been there for a great many years anyway, Marcelline. I heard mamma telling a lady the other day that she never remembered your going away, not even for a day — never since she was born."

"Ah!" said Marcelline, "but, Mademoiselle, we don't always know what even those nearest us do. I might have gone to that country without your mamma knowing. Sometimes we are far away when those beside us think us close to them."

"Yes," said Hugh, looking up suddenly, "that is true, Marcelline."

What she said made him remember Dudu's remark about Jeanne the night before, that she was far, far away, and he began to feel that Marcelline understood much that she seldom alluded to.

But Jeanne took it up differently. She jumped on to Marcelline's knee and pretended to beat her.

"You naughty little old woman," she said; "you very naughty little old woman, to say things like that to puzzle me — just what you know I don't like. Go back to your own country, naughty old Marcelline; go back to your fairyland, or wherever it was you came from, if you are going to tease poor little Jeanne so."

"*Tease* you, Mademoiselle?" Marcelline repeated.

"Yes, tease me," insisted Jeanne. "You know I hate people to go on about things I don't understand. Now you're to tell us a story at once, do you hear, Marcelline?"

Hugh said nothing, but he looked up in Marcelline's face with his grave blue eyes, and the old woman smiled again. She seemed as if she was going to speak, when just then a servant came upstairs to say that Jeanne's mother wished the children to go downstairs to her for a little. Jeanne jumped up, delighted to welcome any change.

"You must keep the story for another day, Marcelline," she said, as she ran out of the room.

"I am getting too old to tell stories," said Marcel
line, half to herself, half to Hugh, who was following
his cousin more slowly. He stopped for a moment.

"Too old?" he repeated.

"Yes, Monsieur Chéri, too old," the nurse replied.
"The thoughts do not come so quickly as they once
did, and the words, too, hobble along like lamesters
on crutches."

"But," said Hugh, half timidly, "it is never —
you would never, I mean, be too old to visit that
country, where there are so many stories to be
found?"

"Perhaps not," said Marcelline, "but even if I
found them, I might not be able to tell them. Go
and look for them for yourself, Monsieur Chéri; you
have not half seen the tapestry castle yet."

But when Hugh would have asked her more she
would not reply, only smiled and shook her head.
So the boy went slowly downstairs after Jeanne,
wondering what old Marcelline could mean, half
puzzled and half pleased.

"Only," he said to himself, "if I get into the
castle, Jeanne really must come with me, especially
if it is to hear stories."

CHAPTER VII.

WINGS AND CATS.

"And all their cattish gestures plainly spoke
They thought the affair they'd come upon no joke."
CHARLES LAMB.

SOME days went on, and nothing more was said by
the children about the adventures which had so
puzzled poor Hugh. After a while he seemed to
lose the wish to talk about them to little Jeanne; or
rather, he began to feel as if he could not, that the
words would not come, or that if they did, they would
not tell what he wanted. He thought about the
strange things he had seen very often, but it was as
if he had read of them rather than as if he had seen
and heard them, or as if they had happened to some
one else. Whenever he saw Dudu and Houpet and
the rest of the pets, he looked at them at first in a
half dreamy way, wondering if they too were puzzled
about it all, or if, being really fairies, they did not
find anything to puzzle them! The only person (for,
after all, he could often not prevent himself from
looking upon all the animals as persons) — the only
person who he somehow felt sure *did* understand
him, was Marcelline, and this was a great satisfaction.
She said nothing ; she almost never even smiled in

what Jeanne called her "funny" way; but there was just a very tiny little undersound in the tone of her voice sometimes, a little wee smile in her eyes more than on her lips, that told Hugh that, fairy or no fairy, old Marcelline knew all about it, and it pleased him to think so.

One night when Hugh was warmly tucked up in bed Marcelline came in as usual before he went to sleep to put out his light.

"There's been no moonlight for a good while, Marcelline, has there?" he said.

"No, Monsieur, there has not," said Marcelline.

"Will it be coming back soon?" asked Hugh.

"Do you like it so much, my child?" said the old nurse. She had a funny way of sometimes answering a question by asking another.

"Yes," said Hugh. "At least, of course when I'm fast asleep it doesn't matter to me if it's moonlight or not. But you know what I like it for, Marcelline, and you said the other day that I hadn't half seen the tapestry castle, and I want very much to see it, Marcelline, only I'd like Jeanne to be with me; for I don't think I could tell her well about the fairy things if she hadn't been with me. She didn't seem to understand the words, and I don't think I could get the right ones to tell, do you know, Marcelline?"

He half sat up in bed, resting his head on his elbow, which was leaning on the pillow, and looking

up in the old woman's face with his earnest blue
eyes. Marcelline shook her head slowly.

"No," she said, "you're right. The words wouldn't
come, and if they did, it would be no use. You're
older than Mademoiselle Jeanne, Monsieur Hugh,
and it's different for her. But it doesn't matter —
the days bring their own pleasures and interests,
which the moonlight wouldn't suit. You wouldn't
have cared for a dinner like what you have every day
when you were listening to the song of the swan?"

"No, certainly not," said Hugh. "I see you do
understand, Marcelline, better than anybody. It
must be as I said; there must be two of me, and
two of Jeanne, and two of you, and —"

"And two of everything," said Marcelline; "and
the great thing is to keep each of the twos in its right
place."

She smiled now, right out, and was turning away
with the light in her hand, when Hugh called after
her,

"*Will* the moonlight nights come again soon,
Marcelline? Do tell me. I'm sure you know."

"Have a little patience," said the old nurse, "you
shall be told. Never fear."

And, a little inclined to be *im*patient, Hugh was
nevertheless obliged to shut his eyes and go to sleep.
There was no moonlight *that* night anyway.

But not many nights after there came a great
surprise.

Curiously enough Hugh had gone to sleep *that* night without any thought of tapestry adventures. He and Jeanne had been very merry indeed; they had been dressing up, and playing delightful tricks — such as tapping at the salon door, and on being told to come in, making their appearance like two very, very old peasants, hobbling along on sticks — Jeanne with a cap and little knitted shawl of Marcelline's, Hugh with a blouse and cotton nightcap, so that Jeanne's mother quite jumped at first sight of the quaint little figures. Then Jeanne dressed up like a fairy, and pretended to turn Hugh into a guinea-pig, and they got Nibble up into the nursery, and Hugh hid in a cupboard, and tried to made his voice sound as if it came from Nibble, and the effect of his ventriloquism was so comical that the children laughed till they actually rolled on the floor. And they had hardly got over the laughing — though Marcelline did her best to make them sit still for half an hour or so before going to bed — when it was time to say good-night and compose themselves to sleep.

"I shan't be able to go to sleep for ever so long," said Hugh; "I shall stay awake all the night, I believe."

"Oh no, you won't," said Marcelline, with a smile, as she went off with the light.

And strange to say, hardly had she shut the door when Hugh did fall asleep — soundly asleep. He knew no more about who he was, or where he was, or anything — he just slept as soundly as a little top, without dreaming or starting in the least, for — dear me, I don't know for how long! — anyway it must have been for several hours, when — in the strange sudden way in which once or twice before it had happened to him to awake in this curious tapestry room, he opened his eyes as if startled by an electric shock, and gazed out before him, as much awake as if he had never been asleep in his life.

What had awakened him, and what did he see? He could hardly have told what had awakened him but for what he *now* saw and heard. A voice, a very well-known little voice, was speaking to him. " Chéri dear," it said, " Chéri, I have come for you. And see what I have got for you." And there before him stood Jeanne — but Jeanne as he had never seen her before. She seemed all glistening and shining — her dress was of some kind of sparkling white, and round her waist was a lovely silver girdle — her sleeves too were looped up with silver bands, and, prettiest of all, two snow-white wings were fastened to her shoulders. She looked like a fairy queen, or like a silvery bird turned into a little girl. And in her hand she held another pair of wings exactly like her own.

Hugh gazed at her.

"Have you been dressing up?" he said, "and in the middle of the night? oh how funny! But O, Jeanne, how pretty you look!"

Two Christmas Angels. — p. 105.

— *Frontispiece.*

Jeanne laughed merrily. "Come, get up quick, then," she said, "and I'll make you pretty too. Only I can't promise you a head-dress like mine, Chéri."

She gave her head a little toss, which made Hugh look at it. And now he noticed that on it she wore something very funny indeed, which at first, being black — for Jeanne's hair, you know, was black too — had not caught his attention. At first he thought it was some kind of black silk hood or cap, such as he had seen worn by some of the peasants in Switzerland, but looking again — no, it was nothing of the kind — the head-dress had a head of its own, and as Hugh stared, it cocked it pertly on one side in a way Hugh would have known again anywhere. Yes, it was Dudu, sitting on Jeanne's smooth little head as comfortably as if he had always been intended to serve the purpose of a bonnet.

"Dudu!" exclaimed Hugh.

"Of course," said Jeanne. "You didn't suppose we could have gone without him, Chéri."

"Gone where?" said Hugh, quite sitting up in bed by this time, but still a good deal puzzled.

"Up into the tapestry castle," said Jeanne, "where we've been wishing so to go, though we had to wait for the moonlight, you know."

The word made Hugh glance towards the window, for, for the first time he began to wonder how it was his room was so bright. Yes, it was streaming in, in a beautiful flood, and the tapestry on the walls had taken again the lovely tints which by daylight were no longer visible.

Hugh sprang out of bed. "Are these for me?" he said, touching the wings which Jeanne held.

"Certainly," she replied. "Aren't they pretty? Much nicer than your wall-climbers, Chéri. I chose them. Turn round and let me put them on."

She slipped them over his head — they seemed to be fastened to a band, and in a moment they had fitted themselves perfectly into their place. They were so light that Hugh was hardly conscious of them, and yet he could move them about — backwards and forwards, swiftly or slowly, just as he chose — and as easily as he could move his arms. Hugh was extremely pleased with them, but he looked at his little night-gown with sudden dismay.

" You said you'd make me look pretty too, Jeanne," he observed. " I don't care for myself — boys never care about being grandly dressed — but I shall look rather funny beside you, shan't I ? "

" Wait a minute," said Jeanne, "you're not ready yet. I'm going to powder you. Shut your eyes."

He did so, and therefore could not see what Jeanne did, but he felt a sort of soft puff fly all over him, and opening his eyes again at Jeanne's bidding, saw, to his amazement, that he too was now dressed in the same pretty shiny stuff as his little cousin. They looked just like two Christmas angels on the top of a frosted Twelfth Night cake.

"There now," said Jeanne, "aren't you pleased? You don't know how nice you look. Now, Dudu, we're quite ready. Are we to fly up to the castle?"

Dudu nodded his wise head. Jeanne took Hugh's hand, and without Hugh's quite knowing how it was managed, they all flew up the wall together, and found themselves standing on the castle terrace. There was no light streaming out from the windows this time, and the peacocks were quite motionless at their post.

"Are they asleep?" said Hugh.

"Perhaps," said Dudu, speaking for the first time. "They lead a monotonous life, you see. But there is no occasion to disturb them."

They were standing just in front of the door, by which, the last time, Hugh had entered the long lighted-up passage. As they stood waiting, the door slowly opened, but to Hugh's great surprise the inside was perfectly different. A very large white-painted hall was revealed to them. The ceiling was arched, and looking up, it seemed so very high, that it gave one more the feeling of being the sky than the roof of a house. This great hall was perfectly empty, but yet it did not feel chilly, and a faint pleasant perfume stole through it, as if not far off sweet-scented flowers and plants were growing.

Hugh and Jeanne stood hand-in-hand and looked around them. The door by which they had entered had closed noiselessly, and when they turned to see

the way by which they had come in, no sign of a
door was there. In the panels of white wood which
formed the walls, it was somehow concealed.

"How shall we ever get out again?" said Hugh.

But Jeanne only laughed.

"We needn't trouble about that," she said. "We
got back all right the last time. What I want to
know is what are we to do next? I see no way out
of this hall, and though it's rather nice, it's not very
amusing. Dudu, I wish you would sit still — you
keep giving little juggles on my head that are very
uncomfortable, and make me feel as if I had a hat on
that was always tumbling off."

"I beg your pardon, Mademoiselle Jeanne," replied Dudu with great dignity. "You really do say
such foolish things sometimes that it is impossible
to restrain one's feelings altogether. No way out of
this hall, do you say, when it is the entrance to
everywhere?"

"But how are we to get to everywhere, or anywhere?" asked Jeanne.

"Really!" said Dudu, as if quite out of patience.
"When you are running up and down the terrace, in
your other life, you don't stand still at one end and
say, 'Dudu, how am I to get to the other?' You
move your feet, which were given you for the purpose. And in present circumstances, instead of your
feet, you naturally —"

"Move our wings," cried Jeanne. "Oh, of course.

We're to fly. But you see, Dudu, we're accustomed to having feet, and to running and walking with them, but having wings is something new."

Dudu still looked rather contemptuous, and Hugh gave a little pull to Jeanne's hand.

"Let's set off," he said.

"But where are we to go to?" asked Jeanne.

Dudu gave a little croak. "Really," he said again. "What am I here for?"

"Oh, to show us the way, of course," said Jeanne. "You're going to steer us, I suppose, on the top of my head. Well, we're quite ready."

Off they set. The flying this time was really quite a pleasure in itself, and the higher up they rose the easier and swifter it seemed to become. The hall was lighted from the roof—at least the light seemed to come down from among the arches so high up that their form was only vaguely seen. But whether it was daylight or what, the children did not know, and perhaps it did not occur to them to think. They just flew softly on, till suddenly Dudu veered to one side and stopped them in front of a low carved door with a step before it just large enough for them to stand on. They had not noticed this door before —the hall was so very large and the door in comparison so small, and the step before it had looked just like a little jutting-out ledge in the carving, till they were close to it.

"Don't turn round," said Dudu, "for fear it

should make you giddy. Push the door and go in at once."

The children did so. The door yielded, and then immediately — they were such well-behaved doors in the tapestry palace — closed behind them. And what the children now saw was a small winding stair, the lowest steps of which were close to their feet.

"Here," said Dudu, "I will leave you. You can't go wrong."

He flew down from Jeanne's head as he spoke. Jeanne gave her head a little shake; she seemed not altogether sorry to be freed from her head-dress, for a head-dress with *feelings* is a somewhat uncomfortable affair.

"I don't mind getting you off my head, Dudu," she said. "But you might take a turn on Chéri's for a change. I think it's rather shabby of you to leave us already."

Hugh looked at Jeanne in surprise. He could not understand how it was that Jeanne ventured to speak so coolly to the raven — she who in their daylight life was so frightened of him that she would hardly go near him for fear he should turn her into a mouse, or in some other way bewitch her!

"I think it's very good-natured of Monsieur Dudu to have come with us so far," he said. "We could never have got into the tapestry castle at all but for him.'

"No," said Dudu, "that you certainly wouldn't." But he didn't seem offended. "Good-bye," he said,

" and if you're in any trouble remember the former arrangement. Whistle three times."

" Good-bye," said Hugh and Jeanne. But as they said it, their looks met each other in astonishment — there was no Dudu there — he had already disappeared.

" What a queer way he has of going off all of a sudden," said Jeanne.

" And what are we to do now?" said Hugh.

" Go up the stairs, of course, till we find where they lead to," said Jeanne.

" It will be rather awkward with our wings," said Hugh. " The stair is so very narrow and twisting."

Jeanne made an exclamation.

" Wings!" she said. " Why, Chéri, your wings are gone!"

" And so are yours!" said Hugh.

Both the children stared at each other and turned round to look at their shoulders, as if they could hardly believe it.

" It's too bad," said Jeanne. " It's all Dudu."

" Never mind," said Hugh. " He wouldn't have taken them away if we had been going to need them again; and really, Jeanne, the more I think of it the more sure I am we could never have got up that stair with our wings on."

" Perhaps not," said Jeanne. " Anyway *I* couldn't have got up it with Dudu on my head. But let's go on, Chéri. Are you frightened? I'm not a bit."

"I'm not, either," said Hugh. "Still, it's a very queer place. I wish Dudu, or Houpet, or some of them, had come with us!"

They set off on their climb up the steep spiral staircase. So narrow it was, that going hand-in-hand was out of the question.

"It's worse than the staircase down to the frogs' country," said Jeanne.

Hugh looked at her triumphantly.

"There now, Jeanne, you *do* remember," he said. "I believe it was just pretence your saying you thought I had dreamt it all."

"No," said Jeanne, "it wasn't. You don't understand, Chéri. I'm moonlight Jeanne, now — when we were having the dolls' feast I was daylight Jeanne. And you know it's never moonlight in the daytime."

"Well, certainly, I *don't* understand," said Hugh. "And one thing particularly — how is it that in the moon-time you remember about the day-time, if in the day you forget all about the other?"

"I don't exactly forget," said Jeanne, "but it spoils things to mix them together. And lots of things would be *quite* spoilt if you took them into the regular daylight. I fancy, too, one can see farther in the moonlight — one can see more ways."

She was standing at the foot of the stair, a step or two higher than Hugh, and the soft light, which still, in some mysterious way, seemed to come down from above — though, looking up the spiral stair, its top seemed lost in gloom — fell on her pretty little face. Her hair had fallen back over her shoulders and lay dark on her pure white shiny dress; there was a look in her eyes which Hugh had never noticed before, as if she could see a long way off. Hugh looked at her earnestly.

"Jeanne," he said, "you're a perfect puzzle. I do wonder whether you're half a fairy, or an angel, or a dream. I do hope you're not a dream when you're in the moonlight. But, oh dear, I cannot understand."

"Do leave off trying to understand, Chéri," said Jeanne, "and let us amuse ourselves. I always love *you*, Chéri, whatever I am, don't I?"

She turned towards him brightly, with such a merry smile on her face that Hugh could not help smiling too.

"Do let us go on quickly," she said; "I do so want to see where this stair goes to."

"Let me go first. I'm a boy, you know, and it's right I should go first in case of meeting anything that might frighten you," said Hugh.

So he stepped up in front of Jeanne, and they slowly made their way.

It was impossible to go fast. Never was there such a twisty little stair. Here and there, too, it got darker, so that they could only just find their way, step by step. And it really seemed as if they had climbed a very long way, when from above came faintly and softly the sound of a plaintive "mew." "Mew, mew," it said again, whoever the "it" was, and then stopped.

The children looked at each other.

"Cats!" they said at the same instant.

"It's just as well," said Hugh, "that none of the animals did come with us, as so many of them are birds."

Another step or two and the mystery was explained. They had reached the top of the turret stair; it led them into a little hall, all, like the great hall below, painted white. It looked perfectly pure and clean, as if it had only been painted the day before, and yet there was a curiously *old* look about it too, and a faint scent of dried rose leaves seemed to be in the air.

There was a door in this little hall, exactly opposite the top of the stair, and at each side of the door was an arm-chair, also all white, and with a white satin cushion instead of a seat. And on each of these chairs sat a most beautiful white cat. The only colour in the hall was the flash of their green eyes, as they turned them full on the two children.

Jeanne crept a little closer to Hugh. But there was no reason for fear. The cats were most amiably disposed.

"Mew!" said the one on the right-hand chair.

"Mew!" said the one on the left-hand chair.

Then they looked at each other for a moment, and

at last, seeming to have made up their minds, each held out his right paw. Something in the way they did it reminded Hugh and Jeanne of Dudu when he stood on one leg, and stuck out the other like a walking-stick.

"Mew!" they said again, both together this time. And then in a clear, though rather mewey voice, the right-hand cat spoke to the children.

"Madame is expecting you," he said.

The children did not know what else to say, so they said, "Thank you."

"She has been waiting a good while," said the left-hand cat.

"I'm very sorry to have kept her waiting," said Hugh, feeling Jeanne nudge him. "I hope she has not been waiting very long?"

"Oh no," said the right-hand cat, "not long; not above three hundred years."

Jeanne gave a start of astonishment.

"Three hundred—" "years," she was going to say, but the left-hand cat interrupted her.

"You are not to be surprised," he said, very hastily, and Jeanne could not quite make out if he was frightened or angry, or a little of both. "You must not *think* of being surprised. Nobody is ever surprised here."

"No one is ever surprised here," repeated the right-hand cat. "This is the Castle of Whiteness, you know. You are sure you have nothing coloured about you?" he added, anxiously.

Instinctively both the children put their hands up to their heads.

" Only our hair," they said.

" Mine's light-brown, you see," said Hugh.

" And mine's bl — " Jeanne was saying, but the cats, both speaking together this time, stopped her with a squeal of horror.

" Oh, oh, oh ! " they said. " Where are your manners ? You must never mention such a word. Your hair, Mademoiselle, is *shadowy*. That is the proper expression."

Jeanne was annoyed, and did not speak. Hugh felt himself bound to defend her from the charge of bad manners.

" You needn't be so sharp," he said to the cats ; " your eyes are as green as they can be."

" Green doesn't count," said the right-hand cat, coolly.

" And how were we to know that ? " said Hugh.

" I don't know," said the left-hand cat.

" Well, but can't you be sensible ? " said Hugh, who didn't feel inclined to give in to two cats.

" Perhaps we might be if we tried," said the right-hand cat. " But — "

A sudden sound interrupted him. It was as if some one had moved a piece of furniture with squeaking castors.

" Madame's turning her wheel," said the left-hand cat. " Now's the time."

Both cats got down from their chairs, and each, standing on their hind legs, proceeded to open his side of the door between the chairs — or "doors" I should almost say, for it was a double-hinged one, opening in the middle, and the funny thing about it was that one side opened outwards, and the other inwards, so that at first, unless you were standing just exactly in the middle, you did not see very clearly into the inside.

CHAPTER VIII.

"THE BROWN BULL OF NORROWA."

> " Delicate, strong, and white,
>   Hurrah for the magic thread !
>   The warp and the woof come right."
>   CHILD WORLD.

THEY were not to be surprised! Both the children remembered that, and yet it was a little difficult to avoid being so.

At first all they saw was just another white room, a small one, and with a curious pointed window in one corner. But when the doors were fully opened there was more to be seen. In the first place, at the opposite corner, was a second window exactly like the other, and in front of this window a spinning-wheel was placed, and before this spinning-wheel sat, on a white chair, a white-haired lady.

She was spinning busily. She did not look up as the children came in. She seemed quite absorbed in her work. So the children stood and gazed at her, and the cats stood quietly in front, the right-hand one before Hugh, the left-hand one before Jeanne, not seeming, of course, the least surprised. Whether I should call the white-haired lady an " old " lady or not, I really do not know. No doubt she was old, as we count old, but yet, except for her hair, she did not look so. She was very small, and she was dressed entirely in white, and her hands were the prettiest little things you ever saw. But as she did not look up, Hugh and Jeanne could not at first judge of her face. They stood staring at her for some minutes without speaking. At last, as they were not allowed to be surprised, and indeed felt afraid of being reproached with bad manners by the cats if they made any remarks at all, it began, especially for Jeanne, to grow rather stupid.

She gave Hugh a little tug.

"Won't you speak to her?" she whispered, very, *very* softly.

Instantly both cats lifted their right paws.

"You see," replied Hugh, looking at Jeanne reproachfully, "they're getting angry."

On this the cats wheeled right round and looked at the children.

"I don't care," said Jeanne, working herself up. "I don't care. It's not our fault. They said she was waiting for us, and they made us come in."

"'*She* is the cat,' so I've been told," said a soft voice suddenly. "And 'don't care;' something was once spun about 'don't care,' I think."

Immediately the two cats threw themselves on the ground, apparently in an agony of grief.

"*She* the cat," they cried. "Oh, what presump-

tion! And who said 'don't care'? Oh dear! oh
dear! who would have thought of such a thing?"

The lady lifted her head, and looked at the cats
and the children. There was a curious expression on
her face, as if she had just awakened. Her eyes were
very soft blue, softer and dreamier than Hugh's, and
her mouth, even while it smiled, had a rather sad
look. But the look of her whole face was very — I
can't find a very good word for it. It seemed to ask
you questions, and yet to know more about you than
you did yourself. It was impossible not to keep
looking at her once you had begun.

"Hush, cats," were the next words she said.
"Don't be silly; it's nearly as bad as being surprised."

Immediately the cats sat up in their places again,
as quiet and dignified as if they had not been at all
put about, and Jeanne glanced at Hugh as much as
to say, "Aren't you glad she has put them down a
little?"

Then the lady looked over the cats to the children.

"It is quite ready," she said; " the threads are all
straight."

What could they say? They had not the least
idea what she meant, and they were afraid of asking.
Evidently the white lady was of the same opinion as
the cats as to the rudeness of being surprised; very
probably asking questions would be considered still
ruder.

Jeanne was the first to pick up courage.

"Madame," she said, "I don't mean to be rude, but I *am* so thirsty. It's with flying, I think, for we're not accustomed to it."

"Why did you not say so before?" said the lady. "I can give you anything you want. It has all been ready a long time. Will you have snow water or milk?"

"Milk, please," said Jeanne.

The lady looked at the cats.

"Fetch it," she said quietly. The cats trotted off; they opened the door as before, but left it open this time, and in another moment they returned carrying between them a white china tray, on which were two cups of beautiful rich-looking milk. They handed them to the children, who each took one and drank it with great satisfaction. Then the cats took away the cups and tray, and returned and sat down as before.

The lady smiled at the children.

"Now," she said, "are you ready?"

She had been so kind about the milk that Hugh this time took courage.

"We are *very* sorry," he said, "but we really don't understand what it is you would like us to do."

"Do?" said the lady. "Why, you have nothing to do but to listen. Isn't that what you came for? To hear some of the stories I spin?"

The children opened their eyes — with pleasure it

is to be supposed rather than surprise — for the white lady did not seem at all annoyed.

"Oh!" said they, both at once. "Is *that* what you're spinning? Stories!"

"Of course," said the lady. "Where did you think they all come from? — all the stories down there?" She pointed downwards in the direction of the stair and the great hall. "Why, here I have been for — no, it would frighten you to tell you how long, by your counting, I have been up here at my spinning. I spin the round of the clock at this window, then I turn my wheel — to get the light, you see — and spin the round again at the other. If you saw the tangle it comes to me in! And the threads I send down! It is not *often* such little people as you come up here themselves, but it does happen sometimes. And there is plenty ready for you — all ready for the wheel."

"How wonderful!" said Hugh. "And oh!" he exclaimed, "I suppose sometimes the threads get twisted again when you have to send them down such a long way, and that's how stories get muddled sometimes."

"Just so," said the white lady. "My story threads need gentle handling, and sometimes people seize them roughly and tear and soil them, and then of course they are no longer pretty. But listen now. What will you have? The first in the wheel is a very, very old fairy story. I span it for your great-great-grandmothers; shall I spin it again for you?"

"Oh, please," said both children at once.

"Then sit down on the floor and lean your heads against my knees," said the lady. "Shut your eyes and listen. That is all you have to do. Never mind the cats, they will be quite quiet."

Hugh and Jeanne did as she told them. They leaned their heads, the smooth black one of the little girl, the fair-haired curly one of the boy, on the lady's white robe. You can hardly imagine how soft and pleasant it was to the touch. A half-sleepy feeling came over them; they shut their eyes and did not feel inclined to open them again. But they did not really go to sleep; the fairy lady began to work the wheel, and through the soft whirr came the sound of a voice — whether it was the voice of the lady or of the wheel they could not tell. And this was the old, old story the wheel spun for them.

"Listen, children," it began.

"We are listening," said Jeanne, rather testily. "You needn't say that again."

"Hush, Jeanne," said Hugh; "you'll stop the story if you're not quiet."

"Listen, children," said the voice again. And Jeanne was quite quiet.

"Once on a time — a very long time ago — in a beautiful castle there lived a beautiful Princess. She was young and sweet and very fair to see. And she

was the only child of her parents, who thought
nothing too rare or too good for her. At her birth
all the fairies had given her valuable gifts — no evil
wishes had been breathed over her cradle. Only the
fairy who had endowed her with good sense and
ready wit had dropped certain words, which had left
some anxiety in the minds of her parents.

"'She will need my gifts,' the fairy had said. 'If
she uses them well, they and these golden balls will
stand her in good need.'

"And as she kissed the baby she left by her pillow
three lovely golden balls, at which, as soon as the
little creature saw them, she smiled with pleasure,
and held out her tiny hands to catch them.

" They were of course balls of fairy make — they
were small enough for the little Princess at first to
hold in her baby hands, but as she grew they grew,
till, when she had reached her sixteenth year, they
were the size of an orange. They were golden, but
yet neither hard nor heavy, and nothing had power
to dint or stain them. And all through her babyhood
and childhood, and on into her girlhood, they were
the Princess's favourite toy. They were never away
from her, and by the time she had grown to be a tall
and beautiful girl, with constant practice she had
learnt to catch them as cleverly as an Indian juggler.
She could whiz them all three in the air at a time,
and never let one drop to the ground. And all the
people about grew used to seeing their pretty Prin-

cess, as she wandered through the gardens and woods near the castle, throwing her balls in the air as she walked, and catching them again without the slightest effort.

"And remembering the words of the fairy who had given them, naturally her father and mother were pleased to see her love for the magic gift, and every one about the palace was forbidden to laugh at her, or to say that it was babyish for a tall Princess to play so much with a toy that had amused her as an infant.

"She was not a silly Princess at all. She was clever at learning, and liked it, and she was sensible and quick-witted and very brave. So no one was inclined to laugh at her pretty play, even if they had not been forbidden to do so. And she was so kind-hearted and merry, that if ever in her rambles she met any little children who stared at her balls with wondering eyes, she would make her ladies stop, while she threw the balls up in the air, higher and yet higher, ever catching them again as they flew back, and laughed with pleasure to see the little creatures' delight in her skill.

"She was such a happy Princess that the bright balls seemed like herself — ready to catch every ray of sunshine and make it prisoner. And till she had reached her sixteenth year no cloud had come over her brightness. About this time she noticed that the king, her father, began to look anxious and grave, and messengers often came in haste to see him from far-off parts of his kingdom. And once or twice she overheard words dropped which she could not understand, except that it was evident some misfortune was at hand. But in their desire to save their daughter all sorrow, the king and queen had given orders that the trouble which had come to the country was not to be told her; so the Princess could find out nothing even by questioning her ladies or her old nurse, who hitherto had never refused to tell her anything she wanted to know.

" One day when she was walking about the gardens, playing as usual with her golden balls, she came upon a young girl half hidden among the shrubs, crying bitterly. The Princess stopped at once to ask her what was the matter, but the girl only shook her head and went on weeping, refusing to answer.

" 'I dare not tell you, Princess,' she said. 'I dare not. You are good and kind, and I do not blame you for my misfortunes. If you knew all, you would pity me.'

" And that was all she would say.

" She was a pretty girl, about the same age and height as the Princess, and the Princess, after speaking to her, remembered that she had sometimes seen her before.

" 'You are the daughter of the gardener, are you not?' she inquired.

" 'Yes,' said the girl. 'My father is the king's gardener. But I have been away with my grandmother. They only sent for me yesterday to come home — and — and — oh, I was to have been married next week to a young shepherd, who has loved me since my childhood!'

" And with this the girl burst into fresh weeping, but not another word would she say.

" Just then the Princess's governess, who had been a little behind — for sometimes in playing with her balls the Princess ran on faster — came up to where the two young girls were talking together. When the governess saw who the Princess's companion was she seemed uneasy.

" ' What has she been saying to you, Princess?' she asked eagerly. ' It is the gardener's daughter, I see.'

" ' Yes,' said the Princess. ' She is the gardener's daughter, and she is in some great trouble. That is all I know, for she will tell me nothing but that she was to have been married next week, and then she weeps. I wish I knew what her sorrow is, for, per-haps, I could be of use to her. I would give her all my money if it would do her any good,' and the Princess looked ready to cry herself. But the girl only shook her head. ' No, Princess,' she said; ' it would do me no good. It is not your fault; but oh, it is very hard on me!'

" The governess seemed very frightened and spoke sharply to the girl, reproving her for annoying the Princess with her distress. The Princess was surprised, for all her ladies hitherto had, by the king and queen's desire, encouraged her to be kind and sympathising to those in trouble, and to do all she could to console them. But as she had also been taught to be very obedient, she made no remonstrance when her governess desired her to leave the girl and return to the castle. But all that day the Princess remained silent and depressed. It was the first time a shadow had come near her happiness.

" The next morning when she awoke the sun was shining brilliantly. It was a most lovely spring day. The Princess's happy spirits seemed all to have returned. She said to herself that she would confide to the queen her mother her concern about the poor girl that she had seen, and no doubt the queen would devise some way of helping her. And the thought made her feel so light-hearted that she told her attendants to fetch her a beautiful white dress trimmed with silver, which had been made for her but the day before. To her surprise the maidens looked at each other in confusion. At last one replied that the queen had not been pleased with the dress and had sent it away, but that a still more beautiful one trimmed with gold should be ready by that evening. The Princess was perplexed; she was not so silly as to care about the dress, but it seemed to her very strange that her mother should not admire what she had thought so lovely a robe. But still more surprised was she at a message which was brought to her, as soon as she was dressed, from the king and queen, desiring her to remain in her own room the whole of that day without going out, for a reason that should afterwards be explained to her. She made no objections, as she was submissive and obedient to her parents' wishes, but she found it strange and sad to spend that beautiful spring day shut up in her rooms, more especially as in her favourite boudoir, a turret chamber which overlooked the castle court-yard, she found the curtains drawn closely, as if it were night, and was told by her governess that this too was by the king's orders; the Princess was requested not to look out of the windows. She grew at this a little impatient.

"'I am willing to obey my parents,' she said, 'but I would fain they trusted me, for I am no longer a child. Some misfortune is threatening us, I feel, and it is concealed from me, as if I could be happy or at rest if sorrow is hanging over my dear parents or the nation.'

"But no explanation was given to her, and all that day she sat in her darkened chamber playing sadly with her golden balls and thinking deeply to herself about the mystery. And towards the middle of the day sounds of excitement reached her from the court-yard beneath. There seemed a running to and fro, a noise of horses and of heavy feet, and now and then faint sounds of weeping.

"'Goes the king a hunting to-day?' she asked her ladies. 'And whose weeping is it I hear?'

"But the ladies only shook their heads without speaking.

"By the evening all seemed quiet. The Princess was desired to join her parents as usual, and the white and golden robe was brought to her to wear. She put it on with pleasure, and said to herself there could after all be no terrible misfortune at hand, for if so there would not be the signs of rejoicing she observed as she passed through the palace. And never had her parents been more tender and loving. They seemed to look at her as if never before they had known how they treasured her, and the Princess was so touched by these proofs of their affection that she could not make up her mind to trouble them by asking questions which they might not wish to answer.

"The next day everything went on as usual in the palace, and it seemed to the Princess that there was a general feeling as if some great danger was safely passed. But this happiness did not last long; about three days later, again a messenger, dusty and wearied with riding fast and hard, made his appearance at the castle; and faces grew gloomy, and the king and queen were evidently overwhelmed with grief. Yet nothing was told to the Princess.

"She wandered out about the gardens and castle grounds, playing as usual with her balls, but wondering sadly what meant this mysterious trouble. And as she was passing the poultry-yard, she heard a sound which seemed to suit her thoughts — some one was crying sadly. The Princess turned to see who it was. This time too it was a young girl about her own age, a girl whom she knew very well by sight, for she was the daughter of the queen's hen-wife, and the Princess had often seen her driving the flocks of turkeys or geese to their fields, or feeding the pretty cocks and hens which the queen took great pride in.

"'What is the matter, Bruna?' said the Princess, leaning over the gate. 'Have the rats eaten any of the little chickens, or has your mother been scolding you for breaking some eggs?'

"'Neither, Princess,' said the girl among her sobs. 'The chickens are never eaten, and my mother seldom scolds me. My trouble is far worse than that, but I dare not tell it to you — to you of all people in the world.'

"And the Princess's governess, who just then came up, looked again very frightened and uneasy.

"'Princess, Princess,' she said, 'what a habit you are getting of talking to all these foolish girls. Come back to the palace at once with me.'

"'I have often talked to Bruna before,' said the Princess gently, 'and I never was blamed for doing so. She is a pretty girl, and I have known her all my life. Some one said she was betrothed to one of my father's huntsmen, and I would like to ask if it is true. Perhaps they are too poor to marry, and it may be for that she is weeping.'

" Bruna heard what the Princess said, and wept still more violently. 'Ah, yes, it is true!' she said, ' but never, never shall I now be married to him.'

"But the Princess's governess would not let her wait to ask more. She hurried her back to the castle, and the Princess — more sure than ever that some mysterious trouble was in question — could get no explanation.

" She did not see the king and queen that night, and the next morning a strange thing happened — her white and golden robe was missing. And all that her attendants could tell her was that it had been taken away by the queen's orders.

" 'Then,' said the Princess, 'there is some sad trouble afloat which is hidden from me.'

" And when she went to her turret room, and found, as before, that the windows were all closed, so that she could not see out, she sat down and cried with distress and anxiety.

" And, again, about mid-day, the same confused noises were to be heard. A sound of horses and people moving about in the courtyard, a tramping of heavy feet, and through all a faint and smothered weeping. The Princess could bear her anxiety no longer. She drew back the curtains, and unfastened the shutters, and leaned out. From her window she could clearly see the courtyard. It was, as she suspected, filled with people; rows of soldiers on horseback lined the sides, and in front, on the steps, the king and queen were standing looking at a strange object. It was an enormous bull: never had the Princess seen such a bull. He was dark brown in colour, and pawed the ground in front of him impatiently, and on his back was seated a young girl whom the Princess gazed at with astonishment. She really thought for a moment it was herself, and that she was dreaming! For the girl was dressed in the Princess's own white and golden robe, and her face could not be seen, for it was covered with a thick veil, and numbers of women and servants standing about were weeping bitterly. And so, evidently, was the girl herself. Then the great bull gave another impatient toss, the girl seized his horns to keep herself from falling, and off he set, with a terrible rush; and a great shout, half of fear, half of rejoicing, as seeing him go, rose from the people about.

"Just at this moment the Princess heard some one approaching her room. She hastily drew the curtains, and sat down playing with her balls, as if she had seen nothing.

"She said not a word to any one, but she had her own thoughts, and that evening she was sent for to her father and mother, who, as usual, received her with caresses and every sign of the tenderest affection. And several days passed quietly, but still the Princess had her own thoughts.

"And one evening when she was sitting with her

mother, suddenly the king entered the room in the greatest trouble, and not seeing the Princess, for it was dusk, he exclaimed,

" ' It has failed again. The monster is not to be deceived. He vows he will not cease his ravages till he gets the real Princess, our beloved daughter. He has appeared again, and is more infuriated than ever, tearing up trees by the roots, destroying the people's houses, tramping over their fields, and half killing all the country with terror. What is to be done ? The people say they can endure it no longer. The girl Bruna was found bruised and bleeding by the wayside a long way from this, and she gives the same account as the gardener's daughter of the monster's rage at finding he had been deceived.'

" The queen had tried to prevent the king's relating all this, but he was too excited to notice her hints, and, indeed, after the first few words, the Princess had heard enough. She started from her seat and came forward. And when he saw her, the king threw up his hands in despair. But the Princess said quietly, ' Father, you must tell me the whole.'

" So they had to tell her the whole. For many weeks past the terrible monster she had seen in the courtyard had been filling the country with fear. He had suddenly appeared at a distant part of the kingdom — having come, it was said, from a country over the sea named ' Norrowa ' — and had laid it waste, for though he did not actually kill or devour,

he tore down trees, trampled crops, and terrified
every one that came in his way, as the king had said.
And when begged to have mercy and to return to his
own country, he roared out with a voice between the
voice of a man and the bellow of a bull, that he would
leave them in peace once the king gave him his
daughter in marriage.

"Messenger after messenger had been sent to the
palace to entreat for assistance. Soldiers in numbers
had been despatched to seize the monster and imprison
him. But it was no use — he was not to be caught.
Nothing would content him but the promise of the
Princess; and as it was of course plain that he was
not a common bull, but a creature endowed with
magical power, the country-people's fear of him was
unbounded. They threatened to rise in revolution
unless some means were found of ridding them of
their terrible visitor. Then the king called together
the wisest of his counsellors, and finding force of no
avail, they determined to try cunning. The giving
the Princess was not to be thought of, but a pretty
girl about her age and size — the gardener's daughter,
the same whom the Princess had found weeping over
her fate — was chosen, dressed in one of her royal
mistress's beautiful robes, and a message sent to the
bull that his request was to be granted. He came.
All round, the castle was protected by soldiers,
though they well knew their power against him was
nothing. The king and queen, feigning to weep over

the loss of their daughter, themselves presented to him the false Princess.

" She was mounted on his back, and off he rushed with her — up hill, down dale, by rocky ground and smooth, across rivers and through forests he rushed, said the girl, faster and faster, till at last, as evening fell, he came to a stand and spoke to her for the first time.

" 'What time of day must it be by this, king's daughter?' he said.

" The girl considered for a moment. Then, forgetting her pretended position, she replied thoughtlessly,

" 'It must be getting late. About the time that my father gathers the flowers to adorn the king's and queen's supper table.'

" 'Throw thee once, throw thee twice, throw thee *thrice*,' roared the bull, each time shaking the girl roughly, and the last time flinging her off his back. ' Shame on thee, gardener's daughter, and thou wouldst call thyself a true Princess.'

" And with that he left her bruised and frightened out of her wits on the ground, and rushed off by himself whither she knew not. And it was not till two days later that the unfortunate gardener's daughter found her way home, glad enough, one may be sure, to be again there in safety.

" In the meantime the ravages and terrors caused by the terrible bull had begun again, and, as before,

messengers came incessantly to the king entreating
him to find some means of protecting his unfortunate
subjects.   And the king and queen were half beside
themselves with anxiety.   Only one thing they were
determined on — nothing must be told to the Princess.

CHAPTER IX.

THE BROWN BULL — (*Continued*).

" And she
Told them an old-world history."

MATTHEW ARNOLD.

" ' SHE is so courageous,' said the queen, ' there is
no knowing what she might not do.'

" ' She is so kind-hearted,' said the king; ' she
might imagine it her duty to sacrifice herself to our
people.'

" And the poor king and queen wept copiously at
the mere thought, and all the ladies and attendants
of the Princess were ordered on no account to let a
breath of the terrible story be heard by her. Yet,
after all, it so happened that her suspicions were
aroused afresh by the sight this time of the weeping
Bruna. For nothing else could be suggested than
again to try to deceive the monster; and Bruna, a
still prettier girl than the gardener's daughter, was
this time chosen to represent the Princess. But all
happened as before. The brown bull rushed off with
his prize, the whole day the unfortunate Bruna was
shaken on his back, and again, as night began to fall,
he stopped at the same spot.

" ' What time must it be by this, king's daughter?' he asked.

" Foolish Bruna, thankful to have a moment's rest, answered hastily,

" ' O brown bull, it must be getting late, and I am sorely tired. It must be about the time that my mother takes all the eggs that have been laid in the day to the king's kitchen.'

" ' Throw thee once, throw thee twice, throw thee *thrice*,' roared the bull, each time shaking the henwife's daughter roughly, at the end flinging her to the ground. 'Shame on thee, thou henwife's daughter, to call thyself a true Princess.'

" And with that off he rushed, furious, and from that day the ravages and terrors began again, and Bruna found her way home, bruised and weeping, to tell her story.

" This was the tale now related to the Princess, and as she listened a strange look of determination and courage came over her face.

" ' There is but one thing to be done,' she said. ' It is childish to attempt to deceive a creature who is evidently not what he seems. Let me go myself, my parents. Trust me to do my best. And, at worst, if I perish, it will be in a good cause. Better it should be so than that our people should be driven from their homes, the whole country devastated, and all it's happiness destroyed.'

" The king and queen had no answer to give but

their tears. But the Princess remained firm, and they found themselves obliged to do as she directed. A messenger was sent to the monster to inform him, for the third time, that his terms were to be agreed to, and the rest of the day was spent in the palace in weeping and lamentation.

"Only, strange to say, the Princess shed no tears. She seemed as cheerful as usual; she played with her golden balls, and endeavoured to comfort her sorrowful parents, and was so brave and hopeful that in spite of themselves the poor king and queen could not help feeling a little comforted.

"'It is a good sign that she has never left off playing with her balls,' they said to each other. 'Who knows but what the fairy's prediction may be true, and that in some way the balls may be the means of saving her?'

"'They and my wits,' said the Princess, laughing, for she had often been told of the fairy's saying.

"And the king and queen and all the ladies and gentlemen of the court looked at her in astonishment, admiring her courage, but marvelling at her having the spirit to laugh at such a moment.

"The next morning, at the usual time, the terrible visitor made his appearance. He came slowly up to the castle courtyard and stood at the great entrance, tossing his enormous head with impatience. But he was not kept waiting long; the doors were flung open, and at the top of the flight of steps leading down

THE BROWN BULL OF NORROWA. — p. 141.

from them appeared the young Princess, pale but
resolute, her fair hair floating over her shoulders, her
golden balls flashing as she slowly walked down the
steps, tossing them as she went. And, unlike the
false princesses, she was dressed entirely in black,
without a single jewel or ornament of any kind —
nothing but her balls, and her hair caught the sunlight as she passed. There were no soldiers this
time, no crowd of weeping friends; the grief of the
king and queen was now too real to be shown, and
the Princess had asked that there should be no one
to see her go.

"The brown bull stood still as a lamb for her to
mount, and then at a gentle pace he set off. The
Princess had no need to catch hold of his horns to
keep herself from falling, his step was so even. And
all along as she rode she threw her balls up softly in
the air, catching them as they fell. But the brown
bull spoke not a word.

"On and on they went; the sun rose high in the
heavens and poured down on the girl's uncovered head
the full heat of his rays. But just as she began to
feel it painfully, they entered a forest, where the green
shade of the summer trees made a pleasant shelter.
And when they came out from the forest again on the
other side the sun was declining; before long he had
sunk below the horizon, evening was at hand. And
as before, the brown bull stopped.

"'King's daughter,' he said, in a voice so gentle,

though deep, that the Princess started with surprise, 'what hour must it be by this? Tell me, king's daughter, I pray.'

"'Brown bull,' replied the Princess, without a moment's hesitation, for those who have nothing to conceal are fearless and ready; 'brown bull, it is getting late. By now must the king and queen, my father and mother, be sitting down to their solitary supper and thinking of me, for at this hour I was used to hasten to them, throwing my pretty balls as I went.'

"'I thank thee, thou true Princess,' said the bull in the same tone, and he hastened on.

"And ere long the night fell, and the poor Princess was so tired and sleepy, that without knowing it her pretty head drooped lower and lower, and at last she lay fast asleep on the bull's broad back, her fair head resting between his horns.

"She slept so soundly that she did not notice when he stopped, only she had a strange dream. Some one lifted her gently and laid her on a couch, it seemed to her, and a kind voice whispered in her ear, 'Goodnight, my fair Princess.'

"But it must have been a dream, she said to herself. How could a bull have arms to lift her, or how could a rough, ferocious creature like him be so gentle and kind? It must have been a dream, for when she awoke she saw the great monster standing beside her on his four legs as usual; yet it was strange, for she found herself lying on a delicious mossy couch, and the softest and driest moss had been gathered together for a pillow, and beside her a cup of fresh milk and a cake of oaten bread were lying for her breakfast. How had all this been done for her? she asked herself, as she ate with a very good appetite, for she had had no food since the morning before. She began to think the bull not so bad after all, and to wonder if it was to Fairyland he was going to take her. And as she thought this to herself she threw her balls, which were lying beside her, up into the air, and the morning sun caught their sparkle and seemed to send it dancing back again on to her bright fair hair. And a sudden fancy seized her.

"'Catch,' she said to the bull, throwing a ball at him as she spoke. He tossed his head, and to her surprise the ball was caught on one of his horns.

"'Catch,' she said again, and he had caught the second.

"'Catch,' a third time. The great creature caught it in his mouth like a dog, and brought it gently to the Princess and laid it at her feet. She took it and half timidly stroked his head; and no one who had seen the soft pathetic look which crept into his large round eyes would have believed in his being the cruel monster he had been described. He did not speak, he seemed without the power to do so now, but by signs he made the Princess understand it was time to continue their journey, and she mounted his back as before.

" All that day the bull travelled on, but the Princess was now getting accustomed to her strange steed, and felt less tired and frightened. And when the sun grew hot the bull was sure to find a sheltered path, where the trees shaded her from the glare, and when the road was rough he went the more slowly, that she should not be shaken.

" Late in the evening the Princess heard a far-off rushing sound, that as they went seemed to grow louder and louder.

" ' What is that, brown bull ? ' she asked, feeling somehow a little frightened.

" The brown bull raised his head and looked round him. Yes, the sun had sunk, he might speak. And in the same deep voice he answered,

" ' The sea, king's daughter, the sea that is to bear you and me to my country of Norrowa.'

" ' And how shall we cross it, brown bull ? ' she said.

" ' Have no fear,' he replied. ' Lay down your head and shut your eyes, and no harm will come near you.'

" The Princess did as he bade her. She heard the roar of the waves come nearer and nearer, a cold wind blew over her face, and she felt at last that her huge steed had plunged into the water, for it splashed on to her hand, which was hanging downwards, and then she heard him, with a gasp and a snort, strike out boldly. The Princess drew herself up on the bull's back as closely as she could; she had no wish to get wet. But she was not frightened. She grew accustomed to the motion of her great steed's swimming, and as she kept her eyes fast shut she did not see how near she was to the water, and felt as if in a peaceful dream. And after a while the feeling became reality, for she fell fast asleep and dreamt she was in her little turret chamber, listening to the wind softly blowing through the casement.

"When she awoke she was alone. She was lying on a couch, but this time not of moss, but of the richest and softest silk. She rubbed her eyes and looked about her. Was she in her father's castle? Had her youth and her courage softened the monster's heart, and made him carry her back again to her happy home? For a moment she thought it must be so; but no, when she looked again, none of the rooms in her old home were so beautiful as this one where she found herself. Not even her mother's great saloon, which she had always thought so magnificent, was to be compared with it. It was not very large, but it was more like Fairyland than anything she had ever dreamt of. The loveliest flowers were trained against the walls, here and there fountains of delicately scented waters refreshed the air, the floor was covered with carpets of the richest hues and the softest texture. There were birds singing among the flowers, gold and silver fish sporting in the marble basins — it was a perfect fairy's bower. The Princess sat up and looked about her. There was no one to be seen, not a sound but the dropping of the fountains and the soft chatter of the birds. The Princess admired it all exceedingly, but she was very hungry, and as her long sleep had completely refreshed her, she felt no longer inclined to lie still. So she crossed the room to where a curtain was hanging, which she thought perhaps concealed a door. She drew aside the curtain, the door behind was already open; she found herself in a second room, almost as beautiful as the first, and lighted in the same way with coloured lamps hanging from the roof. And to her great delight, before her was a table already laid for supper with every kind of delicious fruit and bread, and cakes, and everything that a young Princess could desire. She was so hungry that she at once sat down to the table, and then she perceived to her surprise that it was laid for two!

"'Can the bull be coming to sup with me?' she said to herself, half laughing at the idea. And she added aloud, 'Come if you like, Mr. Bull; I find your house very pretty, and I thank you for your hospitality.'

"And as she said the words, a voice which somehow seemed familiar to her, replied,

"'I thank you, gracious Princess, for your permission. Without it I could not have entered your presence as I do now,' and looking up, she saw, coming in by another door that she had not noticed, a most unexpected visitor.

"It was not the bull, it was a young Prince such as our pretty Princess, who was not without her day-dreams, like other young girls, had sometimes pictured to herself as coming on a splendid horse, with his followers around him in gallant attire, to ask her of her parents. He was well made and manly, with a bright and pleasant expression, and dressed, of course, to perfection. The Princess glanced at her plain black robe in vexation, and her fair face flushed.

"'I knew not,' she began. 'I thought I should see no one but the brown bull.'

"The Prince laughed merrily. He was in good spirits naturally, as any one would be who, after being forced for ten years to wear a frightful and hideous disguise, and to behave like a rough and surly bull, instead of like a well-born gentleman, should suddenly find himself in his own pleasant person again.

"'I *was* the bull,' he said, 'but you, Princess, have transformed me. How can I ever show you my gratitude?'

"'You owe me none,' said the Princess gently. 'What I did was to save my parents and their people. If it has served you in good stead, that for me is reward enough. But,' she added, 'I wish I had brought some of my pretty dresses with me.   It must look so rude to you to have this ugly black one.'

" The Prince begged her not to trouble herself about such a trifle — to him she was beautiful as the day in whatever attire she happened to be. And then they ate their supper with a good appetite, though it seemed strange to the Princess to be quite without attendants, sitting alone at table with a young man whom she had never seen before.

" And after supper a new idea struck her.

" 'Catch,' she said, drawing the first ball out of the little pocket in the front of her dress, where she always carried her balls, and flinging it across the table to the Prince with her usual skill, not breaking a glass or bending a leaf of the flowers with which the dishes were adorned.

" In an instant the Prince had caught it, and as she sent off the second, crying again ' Catch,' he returned her the first, leaving his hand free for the third.

" 'Yes,' said the Princess, after continuing this game for a little while. ' Yes, I see that you are a true Prince,' for strange to say, he was as skilful at her game as she was herself.

" And they played with her balls for a long time throwing them higher and higher without ever missing, and laughing with pleasure, like two merry children.

" Then suddenly the Prince started from his seat, and his face grew sad and grave.

"'I must go,' he said; 'my hour of liberty is over.'

"'Go?' said the Princess in surprise and distress, for she had found the Prince a very pleasant companion. 'You must go? and leave me alone here?'

"She looked as if she were going to cry, and the Prince looked as if he were going to cry too.

" Alas, Princess!' he said, 'in my joy for the moment, I had almost forgotten my sad fate;' and then he went on to explain to her that for many years past he had been under a fairy spell, the work of an evil fairy who had vowed to revenge herself on his parents for some fancied insult to her. He had been forced to take the form of a bull and to spread terror wherever he went; and the power of this spell was to continue till he should meet with a beautiful Princess who of her own free will would return with him to his country and treat him with friendliness, both of which conditions had been now fulfilled.

"'Then all is right!' exclaimed the Princess joyfully. 'Why should you look so sad?'

"'Alas! no,' repeated the Prince, 'the spell is but partly broken. I have only power to regain my natural form for three hours every evening after sunset. And for three years more must it be so. Then, if your goodness continues so long, all will indeed be right. But during that time it will be necessary for you to live alone, except for the three hours I can pass with you, in this enchanted palace of mine. No harm will befall you, all your wants will be supplied by invisible hands; but for a young and beautiful Princess like you, it will be a sad trial, and one that I feel I have no right to ask your consent to.'

"'And can nothing be done?' said the Princess, 'nothing to shorten your endurance of the spell?'

"'Nothing,' said the Prince, sadly. 'Any effort to do so would only cause fearful troubles. I drop my hated skin at sunset, but three hours later I must resume it.'

"He glanced towards the corner of the room where, though the Princess had not before observed it, the brown bull's skin lay in a heap.

"'Hateful thing!' said the Princess, clenching her pretty hands, 'I would like to burn it.'

"The Prince grew pale with fright. 'Hush! Princess,' he said. 'Never breathe such words. Any rash act would have the most fearful consequences.'

"'What?' said the Princess, curiously.

"The Prince came nearer her and said in a low voice, 'For *me* they would be such. In such a case I might too probably never see you more.'

"The Princess blushed. Considering that he had spent ten years as a bull, it seemed to her that the Prince's manners were really not to be found fault with, and she promised him that she would consider the matter over, and by the next evening tell him her decision.

"She felt rather inclined to cry when she found herself again quite alone in the great strange palace, for she was only sixteen, even though so brave and cheerful. But still she had nothing whatever to complain of. Not a wish was formed in her heart but it was at once fulfilled, for this power was still the Prince's. She found, in what was evidently intended for her dressing-room, everything a young Princess could possibly desire in the shape of dresses, each more lovely than the others; shoes of silk or satin, exquisitely embroidered to suit her various costumes; laces and shawls, ribbons and feathers, and jewels of every conceivable kind in far greater abundance than so sensible a young lady found at all necessary. But believing all these pretty things to be provided to please her by the Prince's desire, she endeavoured to amuse herself with them, and found it rather interesting for the first time in her life to have to choose for herself. Her breakfasts and dinners, and everything conceivable in the shape of delicate and delicious food, appeared whenever she wished for anything of the kind; invisible hands opened the windows and shut the doors, lighted the lamps when the evening closed in, arranged her long fair hair more skilfully than any mortal maid, and brushed it softly when at night she wished to have it unfastened. Books in every language to interest her, for the Princess had been well taught, appeared on the tables, also materials for painting and for embroidery, in which she was very clever. Altogether it was impossible to complain, and the next day passed pleasantly enough, though it must be confessed the young Princess often found herself counting the hours till it should be that of sunset.

"Punctual to the moment the Prince made his appearance, but to his guest's distress he seemed careworn and anxious.

"'Has some new misfortune threatened you?' she asked.

"'No,' replied the Prince, 'but I have to-day scarcely been able to endure my anxiety to learn your decision. Never in all these terrible years has my suffering been greater, never have I so loathed the hideous disguise in which I am compelled to live.'

"Tears filled the Princess's eyes. Had anything been wanting to decide her, the deep pity which she now felt for the unfortunate Prince would have done so.

"'I *have* decided!' she exclaimed. 'Three years will soon pass, and I shall be well able to amuse myself with all the charming things with which I am surrounded. Besides, I shall see you every day, and the looking forward to that will help to cheer me.'

"It would be impossible to tell the Prince's delight. He became at once as gay and lively as the day before. The Princess and he had supper together, and amused themselves afterwards with the enchanted balls, and the evening passed so quickly that the Princess could hardly believe more than one hour instead of three had gone, when he started up, saying his time was over. It was sad to see him go, forced, through no fault of his own, to return to his hated disguise; but still it was with a lightened heart that the poor brown bull went tramping about during the next one-and-twenty hours.

"And on her side the Princess's lonely hours were cheered by the thought that she was to be the means of freeing him from the power of the terrible spell, for all that she saw of him only served to increase her sympathy and respect.

"So time went on. The Princess got more and more accustomed to her strange life, and every day more attached to the Prince, who on his side could not do enough to prove to her his gratitude. For many weeks he never failed to enter her presence the instant the sun had sunk below the horizon, and the three hours they spent together made amends to both for the loneliness of the rest of the day. And whenever the Princess felt inclined to murmur, she renewed her patience and courage by the thought of how much harder to bear was the Prince's share of the trial. She was allowed to remain in peaceful security, and to employ her time in pleasant and interesting ways; while he was forced to rove the world as a hateful monster, shunned by any of the human race whom he happened to meet, constantly exposed to fatigue and privation.

"Sometimes they spent a part of the evening in the beautiful gardens surrounding the palace. There, one day, as sunset was approaching, the Princess had betaken herself to await the Prince's arrival, when a sad shock met her. It was past the usual hour of his coming. Several times she had wandered up and down the path by which he generally approached the castle, tossing her balls as she went, for more than once he had seen their glitter from a distance, and known by it that she was waiting. But this evening she waited and watched in vain, and at last, a strange anxiety seizing her, she turned towards the castle to see if possibly he had entered from the other side, and was hurrying back when a low moan reached her ears, causing her heart for an instant almost to leave off beating with terror.

CHAPTER X.

THE END OF THE BROWN BULL.

"'And happy they ever lived after' —
Yes, that was the end of the tale."

"THE Princess collected her courage, and turned in the direction of the sound. It seemed to come from a little thicket of close-growing bushes near which she had been passing. For a minute or two she could distinguish nothing, but another moan guided her in the right direction, and there, to her horror and distress, she saw the poor Prince lying on the ground, pale and death-like. At first she thought he was without consciousness, but when she hastened up to him with a cry, he opened his eyes.

"'Ah!' he said, faintly; 'I never thought I should have escaped alive. How good of you to have come to seek for me, Princess; otherwise I might have died here without seeing you again.'

"'But you must not die,' said the Princess, weeping; 'can nothing be done for you?'

"He tried to sit up, and when the Princess had fetched him some water from one of the numerous springs in the garden, he seemed better. But his right arm was badly injured.

155

"'How did it happen?' asked the Princess. 'I thought no mortal weapon had power to hurt you. That has been my only consolation through these lonely days of waiting.'

"'You are right,' replied the Prince; 'as a bull nothing can injure me, but in my own form I am in no way magically preserved. All day long I have been chased by hunters, who saw in me, I suppose, a valuable prize. I was terrified of the hour of sunset arriving and finding me far from home. I used my utmost endeavour to reach this in time, but, alas! I was overcome with fatigue, from which no spell protects me. At the entrance to these gardens I saw the sun disappear, and I fell exhausted, just as an arrow struck my right arm at the moment of my transformation. All I could do was to crawl in among these bushes, and here I have lain, thankful to escape from my persecutors, and most thankful to the happy thought, Princess, which brought you this way.'

"The Princess, her eyes still full of tears, helped him to the palace, where she bound up his arm and tended him carefully, for, young as she was, she had learnt many useful acts of this kind in her father's castle. The wound was not a very serious one; the Prince was suffering more from exhaustion and fatigue.

"'If I could spend a day or two here in peace,' he said sadly, 'I should quickly recover. But, alas!

that is impossible. I must submit to my cruel fate. But this night I must confine my wanderings to the forests in this neighbourhood, where, perhaps, I may be able to hide from the huntsmen, who, no doubt, will be watching for me.'

" He sighed heavily, and the Princess's heart grew very sad.

" ' I have little more than an hour left,' he said.

" ' Yes,' said the Princess, 'sleep if you can; I will not disturb you.'

" And when she saw that he had fallen asleep she went into the other room, where in a corner lay the bull's skin, which the Prince had dragged behind him from the spot where it had fallen off as the sun sank.

" The Princess looked at it with a fierce expression, very different to the usual gentle look in her pretty eyes.

" ' Hateful thing!' she said, giving it a kick with her little foot; 'I wonder how I could get rid of you. Even if the Prince did risk never seeing me again, I am not sure but that it would be better for him than to lead this dreadful life.'

" And as her fancy pictured her poor Prince forced in this monstrous disguise to wander about all night tired and shelterless, her indignation rose beyond her control. She forgot where she was, she forgot the magic power that surrounded her, she forgot everything except her distress and anxiety.

"'Hateful thing!' she repeated, giving the skin another kick; 'I wish you were burnt to cinders.'

"Hardly had she said the words when a sudden noise like a clap of thunder shook the air; a flash of lightning seemed to glance past her and alight on the skin, which in an instant shrivelled up to a cinder like a burnt glove. Too startled at first to know whether she should rejoice or not, the Princess gazed at her work in bewilderment, when a voice of anguish, but, alas! a well-known voice, made her turn round. It was the Prince, hastening from the palace with an expression half of anger, half of sorrowful reproach on his face.

"'O Princess, Princess,' he cried, 'what have you done? But a little more patience and all might have been well. And now I know not if I shall ever see you again.'

"'O Prince, forgive me, I did not mean it,' sobbed the poor Princess. 'I *will* see you again, and all shall yet be well.'

"'Seek for me across the hill of ice and the sea of glass,' said the Prince; but almost before the words had passed his lips a second thunderclap, louder and more terrific than the first, was heard. The Princess sank half fainting on the ground. When she again opened her eyes, Prince, palace, everything had disappeared. She was alone, quite alone, on a barren moorland, night coming on, and a cold cutting wind freezing the blood in her veins. And she was clothed in the plain black dress with which she had made her strange journey riding on the brown bull.

"It must be a dream, she thought, a terrible dream, and she shut her eyes again. But no, it was no dream, and soon her courage revived, and she began to ask herself what she should do.

"'Seek me beyond the hill of ice and the sea of glass,' the Prince had said; and she rose up to begin her weary journey. As she rose her hand came in contact with something hard in the folds of her dress; it was her golden balls. With the greatest delight she took them out of her pocket and looked at them. They were as bright and beautiful as ever, and the fairy's prophecy returned to the Princess's mind.

"'With my balls and my ready wit I shall yet conquer the evil powers that are against my poor Prince,' she said to herself cheerfully. 'Courage! all will be well.'

"But there were sore trials to go through in the first place. The Princess set off on her journey. She had to walk many weary miles across the moor, the cold wind blowing in her face, the rough ground pricking her tender feet. But she walked on and on till at last the morning broke and she saw a road before her, bordered on one side by a forest of trees, for she had reached the extreme edge of the moor. She had gone but a little way when she came to a small and miserable hovel, from which issued feeble sounds of distress. The Princess went up to the door and looked in — a very old woman sat huddled up in a corner weeping and lamenting herself.

"'What is the matter, my friend?' asked the Princess.

"'Matter enough,' replied the old woman. 'I cannot light my fire, and I am bitterly cold. Either the sticks are wet, or the strength has gone out of my poor old arms.'

"'Let me help you,' said the Princess. 'My arms are strong enough.'

"She took the sticks and arranged them cleverly in the fireplace, and just as she was choosing two of the driest to rub together to get a light, one of her balls dropped out of her pocket. It fell on to the piled-up wood, and immediately a bright flame danced up the chimney. The Princess picked up her ball and put it back in her pocket, cheered and encouraged by this proof of their magic power. The old woman came near to the fire, and stretched out her withered hands to the blaze.

"'What can I do for you, my pretty lady,' she said, 'in return for your good-nature?'

"'Give me a cup of milk to refresh me for my journey,' said the Princess. 'And perhaps, too, you can tell me something about my journey. Are the hill of ice and the sea of glass anywhere in this neighbourhood?'

"The old woman smiled and nodded her head two or three times.

" 'Seven days must you travel,' she said, ' before you see them. At the foot of the hill of ice lies the sea of glass. No mortal foot unaided has ever crossed the one or ascended the other. Here, take these shoes — with them you can safely walk over the sea of glass, and with this staff you can mount the hill of ice,' and as she spoke she handed to the Princess a pair of curiously carved wooden shoes and a short sharp-pointed stick. The Princess took them gratefully, and would have thanked the old woman, whom she now knew to be a fairy, but she stopped her.

" 'Think not,' she said, ' that your difficulties will be over when you have reached the summit of the hill of ice. But all I can do for you more is to give you this nut, which you must open in your moment of sorest perplexity.'

"And as the Princess held out her hand for the nut the old woman had disappeared.

"But refreshed and encouraged the Princess left the cottage, carrying with her her three gifts, and prepared to face all the perils of her journey with an undaunted heart.

"It would be impossible to describe all she went through during the seven days which passed before she reached the sea of glass. She saw some strange and wonderful sights, for in those days the world was very different from what it is now. She was often tired and hungry, thankful for a cup of milk or crust of bread from those she happened to meet on the way. But her courage never failed her, and at last, on the morning of the eighth day, she saw shining before her in the sunlight the great silent sea of glass of which she had been told.

"It would have been hopeless to attempt to cross it without fairy aid, for it was polished more brightly than any mirror, and so hard that no young Princess's bones could have borne a fall on its cruel surface. But with the magic shoes there was less than no difficulty, for no sooner had the Princess slipped her feet into them than they turned into skates, and very wonderful skates, for they possessed the power of enabling their wearer to glide along with the greatest swiftness. The Princess had never skated in her life, and she was delighted.

"'Next to flying,' she said to herself, 'nothing could be pleasanter,' and she was almost sorry when her skim across the sea of glass was over, and she found herself at the foot of the hill of ice.

"She looked upwards with something like despair. It was a terrible ascent to attempt, for the mountain was all but straight, so steep were its sides of hard, clear, sparkling ice. The Princess looked at her feet, the magic shoes had already disappeared; she looked at the staff she still held in her hand — how could a stick help her up such a mountain? and half impatiently, half hopelessly, she threw it from her. Instantly it stretched itself out, growing wider and wider, the notches in the wood expanding, till it had taken the shape of a roughly-made ladder of irregular steps, hooked on to the ice by the sharp spike at its end, and the Princess, ashamed of her discouragement, mounted up the steps without difficulty, and as she reached the top one, of itself the ladder pushed up before her, so that she could mount straight up without hesitation.

"She stepped forward bravely. It took a long time, even though she had the fairy aid, and by the time she reached the top of the hill night had fallen, and but for the light of the stars, she would not have known where to step. A long plain stretched before her — no trees or bushes even broke the wide expanse. There was no shelter of any kind, and the Princess found herself obliged to walk on and on, for the wind was very cold, and she dared not let herself rest. This night and the next day were the hardest part of all the journey, and seemed even more so, because the Princess had hoped that the sea of glass and the hill of ice were to be the worst of her difficulties. More than once she was tempted to crack the nut, the last of the old woman's presents, but she refrained, saying to herself she might yet be in greater need, and she walked on and on, though nearly dead with cold and fatigue, till late in the afternoon. Then at last, far before her still, she saw gleaming the lights of a city, and, encouraged by the sight, she gathered her courage together and pressed on, till, at the door of a little cottage at the outskirts of the town, she sank down with fatigue. An old woman, with a kind face, came out of the house and invited her to enter and rest.

" ' You look sorely tired, my child,' she said. ' Have you travelled far ? '

" ' Ah yes ! ' replied the poor Princess, ' very far. I am nearly dead with fatigue ; ' and indeed she looked very miserable. Her beautiful fair hair was all tumbled and soiled, her poor little feet were scratched and blistered, her black dress torn and draggled — she looked far more like a beggar-maiden than like a princess. But yet, her pretty way of speaking and gentle manners showed she was not what she seemed, and when she had washed her face and combed her hair, the old woman looked at her with admiration.

" ' 'Tis a pity you have not a better dress,' she said, ' for then you could have gone with me to see the rejoicings in the town for the marriage of our Prince.'

" ' Is your Prince to be married to-day ? ' asked the Princess.

" ' No, not to-day — to-morrow,' said the old woman. ' But the strange thing is that it is not yet known who is to be his bride. The Prince has only lately returned to his home, for, for many years, he has been shut up by a fairy spell in a beautiful palace in the north, and now that the spell is broken and he is restored to his parents, they are anxious to see him married. But he must still be under a spell of some kind, they say, for though he has all that heart can wish, he is ever sad and silent, and as if he were thinking of something far away. And he has said that he will marry no princess but one who can catch three golden balls at a time, as if young princesses were brought up to be jugglers! Nevertheless, all the princesses far and wide have been practising their best at catching balls, and to-morrow the great feasts are to begin, and she who catches best is to be chosen out of all the princesses as the bride of our Prince.'

" The poor Princess listened with a beating heart to the old woman's talk. There could be no doubt as to who the Prince of this country was.

" ' I have come but just in time,' she said to herself, and then she rose, and thanking her hostess for her kindness, said she must be going.

" ' But where are you going, you poor child?' said the old woman. ' You look far too tired to go farther, and for two or three days all these rejoicings will make the country unpleasant for a young girl to travel through alone. Stay with me till you are rested.'

" The Princess thanked her with tears in her eyes for her kindness. ' I have nothing to reward you with,' she said, ' but some day I may be able to do so,' and then she thankfully accepted her offer.

" ' And to-morrow,' said the old woman, ' you must smarten yourself up as well as you can, and then we shall go out to see the gay doings.'

"But the Princess lay awake all night thinking what she should do to make herself known to her faithful Prince.

"The next day the old woman went out early to hear all about the festivities. She came back greatly excited.

"'Come quickly,' she said. 'The crowd is so great that no one will notice your poor clothes. And, indeed, among all the pretty girls there will be none prettier than you,' she added, looking admiringly at the Princess, who had arranged her beautiful hair and brushed her soiled dress, and who looked sweeter than ever now that she was rested and refreshed. 'There are three princesses who have come to the feast,' she went on, 'the first from the south, the second from the east, the third from the west, each more beautiful than another, the people say. The trial of the golden balls is to be in the great hall of the palace, and a friend of mine has promised me a place at one of the windows which overlook it, so that we can see the whole;' and the Princess, feeling as if she were in a dream, rose up to accompany the old woman, her balls and her precious nut in her pocket.

"They made their way through the crowd and placed themselves at the window, as the old woman had said. The Princess looked down at the great hall below, all magnificently decorated and already filled with spectators. Suddenly the trumpet sounded, and the Prince in whose honour was all the rejoicing entered.   At sight of him — her own Prince indeed, but looking so strangely pale and sad that she would hardly have recognised him — the Princess could not restrain a little cry.

" ' What is it ? ' said the old woman.

" ' A passer-by trod on my foot,' said the Princess, fearful of attracting attention.   And the old woman said no more, for at this moment another blast of trumpets announced the arrival of the princesses, who were to make the trial of the balls.   The first was tall and dark, with raven tresses and brilliant, flashing eyes.   She was dressed in a robe of rich maize colour, and as she took her place on the dais she looked round her, as if to say, ' Who can compete with me in beauty or in skill ? '   And she was the Princess of the south.

" The second was also tall, and her hair was of a deep rich brown, and her eyes were sparkling and her cheeks rosy.   She was dressed in bright pink, and laughed as she came forward, as if sure of herself and her attractions.   And she was the Princess of the east.

" The third moved slowly, and as if she cared little what was thought of her, so confident was she of her pre-eminence.   She wore a blue robe, and her face was pale and her eyes cold, though beautiful. And her hair had a reddish tinge, but yet she too was beautiful.   And she was the Princess of the west.

" The Prince bowed low to each, but no smile lit up his grave face, and his glance rested but an instant on each fair Princess as she approached.

" ' Are these ladies all ? ' he asked, in a low voice, as if expecting yet more. And when the answer came, ' Yes, these are all,' a still deeper melancholy settled on his face, and he seemed indifferent to all about him.

" Then the trial began. The Prince had three golden balls, one of which he offered to each Princess. They took them, and each threw one back to him. Then one after another, as quick as lightning, he threw all three to the yellow Princess. She caught them all and threw them back ; again he returned them, but the first only, reached her hand, the second and third fell to the ground, and with another low bow the Prince turned from her, and her proud face grew scarlet with anger. The pink Princess fared no better. She was laughing so, as if to show her confidence, that she missed the third ball, even at the first throw, and when the Prince turned also from her she laughed again, though this time her laughter was not all mirth. Then the cold blue Princess came forward. She caught the balls better, but at the third throw, one of them rising higher than the others, she would not trouble herself to stretch her arm out farther, so it fell to the ground, and as the Prince turned from her likewise, a great silence came over the crowd.

" Suddenly a cry arose. 'A fourth Princess,' the people shouted, and the old woman up at the window was so eager to see the new-comer that she did not notice that her companion had disappeared. She had watched the failure of the two first Princesses, then seeing what was coming she had quietly made her way through the crowd to a hidden corner behind the great pillars of the hall. There, her hands trembling with eagerness, she drew forth from the magic nut, which she had cracked with her pretty teeth, a wonderful fairy robe of spotless white. In an instant her black dress was thrown to her feet, and the white garment, which fitted her as if by magic, had taken its place. Never was Princess dressed in such a hurry, but never was toilette more successful. And as the cry arose of ' A fourth Princess ' she made her way up the hall. From one end to the other she came, rapidly making her way through the crowd, which cleared before her in surprise and admiration, for as she walked she threw before her, catching them ever as she went, her golden balls. Her fair hair floated on her shoulders, her white robe gleamed like snow, her sweet face, flushed with hope and eagerness, was like that of a happy child, her eyes saw nothing but the one figure standing at the far end of the hall, the figure of the Prince, who, as the cry reached his ears, started forward with a hope he hardly dared encourage, holding out his hands as she came nearer and yet nearer in joyfulness of welcome.

"But she waved him back — then, taking her place where the other Princesses had stood, she threw her balls, one, two, three; in an instant they were caught by the Prince, and returned to her like flashes of lightning over and over again, never failing, never falling, as if attached by invisible cords, till at last a great cry arose from the crowds, and the Prince led forward, full in the view of the people, his beautiful bride, his true Princess.

"Then all her troubles were forgotten, and every one rejoiced, save perhaps the three unsuccessful Princesses, who consoled themselves by saying there was magic in it, and so possibly there was. But there is more than one kind of magic, and some kinds, it is to be hoped, the world will never be without. And messengers were sent to summon to the wedding the father and mother of the Princess, who all this time had been in doubt and anxiety as to the fate of their dear child. And the kind old woman who had sheltered her in her poverty and distress was not forgotten."

The voice stopped — for a minute or two the children sat silent, not sure if they were to hear anything else. Strangely enough, as the story went on, it seemed more and more as if it were Marcelline's voice that was telling it, and at last Hugh looked up to see if it was still the white lady, whose knee his head was resting on. Jeanne too looked up at the same moment, and both children gave a little cry of surprise. The white lady had disappeared, and it was indeed Marcelline who was in her place. The white room, the white chairs, the white cats, the spinning-wheel, and the pointed windows, had all gone, and instead there was old Marcelline with her knitting-needles gently clicking in a regular way, that somehow to Hugh seemed mixed up with his remembrance of the soft whirr of the wheel, her neatly frilled cap round her face, and her bright dark eyes smiling down at the children. Hugh felt so sorry and disappointed that he shut his eyes tight and tried to go on dreaming, if indeed dreaming it was. But it was no use. He leant his face against Marcelline's soft white apron and tried to fancy it the fairy lady's fairy robe; but it was no use. He had to sit up and look about him.

"Well," said Marcelline, "and didn't you like the story?"

Hugh looked at Jeanne. It couldn't be a dream then — there *had* been a story, for if he had been asleep, of course he couldn't have heard it. He said nothing, however — he waited to see what Jeanne would say. Jeanne tossed back her head impatiently.

"Of course I liked it," she said. "It's a beautiful story. But, Marcelline, how did you turn into yourself — *was* it you all the time? Why didn't you leave us with the white lady?"

Hugh was so pleased at what Jeanne said that he didn't mind a bit about Marcelline having taken the

place of the white lady. Jeanne was the same as he
was — that was all he cared about. He jumped up
eagerly — they were in Jeanne's room, close to the
fire, and both Jeanne and he had their little red
flannel dressing-gowns on.

"How did these come here?" he said, touching
the sleeve of his own one.

"Yes," said Jeanne. "And where are our wings,
if you please, Mrs. Marcelline?"

Marcelline only smiled.

"I went to fetch you," she said, "and of course I
didn't want you to catch cold on the way back."

But that was *all* they could get her to say, and
then she carried them off to bed, and they both slept
soundly till morning.

CHAPTER XI.

"It was not a story, however,
But just of old days that had been."
CHILD NATURE.

IT was queer, but so it was. The children said
very little to each other the next day of their new
adventures. Only Hugh felt satisfied that this time
little Jeanne had forgotten nothing; daylight Jeanne
and moonlight Jeanne were the same. Yet he had a
feeling that if he said much about it, if he persisted
in trying to convince Jeanne that he had been right
all through, he might spoil it all. It would be like
seizing the fairy lady's cobweb threads roughly, and
spoiling them, and finding you had nothing left. He
felt now quite content to let it all be like a pretty
dream which they both knew about, but which was
not for everyday life.

Only one impression remained on his mind. He
got the greatest wish to learn to throw balls like the
Princess of the Brown Bull story, and for some days
every time they went out, he kept peering in at the
toy-shop windows to see if such a thing as golden
balls was to be had. And at last Jeanne asked him
what he was always looking for, and then he told her.

173

She agreed with him that golden balls would be a very pretty play, but she was afraid such a thing could not be found.

"They were fairy balls, you know, Chéri," she said, gravely.

"Yes," Hugh replied, "he knew they were; he did not expect such balls as they were, of course, but still he didn't see why they might not get some sort of gold-looking balls. There were red and blue, and green ones in plenty. He didn't see why there should be no gold ones."

"Gold is so very dear," said Jeanne.

"Yes, real gold is, of course," said Hugh; "but there are lots of things that look like gold that can't be real gold — picture frames, and the edges of books, and lots of other things."

"Yes," said Jeanne, "but still, I don't see that the stuff any of those are made of would do to make balls of."

However, she joined Hugh in the search, and many a day when they were out they peeped together not only into the toy-shops, but into the windows of the queer old curiosity shops, of which, in the ancient town which was Jeanne's home, there were many. And at last one day they told Marcelline what it was they were so anxious to find. She shook her head. There was no such toy in *this* country, she said, but she did not laugh at them, or seem to think them silly. And she advised them to be content with the prettiest balls they *could* get, which were of nice smooth buff-coloured leather, very well made, and neither too soft nor too hard. And in the sunlight, said Jeanne, they really had rather a shiny, goldy look.

For several days to come these balls were a great interest to the children. Early and late they were practising at them, and, with patience and perseverance, they before long arrived at a good deal of skill. Jeanne was the quicker in the first place, but Hugh was so patient that he soon equalled her, and then the interest grew still greater.

" I really think, Chéri," said Jeanne, one evening, when they had been playing for a good while, " I really think our balls are *getting* to be rather like fairy ones. Every day they go better and better."

" Perhaps it is our hands that are getting to be like fairy ones," said Hugh. " But it is growing too dark to see to play any more."

They were playing in the tapestry room, for Marcelline had told them they would have more space there, as it was large, and Hugh's little bed in the corner did not take up much room. It was getting dusk, for the days were not yet very long, though winter was almost over, and they had been playing a good while. As Hugh spoke he gave the last ball a final throw high up in the air, higher than usual, for though Jeanne sprang forward to catch it, she missed it somehow. It dropped to the ground behind her.

"O Chéri!" she cried, reproachfully, "that is the first time I have missed. Oh dear, where can the ball have gone to?"

She stooped down to look for it, and in a minute Hugh was down beside her. They felt all about, creeping on their hands and knees, but the missing ball was not to be so easily found.

"It must have got behind the tapestry," said Hugh, pulling back as he spoke, a corner of the hangings close to where he and Jeanne were, which seemed loose. And at the same moment both children gave a little cry of astonishment. Instead of the bare wall which they expected to see, or to feel rather, behind the tapestry, a flight of steps met their view —a rather narrow flight of steps running straight upwards, without twisting or turning, and lighted from above by a curious hanging lamp, hanging by long chains from a roof high up, which they could not see.

"Why, this is a new part of the house?" cried Hugh. "Jeanne, did you know there were stairs behind the tapestry?"

"No, of course not," said Jeanne. "It must be a part of our house, I suppose, but I never saw it before. Shall we go up, Chéri, and see where it takes us to? Perhaps it's another way to the white lady's turret, and she'll tell us another story."

"No," said Hugh, "I don't believe it leads to her turret, and I don't think we could find our way

"Is this a New Part of the House?" —p. 176.

there again. She seemed to mean we could never go again, I think. But we may as well go up this stair, and see what we do find, Jeanne."

And just at that moment a funny thing happened. They heard a little noise, and looking up, there — hopping down the stair before them, step by step, as if some one had started it from the top, came the lost ball, or what the children thought the lost ball, for with an exclamation Hugh darted forward to pick it up, and held it out to Jeanne. But Jeanne looked at it with astonishment.

"Why, Chéri," she cried, "it's turned into gold."

So it was, or at least into something which looked just like it.

"Chéri," Jeanne went on, her eyes dancing with excitement, "I do believe this is another way into Fairyland, or into some other queer place like what we've seen. Come on, quick."

The children seized hold of each other's hands, and hurried up the stair. The steps were easier to mount than those of the corkscrew staircase up to the white lady's turret, and very soon the children found themselves at the top of the first flight. There, looking upwards, they could see the roof. It was a sort of cupola; the chains from which the lamps hung were fastened to the centre, but the rest of the roof was of glass, and through it the children saw the sky, already quite dark, and with innumerable stars dotting its surface.

"Come on, Chéri," said Jeanne; "I believe this stair leads out on to the roof of the house."

So it did. A door at the top opened as they ran up the last steps, and a familiar figure stepped out.

"Dudu!" exclaimed Jeanne, in a tone of some dis-appointment.

"Did you not expect to see me?" said the raven. "Why, I thought it would amuse you to come up here and see the stars."

"So it will," said Hugh, anxious to make up for Jeanne's abruptness. "But, you see, we thought — at least we hoped — we should find some new advent-ures up here, especially when the ball hopped down the stairs, all gold."

"What did you expect?" said Dudu, cocking his head. "Fairies, I suppose, or enchanted princesses, or something of that kind. What creatures children are for wonders, to be sure."

"Now, Dudu," said Jeanne, "you needn't talk that way. Whether we're fond of wonders or not, anyhow it's you that's given us them to be fond of. It was you that sent us to the frogs' country, and all that, and it was you that took us to hear the white lady's story. So you're not to laugh at us, and you must find us some more adventures, now you've brought us up here."

"Adventures don't grow on every tree, Mademoi-selle Jeanne," remarked Dudu.

"Well, *Dudus* don't either," replied Jeanne; "but

as we've got *you*, you see, it all depends on you to get us the adventures. I know you can, if you like."

Dudu shook his head.

"No," he said, "there are many things I can't do. But come out on to the roof, we can talk there just as well."

He just turned towards the door by which he had entered, and it opened of itself. He hopped through, and the children followed him. They found themselves, as Dudu had said, on the roof of the house, of a part of the house, that is to say. It seemed more like the roof of a little tower or turret.

Hugh and Jeanne stood for a moment or two in silence, looking up at the brilliant show of stars overhead. It was not cold, the air seemed peculiarly fresh and sweet, as if it were purer and finer than that lower down.

"It's rather nice up here, eh?" said Dudu.

"Yes, very," replied Hugh. "We're very much obliged to you for bringing us up here. Aren't we, Jeanne?"

"Yes," said Jeanne, "not counting fairies and adventures that's to say, it's very nice up here."

"I often come up here at night," said Dudu. "I wonder how many thousand times I've been up here."

"Are you so very old Dudu?" said Jeanne, "as old as the white lady?"

"I daresay," said Dudu, vaguely — he seemed to

be thinking to himself. " Yes," he continued, cocking his head on one side, "I suppose I am what *you* would call very old, though the white lady would consider me quite a baby. Yes, I've seen queer things in my time."

"*What?*" said the children both together, eagerly, "oh, do tell us some of them. If you would tell us a story, Dudu, it would be as nice as an adventure."

"Stories," said Dudu, "are hardly in my line. I might tell you a little of some things I've seen, but I don't know that they would interest you."

"Oh yes! oh yes!" cried the children, "of course they would. And it's so nice and warm up here, Dudu — much warmer than in the house."

"Sit down, then," said Dudu, "here, in this corner. You can lean against the parapet," — for a low wall ran round the roof — "and look at the stars while you listen to me. Well — one day, a good long while ago you would consider it, no doubt — "

"Was it a hundred years ago?" interrupted Jeanne.

"About that, I daresay," said the raven carelessly. "I cannot be quite exact to twenty or thirty years, or so. Well, one day — it was a very hot day, I remember, and I had come up here for a little change of air — I was standing on the edge of the parapet watching our two young ladies who were walking up and down the terrace path down there, and thinking how nice they looked in their white dresses and blue sashes tied close up under their arms, like the picture of your great-grandmother as a young girl, in the great salon, Mademoiselle Jeanne."

"Oh yes, I know it," said Jeanne. "She has a nice face, but *I* don't think her dress is at all pretty Dudu."

"And I don't suppose your great-grandmother would think yours at all pretty, either, Mademoiselle Jeanne," said Dudu, with the queer sort of croak which he used for a laugh. "It is one of the things that has amazed me very much in my observations — the strange fancies the human race has about clothes. Of course you are not so fortunate as we are in having them ready-made, but still I cannot understand why you don't do the best you can — adopt a pattern and keep to it always. It would be the next best thing to having feathers, *I* should say."

"I don't think so," said Jeanne. "It would be very stupid every morning when you got up, and every time you were going out, or friends coming to see you, or anything like that — it would be *very* stupid never to have to think, 'What shall I put on?' or to plan what colours would look nice together. There would hardly be any use in having shops or dressmakers, or anything. And *certainly*, Monsieur Dudu, I wouldn't choose to be dressed like you, never anything but black — as if one were always going to a funeral."

"It is all a matter of taste, Mademoiselle," replied

Dudu, so amiably that Hugh wondered more and more at his politeness to Jeanne, who was certainly not very civil to him. "For my part, I confess I have always had a great fancy for white — the force of contrast, I suppose — and this brings me back to telling you how very nice your great-grandmother and her sister looked that day walking up and down the terrace path in their white dresses."

"My great-grandmother!" exclaimed Jeanne. "Why, you said ' our young ladies.' "

"So they were our young ladies," replied Dudu. "Even though one was your great-grandmother, Mademoiselle, and not yours only but Monsieur Chéri's too, and the other, of course, your great-grandaunt. There have been many ' our young ladies ' that I can remember in this house, which has so long been the home of one family, and my home always. In three or four hundred years one sees a great deal. Ah yes! Well, as I was saying, I was standing on the edge of the parapet looking over at the young ladies, and admiring them and the sunshine and the flowers in the garden all at once, when I suddenly heard a window open. It was not one of the windows of our house. I have very quick ears, and I knew that in an instant, so I looked about to see what window it was. In those days there were not quite so many houses behind our garden as there are now. Your great-great-grandfather sold some of the land about that time, and then houses were built, but just then there were only two or three that overlooked one side of the garden. One of them was a large high house, which was let in flats to various families, often visitors to the town, or strangers who had come for a short time for the education of their children, or some other reason. It was not long before I discovered that the window I had heard open was in this house. It was one on the second story, looking on to a little balcony which at one end was not very high above the terrace walk. I watched to see who had opened the window, and in a few moments I saw peeping out half timidly the pretty fair face of a little girl. Quite a little girl she was, not much older than you, Mademoiselle Jeanne, but not like you, for she had light hair and soft blue eyes, and a fair face like Monsieur Chéri. She was a little English girl. She peeped out, and then, seeing that no one was observing her, she came quietly on to the balcony, and, creeping down into a corner where she could scarcely be seen, she sat watching our two pretty young ladies with all her eyes. No wonder, I thought; they were very pretty young ladies, and it was nice to see them together, walking up and down with arms intertwined, and talking eagerly, their talk sometimes interrupted by merry bursts of soft girlish laughter. And all the time the lonely little creature on the balcony sat and watched them longingly, her little pale face pressed against the bars, her plain black dress almost hiding her from notice.

" ' How happy they look, those pretty young ladies,' the lonely little girl said to herself. 'How happy I should be if I had a sister, for I have no one to talk to, no one to kiss me and play with me, and if ever I say I am sad my aunt is angry. O mother! why did you go away and leave me?' "

"Could you hear all that from up here on the roof?" said Jeanne. "Dear me, Dudu, you must have good ears."

"Of course I have; I told you so, Mademoiselle," said Dudu drily. "I had better ears than your great-grandmother and her sister, for they heard nothing, not even when the poor little girl took courage to push her face farther forward between the railings, and to say very softly and timidly,

" 'Mesdemoiselles, Mesdemoiselles, *might* I come and walk with you? I am so tired of being here all alone.'

"They did not hear her. They were talking too busily about the fête of their mother, I think, which was to be in a few days, and of what they were to prepare for her. And the poor little girl sat up there for more than an hour, watching them with longing eyes, but not daring to call out more loudly. It made me quite melancholy to see her, and when at last our young ladies went in, and she had to give up hopes of gaining their attention, it made me more melancholy still, she looked so disappointed, and her eyes were full of tears; and I felt quite upset about her, and kept turning over in my head what I could do to make her happier. I thought about it for some time, and at last I decided that the first thing to do was to find out more about the little stranger and the cause of her grief. For this purpose I stationed myself the next morning just below the window of the kitchen of her house, which, by hopping from the balcony, I was easily able to do, and by listening to the conversation of the servants I soon learned all I wanted to know. She was, as I had supposed, a little English girl. Her mother had died in Italy but a short time before, and she was now in the charge of her mother's aunt, an elderly and severe lady, who understood nothing about children, and took no pains to make poor little Charlotte happy. So it was a sad life for the child, whose father also was dead; and as from the talk of the servants I gathered that she was a good and gentle little girl, I felt more sorry for her than before; and as I hopped back on to the balcony I looked to see if she was again at the window. Yes, there she was, her face pressed against the glass, staring out in the direction of the terrace walk, watching, no doubt, to see if our young ladies were coming out again. I hopped in front of the window backwards and forwards two or three times to catch her attention, and a smile lit up her little pale face when she saw me.

"'Good day, Mr. Raven,' she said politely. 'Have you come to see me? It is very kind of you if you have, for I have nobody to play with. But, oh! if you could tell those pretty young ladies how I should like to walk about their garden with them, how pleased I should be.'

"I bowed to her in token of understanding what she said, but I was not sure that she noticed it, for she just went on chattering in her soft little voice.

"'Poor old raven,' she said. 'What a pity you can't speak, for if you could I might send a message by you to those pretty young ladies;' and though I walked slowly backwards and forwards on the balcony, and bowed most politely each time I passed her, yet she did not seem to understand."

"Why didn't you speak?" interrupted Jeanne. "You can speak quite well to Chéri and me. Had you not learned to speak at that time, Dudu?"

The raven hemmed and hawed and cleared his throat.

"It is not to the point, Mademoiselle," he said, "to enter into all these explanations. If you would have the goodness to let me continue my reminiscences without interrupting me, I should really be obliged. I warned you I had not any amusing stories to tell, merely recollections of scenes in my past life. If you would prefer my leaving off, you have only to say so."

"Oh no, no. Please go on," exclaimed Jeanne, seeing that the raven was really ruffled. "I think it's *very* interesting, and I'll promise not to interrupt you any more."

"Well," continued Dudu, "I bowed, as I told you, very politely two or three times, and at last I hopped away, still revolving in my mind how I could serve the poor little girl. That afternoon our young ladies came again on to the terrace, but they did not stay long, and the little girl was not to be seen on the balcony, though I daresay she was peering out through the window to see as far as she could. And the next day and the day after were very rainy, so there was nothing I could do. But after that again there came a very fine day — a beautiful sunny day it was, I remember it well — and our young ladies came out like the flowers and the birds to enjoy it. Out, too, came the forlorn little black figure, hiding itself as before behind the railings of the balcony, but looking with longing eyes at the garden below, which to her must have seemed a kind of Paradise. I directed my steps to the terrace, and walked slowly in front of the young ladies, slowly and solemnly straight in front of them, for I wanted to attract their attention.

"'How particularly solemn Dudu looks to-day,' said one of them to the other.

"'Yes,' she replied, 'quite as if he had something on his mind. Have you been doing anything naughty, Dudu?'

"I turned and looked at her reproachfully. I was not offended, I knew she was only joking, my character stood far above any imputation; but still, there are subjects on which jokes are better avoided, and there *was* a cousin of mine whose honesty, I am sorry to say, had been more than once suspected; altogether, I hardly thought the remark in good taste, and Mademoiselle Eliane was not slow to perceive it.

"'Poor old Dudu,' she cried; 'have I hurt your feelings? But tell me what are you looking so solemn about?'

"I looked at her again, and then, sure that she and her sister were both watching me with attention, I sprang up the side of the wall next the little stranger's house, hopped over the balcony railings, and finding, as I expected, my little friend crouched down in the corner, I gave a loud, sharp croak, as if something were the matter. Charlotte started up in a fright, and the young ladies, watching me curiously, for the first time observed her little figure.

"'Why, Dudu has a friend up there!' exclaimed Mademoiselle Jeanne — your great-grandmother, my dears. 'Mademoiselle,' she called out to the little girl, whose small black figure did not look very much bigger than mine as we stood up there side by side; 'Mademoiselle, do not be frightened of our old raven. He will not hurt you.'

"'I am not frightened, thank you,' said the little girl's gentle voice. 'He has been to see me before. I was only startled when he made that funny noise. But O Mesdemoiselles,' she continued, clasping her hands in entreaty, 'you do not know how I should like to come down into your garden and play with you, or at least,' as she suddenly recollected that such tall young ladies were rather past the age for mere 'playing,' 'walk about and talk with you. I have watched you so many days, and I am so lonely. But I did not like to speak to you unless you spoke to me.'

"'We never saw you,' said Mademoiselle Eliane. 'We should not have seen you now but for the funny way Dudu has been going on, as if he wanted to introduce us to each other.'

"I felt quite proud when Mademoiselle Eliane said that. It has always been a gratification to me to find myself understood. And I felt still prouder when the little girl replied, looking at me gratefully,

"'How nice of him! He must have understood what I said to him in fun the other day. But O Mesdemoiselles,' she went on, '*may* I come down to you?'

"'How can you get down?' said Mademoiselle Jeanne; 'and are you sure your mother would not mind?'

"'I have no mother,' said the little girl sadly, 'and my aunt would not mind, I know. She never minds what I do, if I don't make a noise.'

"'But how can you get down?' repeated Mademoiselle Jeanne, 'unless Dudu can take you on his back and fly down with you!'

"'Oh, I can easily get down,' said the little girl; 'I have often planned it. I can climb over the railings at this end — look, there is a jutting-out ledge that I can put my foot on. Then I can stand a minute outside and jump — if you will come close to, so that I shall not roll down the terrace bank.'"

CHAPTER XII.

"One after another they flew away
  Far up to the heavenly blue,
  To the better country, the upper day — "
                                    JEAN INGELOW.

"LITTLE Charlotte climbed over the railings," continued Dudu, "but she did not jump down on the
other side, for Mademoiselle Eliane, who was tall,
found that by standing half-way up the bank she
could reach the child and hand her down to Mademoiselle Jeanne, a little way below. There was a
good deal of laughing over it all, and this helped
them to make friends more quickly than anything
else would have done. But indeed Charlotte was not
a shy child, she had travelled too much and seen too
many people to be so, and our young ladies, besides,
were so kind and merry that no little girl could long
have been strange with them. She ran about the
garden in the greatest delight; her new friends showed
her all their favourite nooks, and allowed her to make
a bouquet of the flowers she liked best; and when
they were tired of standing about they all sat down
together on a bank, and Charlotte told to the young
ladies the story of her short life. It was a sad little

191

story; her father had died when she was very young, and her mother, whose health had never been good after the shock of his death, had gone to Italy with the aunt who had brought her up, in hopes of growing stronger. But through two or three years of sometimes seeming better and sometimes worse, she had really been steadily failing, and at last she died, leaving her poor little girl almost alone, 'for the old aunt was now,' said Charlotte, 'always ill, and not ill as mamma used to be,' she added, for however tired *she* was, she always liked her little girl to be beside her, and never wearied of listening to all she had to say.

" 'But now,' said the child, 'I am always alone, and it is *so* sad. And I have watched you so often from the balcony, and wished I might come down to you. And now, if you will let me come to see you every day, I shall be *so* happy.'

" She was a dear little girl, so sweet, and simple, and loving. She quite gained our young ladies' hearts with her pretty ways and her funny little English accent. They kissed her on both cheeks, and told her they would be very pleased for her to come to them in the garden whenever she saw them from the balcony, as she was so sure her aunt would not object to it. They could not invite her to the house, they explained, unless their mother and her aunt had made acquaintance. Of course it would not have done, as little Charlotte quite understood; for in those days," Dudu observed in passing, "politeness and ceremony were much more observed than is at present, I am sorry to say, the case.

"The little English girl, however," he went on, "was only too delighted to have received permission to visit them in their garden. And not many days passed on which she did not join them there. It was a lovely summer that year — I remember it so well. Never now does the sun seem to me to shine quite so brightly as in those days. Perhaps it is that I am growing old, perhaps the sad days that soon after followed left a cloud on my memory and a mist on my spirit which have never since entirely cleared away; however that may be, I never remember so bright and beautiful a summer as the one I am telling you of. And little Charlotte's merry laugh was often heard on the terrace walk, as she ran races with Mademoiselle Eliane's dog, or made daisy wreaths for Mademoiselle Jeanne's dark hair. Kindness and companionship were all she required to make her a bright and happy child. But the pleasant summer faded, and with the first autumn days came a fresh sorrow for the little girl. One morning, before the usual time for meeting in the garden, I caught sight of her on the balcony, her face looking again like the little pale Charlotte I had first known her, her eyes red with weeping. And as by good chance the young ladies came out soon the reason was soon explained.

"'I am going away, my dear young ladies,' cried

Charlotte, as she threw herself into their arms. 'My
aunt has just told me. We return to England in a
few days. To England, where I have no friends,
where I shall be again all alone. O Mademoiselle
Eliane! O Mademoiselle Jeanne! what shall I do
without you, and your pretty garden, and your kindness, and poor old Dudu, and the flowers, and everything?'

"They consoled her as well as they could, my
kind young ladies, whose hearts were always full of
sympathy. But the tears came to their own eyes
when they saw how real and acute was the little
girl's grief.

"'You will come back to see us again, little Charlotte, perhaps,' they said. 'Your aunt has travelled so
much, very likely she will not wish to remain always
in England. And you would always find us here —
in the winter at any rate; generally in the summer
we spend some months at our château, though this
summer our father had business which obliged him
to stay here. But for that we should not have seen
you so much.'

"But Charlotte was not to be consoled. Her
aunt, she was sure, would never travel any more.
She had said only that very morning, that once she
got back to England she would stay there for the
rest of her life, she was too old to move about any
more.

"'And I,' added Charlotte, with a fresh burst of

weeping, 'I am to be sent to an English school as soon as aunt can settle about it.'

"'But you will be happier at school, dear,' said Mademoiselle Eliane. 'You will have friends of your own age.'

"'I don't want friends of my own age. I shall never love *any* friends as much as my dear Mademoiselle Jeanne and my dear Mademoiselle Eliane,' sobbed Charlotte; and the only thing that consoled her at all was when the two young ladies found for her among their little treasures a very prettily painted 'bonbonnière,' and a quaint little workcase, fitted with thimble, scissors, and all such things, which she promised them she would always keep, *always*, as souvenirs of their kindness.

"And in return, the poor little thing went out with her aunt's maid the next morning and bought two little keepsakes — a scent-bottle for Mademoiselle Jeanne, and a fan for Mademoiselle Eliane. She spent on them all the money she had; and at this very moment," added Dudu, "the scent-bottle is downstairs in your mother's large old dressing-case, the dressing-case she got from her grandfather. What became of the fan I cannot say.

"Well, the few remaining days passed, and one cold, dreary morning poor Charlotte clambered over the railings for the last time, to embrace her friends and bid them farewell. She might have come in by the door and seen them in the salon; of course neither her aunt nor our young ladies' mother would have objected to such a thing, as she was going away, even though no visits of ceremony had been exchanged between the families. But this would not have suited Charlotte; it was in the garden she had first seen her friends, and in the garden must she bid them good-bye. I assisted at the interview," continued Dudu, "and very touching it was. Had I been of a nature to shed tears, I really think my feelings would have been too much for me. And Charlotte would have kissed and hugged me too, no doubt, had I encouraged anything of the kind. But, fortunately perhaps for the preservation of my feathers and my dignity, I am not, and never have been, of a demonstrative disposition."

Dudu cleared his throat and stopped to rest for a moment. Then he continued —

"The parting was over at last, and little Charlotte was away — quite away over the sea in cold, rainy England. Cold and rainy it must have been that winter in any case, for it was cold and rainy even here, and many changes happened, and shadows of strange events were already faintly darkening the future. It was the next year that our pretty Mademoiselle Jeanne married and went away with her husband from the old house, which yet was to be her home, and the home of her children in the end, for Mademoiselle Eliane never married, and so all came to be inherited by her sister's sons. But with that we have nothing to do at present. I wished only to tell you what concerns our young ladies' friendship with the little stranger. Years went on, as they always do, whether they leave the world happy or miserable, and the shadows I have told you of grew darker and darker. Then, at last, the terrible days began — the storm burst forth, our happy, peaceful home, with hundreds and thousands of others, was broken up, and its kindly inhabitants forced to flee. Mademoiselle Jeanne came hurrying up from her husband's home, where things were even worse than with us, with her boys, to seek for shelter and safety, which, alas! could not be given her here. For all had to flee — my poor old master, frail as he was, his delicate wife, our young ladies, and the boys — all fled together, and after facing perils such as I trust none of their descendants will ever know, they reached a safe refuge. And then they had to endure a new misery, for months and months went by before they had any tidings of poor Mademoiselle Jeanne's husband, your great-grandfather, my children, who, like all of his name — a name you may well be proud of, my little Mademoiselle Jeanne — stayed at the post of danger till every hope was passed. Then at last, in disguise, he managed to escape, and reached this place in safety, hoping here to find something to guide him as to where his wife and children were. But he found nothing — the house was deserted, not a servant or retainer of any kind left except myself, and what, alas! could *I* do? He was worn out and exhausted, poor man; he hid in the house for a few days, creeping out at dusk in fear and trembling to buy a loaf of bread, trusting to his disguise and to his not being well known in the town. But he would have died, I believe, had he been long left as he was, for distress of mind added to his other miseries, not knowing anything as to what had become of your great-grandmother and his children.

"She was a good wife," continued Dudu, after another little pause. "Our Mademoiselle Jeanne, I mean. Just when her poor husband was losing heart altogether, beginning to think they must all be dead, that there was nothing left for him to do but to die too, she came to him. She had travelled alone, quite alone, our delicate young lady — who in former days had scarcely been allowed to set her little foot on the pavement — from Switzerland to the old home, with a strange belief that here if anywhere she should find him. And she was rewarded. The worst of the terrible days were now past, but still disguise was necessary, and it was in the dress of one of her own peasants — the dress in which she had fled — that Mademoiselle Jeanne returned. But he knew her — through all disguises he would have known her — and she him. And the first evening they were together in the bare, deserted house, even with all the terrors behind them, the perils before them, the husband and wife were happy."

Dudu paused again. The children, too interested to speak, listened eagerly.

"Go on, dear Dudu," whispered Jeanne at last, softly.

"How were they to get away to safety? That was the question," continued Dudu. "They dared not stay long where they were; yet they dared not go. Monsieur was far too feeble to stand much fatigue, and the two of them journeying together might attract notice.

"'If we could get to the sea,' said Mademoiselle Jeanne — Madame I should call her, but it never comes naturally — there we might find a ship to take us to England or Holland, and thence find our way to our dear ones again.'

"But Monsieur shook his head. 'Impossible,' he said. 'I have not the strength for even the four leagues' walk to the sea, and finding a ship that would take us is a mere chance. We have almost no money. Here at least we have shelter, and still some sous for bread. Jeanne, my beloved, you must make up your mind to leave me again — alone and unhindered you might find your way back in safety.'

"'I will never leave you,' said Jeanne. 'We will die together, if it must be so. The boys are safe — my father and mother and Eliane will care for them. I will never leave you.'

"And Monsieur said no more; but in his own mind I could see that he thought himself fast dying, that want of comforts and nourishment much longer would exhaust his little strength, and that his poor Jeanne would, in the end, be forced to attempt the journey back alone. They were sitting at the end of the terrace walk that evening — the end near little Charlotte's balcony; it was a mild, still evening — it seemed less dreary and miserable than in the house; from the distance came the sound of the children playing in the old streets, and near at hand some birds were singing still — for children will play and birds will sing whatever happens. Suddenly a sound close at hand made Mademoiselle Jeanne look up. And I too, for I was close beside them on the terrace, I looked up in amazement, half imagining it must be a dream. For we heard — both Mademoiselle Jeanne and I knew it again — the sound of the window on to the balcony opening, the window through which the little English girl used to come out to meet her friends. We looked and could scarcely believe our eyes. Out on to the balcony stepped a young lady, a young girl rather she seemed, for she was tall and slight and had fair curls about her sweet fresh face. She stood for one instant looking at us all as if bewildered, then, with a sudden cry, almost before we knew what she was doing, she was over the railings and down the bank.

"'Mademoiselle Jeanne or Mademoiselle Eliane!' she cried, 'which of you is it? for it is one of you, I know! And you are *not* dead — not all dead and gone — and there is Dudu, too. Oh, how glad, how very glad, I am that I came!'

"Laughing and crying both at once, she threw herself into Madame's arms, while Monsieur looked on in amazement.

"'You know me?' she cried — 'your little English Charlotte. See, here is the bonbonnière,' feeling for it in her pocket as she spoke. 'And you are Mademoiselle Jeanne. I know you now — if you had twenty peasant caps on I should know you. But how thin and pale you are, my poor Jeanne! And is this your husband? I knew you were married. I saw it in the newspapers ever so many years ago. Do you know it is fifteen years since I went away? And I am married, too. But tell me first how it is you are here and dressed like that, and why you look so sad and Monsieur so ill. Tell me all. You may trust me, you may indeed, and perhaps my husband and I may be able to be of some use. You may trust me,' seeing that Madame and her husband looked at each other in bewilderment; 'may they not, Dudu?' she added, turning to me. 'Tell Mademoiselle Jeanne that she can indeed trust me.'

"I flapped my wings and croaked.

"'You see,' said Charlotte, and at that they all laughed.

"'It is not that we do not trust you, my dear friend,' said Madame; 'and indeed you see all in seeing us here as you do. There is nothing to tell but the same sad story that has been to tell in so many once happy French homes. But explain to me, my dear Charlotte, how you are here. It is so strange, so extraordinary.'

" And Charlotte explained. Her husband was a sailor. To be near him, she had been in Spain at the outbreak of the revolution, and had remained there till he was ordered home. Now that the terror was subsiding, there was — for them, as foreigners — but little risk. She had persuaded her husband, whose vessel, owing to some slight accident at sea, had been obliged to put in at the neighbouring port, to let her come to have a look at the old town, at the old house, or garden rather, she still loved so dearly. ' The house we used to live in,' she said, ' was empty. I easily found my way in, and out on to the balcony, as you saw. I had a sort of wild idea that perhaps I might see or hear something of you. Yet I was almost afraid to ask, such terrible things have happened,' added Charlotte, with a shudder.

" But nothing more terrible was in store for our young ladies, I am glad to say," continued Dudu. " The faithful-hearted Charlotte and her husband were able to be of the greatest service to Mademoiselle Jeanne and *her* husband. They conveyed them in safety to the port and saw them on board a friendly vessel, and not many weeks passed before they were again with their children and the old Monsieur and

Madame and Mademoiselle Eliane in their home for the time in Switzerland."

"Oh, how glad I am!" exclaimed Jeanne. "I was dreadfully afraid your story was going to end badly, Dudu."

"It is not ended yet," said Dudu.

"Isn't it?" cried Jeanne. "Oh dear, then go on quick, please. I *hope* Mademoiselle Jeanne's poor husband—"

"Your great-grandfather, you mean," corrected Dudu.

"Oh, well then, my great-grandfather, *our* great-grandfather, for he was Chéri's, too, you said. I do so hope he got better. Did he, Dudu?"

"Yes," said Dudu, "he got better, but never quite well again. However, he lived some years, long enough to see his boys grown up and to return—after the death of our old Monsieur and Madame—to return to his own country with his wife and sister-in-law. But before very long, while still far from an old man, he died. Then our young ladies, young no longer, came back, after a time, to their childish home; and here they lived together quietly, kind and charitable to all, cheered from time to time by the visits of Madame's two sons, out in the world now and married, and with homes of their own. And time went on gently and uneventfully, and gradually Madame's hair became white, quite white, and Mademoiselle Eliane took to limping a little in her walk with the rheumatism, and when they slowly paced up and down the terrace it was difficult for me to think they were really my pretty young ladies with the white dresses and blue ribbons of half a century ago. For it was now just thirty-five years since the last visit of their English friend. She too, if she were alive, must be a woman of more than sixty. They had never heard of her again. In the hurry and anxiety of their last meeting they had forgotten to ask and she to give her exact address, so they could not write. She might have written to them to the old house perhaps, on the chance of it finding them; but if so, they had never got the letter. Yet they often spoke of her, and never saw the balcony at the end of the terrace without a kindly thought of those long ago days.

"One evening — an autumn evening — mild and balmy, the two old ladies were slowly pacing up and down their favourite walk, when a servant came out to say that they were wanted — a lady was asking for them. But not to disturb them, he added, the visitor would be glad to see them in the garden, if they would allow it. Wondering who it could be, Madame and her sister were hesitating what to do, when a figure was seen approaching them from the house.

"'I could not wait,' she said, almost before she reached them. 'I wished so much to see you once more in the old spot, dear friends;' and they knew her at once. They recognised in the bowed and worn but still sweet and lovely woman, their pretty child-friend of fifty years ago. She had come to bid them farewell, she said. She was on her way to the south — not to live but to die, for she had suffered much and her days were numbered.

"'My dear husband is dead some years ago,' she said. 'But we were very happy together, which is a blessed thought. And my children — one after another they faded. So I am an old woman now and quite alone, and I am glad to go to them all. My friends wished me to go to the south, for I have always loved the sunshine, and there my little daughter died, and perhaps death will there come to me in gentler shape. But on my way, I wished to say good-bye to you, dear friends of long ago, whom I have always loved, though we have been so little together.'

"And then they took each others' hands, gently and quietly, the three old ladies, and softly kissed each other's withered cheeks, down which a few tears made their way; the time was past for them for anything but gentle and chastened feelings. And whispering to their old friend not good-bye, but 'Au revoir, au revoir in a better country,' my ladies parted once more with their childish friend.

"She died a few months later; news of her death was sent them. *They* lived to be old — past eighty both of them, when they died within a few days of each other. But I never hobble up and down the terrace walk without thinking of them," added Dudu, "and on the whole, my dears, even if I had my choice, I don't think I should care to live another two or three hundred years in a world where changes come so quickly."

Hugh and Jeanne were silent for a moment. Then "Thank you, dear Dudu," they said together.

And Dudu cocked his head on one side. "There is Marcelline calling you," he said, in a matter-of-fact tone. "Run downstairs. Take a look at the beautiful stars overhead before you go. Good-bye, my dears."

"Good-night, Dudu, and thank you again," said the children, as they hastened away.

They found their way back to the tapestry room without difficulty. They were standing in the middle of the room, half puzzled as to how they had got there, when Marcelline appeared.

"We have been with Dudu," they told her, before she had time to ask them anything. "He has told us lovely stories — nicer even than fairy adventures." And Marcelline smiled and seemed pleased, but not at all surprised.

"A strange thing has happened," said Jeanne's father the next day. "I feel quite distressed about it. Old Dudu the raven has disappeared. He is nowhere to be found since yesterday afternoon, the gardener tells me. They have looked for him every·

where in vain. I feel quite sorry — he has been in the family so long — how long indeed I should be afraid to say, for my father remembered him as a child."

The children looked at each other.

" Dudu has gone ! " they said softly.

" We shall have no more stories," whispered Hugh.

" Nor fairy adventures," said Jeanne.

" He may come back again," said Hugh.

"I think not," said Jeanne, shaking her smooth little black head. "Don't you remember, Chéri, what he said about not wishing to stay here longer?"

" And he said 'good-bye,'" added Hugh sadly. "I fear he will not come back."

But if he *ever* does, children dear, and if you care to hear what he has to tell, you shall not be forgotten. I promise you.

THE END.